# Little Shop
# of Homicide

**Center Point
Large Print**

Also by Denise Swanson and available from
Center Point Large Print:

Scumble River Mysteries
  *Murder of a Creped Suzette*
  *Murder of a Bookstore Babe*
  *Murder of a Wedding Belle*

**This Large Print Book carries the
Seal of Approval of N.A.V.H.**

# Little Shop of Homicide

## A Devereaux's Dime Store Mystery

# Denise Swanson

CENTER POINT LARGE PRINT
THORNDIKE, MAINE

This Center Point Large Print edition
is published in the year 2012 by arrangement with
NAL Signet, a member of Penguin Group (USA) Inc.

The text of this Large Print edition is unabridged.
In other aspects, this book may vary
from the original edition.
Printed in the United States of America
on permanent paper.
Set in 16-point Times New Roman type.

ISBN: 978-1-61173-397-6

Library of Congress Cataloging-in-Publication Data

Swanson, Denise.
Little shop of homicide : a Devereaux's dime store mystery / Denise
Swanson. — Large print ed.
p. cm. — (Center Point large print edition)
ISBN 978-1-61173-397-6 (lib. bdg. : alk. paper)
1. Merchants—Fiction. 2. Murder—Fiction. 3. Large type books.
   I. Title.
PS3619.W36L58 2012
813'.6—dc23

2012003316

For Kelle Z. Riley
Because she is always there to help me brainstorm, listen to my plots, and tell me when I'm going in the wrong direction.
Because she tolerates my whining, but never lets me sink into the quagmire of writer's depression—especially when I think I might have committed career suicide.
But, mostly, because she writes amazing stories with life-affirming happy endings that everyone is going to love once some smart editor snaps them up.
Never give up the dream!

# Acknowledgments

After so many books, I sometimes forget to thank the two people who have had such a huge part in making those books possible. However, with a new series starting, it reminded me how much I owe my agent, Laura Blake Peterson, and my editor, Ellen Edwards. So, thank you for all you've done, and for being with me for the long haul!

Thanks also to my Facebook peeps. Your generosity in answering all my "research" questions, and your support of my books (and me) help in ways you can't imagine—especially on the days that I wonder why I ever wanted to be a writer.

# CHAPTER 1

Stepping back from the old kitchen table I used as a workbench, I contemplated my creations. Both evoked strong feelings. The one on my left called up memories of a simpler time, filled with sunlight and innocence, while the one on my right summoned thoughts of sensual darkness and guilty pleasures.

As I examined the nostalgia basket, the one for the Gerbers' sixtieth anniversary, I smoothed the 1952 *Saturday Evening Post*, straightened the fifties music CD, and pinned an I LIKE IKE button to the sock monkey's hat. Once I tucked in the sacks of peppermint sticks and licorice whips, a mesh bag of marbles, and a kazoo, I was ready to place my trademark—the one perfect book—in the center. *Norman Rockwell's Faith of America* had been the clear choice.

Happy with the Gerbers' basket, I turned my attention to the one for the Cusslers, who were celebrating their first anniversary. I studied my handiwork. It needed something to be amazing. They had asked for heat and passion; so which would sizzle more, a crimson silk blindfold or a pair of black satin panties? Already nestled in the folds of an ebony lace shawl were a bottle of cinnamon massage oil, a box of chocolate-

9

dipped strawberries, and a lushly illustrated copy of the *Kama Sutra*.

Closing my eyes, I visualized the couple receiving the gift. He was the golf pro at the local country club and she was a PE teacher. Both were extremely athletic. It was a shame a trapeze bar wouldn't fit into the basket.

My deliberation was interrupted by the jingling of sleigh bells. *Shoot!* The front door was supposed to be locked. On Mondays, Devereaux's Dime Store and Gift Baskets didn't open until noon, by which time all the naughty bits and pieces would be safely tucked out of sight, and I would be working on a Birthday Bonanza toy box featuring a first edition of *Lassie Come Home* for dog lover Timmy Harper.

Not that I was ashamed of my erotic creations, but like the sour-looking middle-aged man who had just entered the store, there were a lot of people with whom I didn't want to discuss my artistic vision. The way my luck had been running lately, this guy was probably the town's new minister, or worse, a reporter who hadn't gotten the message that I was old news.

When the man's unblinking muddy brown eyes skimmed my worktable and his lips pressed together in a disapproving thin white line, I said hastily, "Sorry. We're closed."

He grunted, lumbering past the paperback bookrack, the three-stool soda fountain, and the glass candy case, straight toward me. He walked as if each step was drawn on the floor, and nothing short of an act of God would stop him. The fact that he hadn't even glanced at the enticing display of fudge, truffles, and other mouthwatering confections was worrisome. What kind of person didn't notice chocolate?

"We're closed," I repeated. "You'll have to come back at twelve." He was starting to scare me.

He ignored my statement and flipped open the counter's hinged panel.

Alarmed, I said sharply, "You can't come back here." With his egg-shaped torso, pedantic movements, and acerbic expression he resembled Humpty Dumpty's evil twin.

As I frantically searched my jeans pockets for my cell phone, which unfortunately seemed to be AWOL, Humpty continued to advance until the only thing between us was my worktable.

Putting both hands on the Formica surface, he demanded, "Devereaux Sinclair?"

For a second, when he leaned forward, he seemed familiar, but if I'd known him he wouldn't have had to ask my name. Unless . . . *Damn!* Was he a process server? I'd certainly met my share of them when I was going through all the crap from my old job.

Before I could decide on an answer, a scowl twisted his heavy features, and he repeated, "Devereaux Sinclair?"

"Yes." What in the world did this guy want? To cover my consternation, I put on my best don't-mess-with-me expression, the one I'd learned while working in the cutthroat investment consulting business, and asked, "How may I help you?"

"I'm Detective Woods."

Okay, that would explain the ill-fitting cheap navy suit and the highly polished black shoes. "May I see some identification, please?" I was fairly sure that the police department in my hometown didn't employ a detective. Especially since I knew the chief and all the officers on the force. So where was this guy from, and what was he doing in Shadow Bend, Missouri, population 4,028?

Woods reached into the inside pocket of his jacket and retrieved a worn leather wallet. He flipped it open, displaying a Kansas City police ID card on one side and a gold badge on the other.

I stopped searching for my phone. Kansas City was forty miles away, and during morning rush hour the trip took a good hour or more. What had I done to merit a visit from KC's finest?

Impassively, he stated, "I understand you made a gift basket for Joelle Ayers."

"That's correct," I answered slowly, struggling to fathom why a cop would be interested in either the basket or Joelle. "It was a Valentine's Day present for her fiancé. She picked it up Saturday afternoon. They were going to spend a romantic weekend in the city." Was there some kind of morality law in Kansas City that prohibited sex toys?

"How well do you know Ms. Ayers?"

"Not very." Which was true, at least technically. "I met her for the first time when she came in to place her order." What I didn't add was that in a rural community like Shadow Bend, it was hard not to have heard plenty about someone like Joelle. She had swept into our town last summer, and by Christmas she had snapped up its most eligible bachelor. "Did something happen to her?"

Detective Woods ignored my question. "But you *do* know her fiancé a whole lot better, don't you?"

"We went to high school together." Had something happened to Noah? Even after the awful way he'd treated me all those years ago, I felt my stomach clench. "Why are you asking me about Dr. Underwood? Were he and Joelle in an accident?"

"You sound pretty worried about someone who was *just* your classmate," Detective Woods said in an insinuating purr. "But then, you two were much more than that. Weren't you?"

"We dated when we were teenagers." I didn't have to ask how he had learned about my

13

relationship with Noah. There aren't many secrets in a small town, where the past is never fully forgiven or forgotten. No doubt someone had been happy to tell Detective Woods all about Noah and me.

"Until your father"—he consulted a small notepad—"one Kern Sinclair, went to prison." Woods's resemblance to Humpty had faded, and now he looked more like a banty rooster, particularly when he thrust out his chin. "That's when Noah Underwood dumped your ass, and from what I hear, you've been carrying a torch for him ever since."

"That's ridiculous." I tugged at the neck of my green sweatshirt, suddenly wishing I had on one of the power suits I had donated to the Salvation Army after I quit my previous job. "It became clear a long time ago that we were too young to have any kind of serious relationship. I've gone out with lots of guys since then." I clasped my hands together to stop them from shaking as I remembered the pain of the day that had changed my life forever. The day my father was convicted of manslaughter and possession of a controlled substance, my mother abandoned me, and the boy who had vowed to love me for all eternity walked away.

"Still, you're nearly thirty and never been married." Woods's expression reminded me of my grandmother's Siamese cat—right after it

14

had finished eating my beloved pet gerbil. He prodded. "It had to gall you, making a 'do me' basket for your rival."

If he thought using crude language would bother me, he had no idea what I'd been exposed to in my past profession. Still, I glanced longingly at the rear exit, wishing I could just run away, or better yet, disappear. But I hadn't gotten an MBA from a top university, and survived working under a vicious man who considered the glass ceiling his protective barrier, to crumble that easily.

"First," I said, in my stop-screwing-around-with-me voice, "my marital status is none of your business. And second, I'm finished answering questions until you tell me what this is all about."

"We can do this at my police station if you prefer."

"Fine." Brass tacks were something two could use to pound home a point. "I'll call my attorney and have him meet us there." I'd never liked bullies, and this one was ticking me off big time.

Minutes went by as we stared at each other, and when I didn't break the growing silence, he blew out an angry breath. "Joelle Ayers was found dead Saturday night."

"Oh, my God!" Considering that he'd been asking about her and identified himself as a detective, I was prepared for something bad, but not that.

As I struggled to comprehend that someone I had spoken to less than forty-eight hours ago was no longer alive, Woods hit me with another bombshell. "You used to work at Stramp Investments."

"Yes." *Damn!* If he knew that, he'd obviously been checking up on me. What else had he found out? "I quit last May and bought this business."

"So, your departure had nothing to do with your boss stealing investors' life savings?" His nostrils flared. "Or was the cash to buy this store your payoff for keeping your mouth shut about his criminal activities?"

"No!" I was becoming more worried by the second. It was common knowledge that a lot of people thought Ronald Stramp's employees were as guilty as he was, and having left several months before he was exposed had not spared me from the accusations or the venom. "I had no idea what he was doing."

"Are you telling me that you quit a high-powered, high-paying job to run a little country store for no good reason?" His pupils dilated.

"I thought I wanted a career—turned out I just wanted a paycheck," I joked. When he didn't smile, I tried again. "If at first you don't succeed, redefine success."

"Are you mocking me, Miss Sinclair?" His fist came down on the worktable's surface and a bottle of Merlot crashed to the floor.

I jumped. *Oops!* Evidently Woods didn't appreciate my twisted sense of humor. So as I cleaned up the broken glass and spilled wine, I quit trying to lighten the mood and said, "The commute from here into the city was brutal, and I needed to spend more time with my grandmother."

"Right." My alarm seemed to pacify him, and he squared his shoulders. "You're just a dutiful granddaughter willing to give up a six-figure salary to take care of Granny."

"It took me a while to see that making a living isn't the same thing as making a life." I knew it sounded corny, but it was the truth.

Woods snorted, then lobbed another grenade. "Is that why you killed Joelle Ayers? She got in the way of your plans for a fresh start. A fresh start that was supposed to include marrying Noah Underwood."

"No!" I didn't like how my voice squeaked, or the fact that my knees had started shaking, but there wasn't anything I could do about either one. "You're saying Joelle was murdered?"

"Don't act so surprised." His tone was hard. "Your fingerprints were all over the murder weapons."

"But how—" I controlled my voice with an effort. "I mean, that's not possible." I regrouped. "Either you tell me the whole story or I'm not saying another word until I speak to my lawyer."

"If that's how you want to play this." His eyes

17

burned with resentment, and he appeared to be involved in some intense internal debate, which he seemed to be losing. Finally he ground out, "Since the room service asshole who found the vic took pictures with his cell phone and they're already on the Internet . . ." He trailed off, then twitched his shoulders as if angry for explaining himself to me. Finally, he continued. "She was handcuffed to the bed, a champagne bottle stuffed down her throat, and a five-and-a-half-inch metal-tipped stiletto high heel rammed into her heart."

"Oh, my God!" Velvet-lined handcuffs and pink champagne bottle—I mentally checked them off the list of playthings in the Strawberry Seduction gift basket I'd put together for Joelle, but I was sure high heels hadn't been included. "My prints couldn't have been on the shoe."

Woods stared at me without responding.

Finally I asked, "Who would do something like that?"

"How about her fiancé's jealous ex-girlfriend?" His dark, predatory eyes studied me for another long moment. "Where were you Saturday night between six and seven?"

Beads of sweat formed on my upper lip as I struggled not to show my panic. A flashback of my one and only visit to my father a year after he'd gone into the penitentiary nearly paralyzed me. I was seventeen, with too much imagination for my own good, and I'd been terrified that when visiting hours were over, they wouldn't let me leave. What if this man made that nightmare come true?

"What in the hell? Are you taking a nap?" Woods's ruddy complexion turned a livid purple. "It's a simple question. Do you or do you not have an alibi?"

Ignoring the sharp pain behind my left eye, I lifted my chin and said with as much conviction as I could muster, "Yes, I do. I was home all evening with my grandmother, Birdie Sinclair."

What I failed to mention was that Gran generally fell asleep in her chair right after supper and woke up only long enough to watch the weather at the end of the ten o'clock news before going to bed. That, and the fact that although she could tell you exactly what dress she wore on her first date with Grandpa, her short-term memory was a little shaky at times.

"Grandmothers have been known to lie for their grandchildren. Anybody else see you? Any calls?"

"No." Hoping to convince him, I added, "But I can tell you the plot of all the shows I watched."

Woods sneered. "Ever heard of TiVo?"

*Crap!* On to plan B. "I have no reason to kill Joelle. My *brief* relationship with Dr. Underwood ended over thirteen years ago and I barely knew his fiancée."

"Maybe. Maybe not." Woods plucked a black satin whip off the table and stroked it. "But how about those fingerprints I mentioned?"

"Fu—" I stopped myself. I had given up using the F bomb when I left my job in the city. "Of course my prints were on everything. As you pointed out, I made the basket they were taken from."

Woods smirked. "All that proves is pre-meditation."

What was up with this guy? "Weren't there any fingerprints other than mine?" It was almost as if he wanted me to be the guilty party.

"Look—let's make this easy for both of us. Just tell me what happened." Sincerity oozed from his voice. "Juries are suckers for crimes of passion. With a good lawyer, you'll probably serve less time than your old man."

After I quit hyperventilating, it hit me. If he could make a case, he would have already taken me into custody. He was on a fishing expedition, but I was no longer taking the bait.

"Which would be great if I were guilty, but I didn't do it." I crossed my arms and leaned a hip nonchalantly against the table edge. "So, unless you're ready to arrest me, get out of my store."

"Who do you think you are?" His expression darkened, and I became increasingly aware that we were alone. "You can't order me around."

"I apologize. I didn't mean it that way." I

backed up, putting more space between us. "Uh, don't police officers usually travel in pairs? Where's your partner?"

"I sent him on an errand." Woods moved toward me. "I wanted to do this by myself."

His smile sent a chill up my back, and I was about to make a run for it when I finally spotted my cell hiding beneath a pair of black lace stockings. I snatched it up and sent a quick text.

Woods tried to grab my phone, but I said, "Too late. I already notified my attorney that you're harassing me and he'll be here any second."

"You haven't heard the last of this." His eyes glittered with malice. "This time I'm putting you behind bars, where you belong." He whirled around and marched down the length of the shop, snarling as he went, "You and your boss made a fool out of me once, but you won't get away with it again."

As soon as he stepped out the door, I locked it behind him, breathing deeply, as though the coffee-and-fudge-scented air might ease the thundering in my head. A few steps later, I sank to the floor and leaned my cheek on my knees.

During my years working in the investment business, I'd developed a way of shutting off my feelings. In such a high-stress profession, emotional disengagement was often the only way to survive situations in which your decisions could ruin people's lives.

At first, it had taken a lengthy period of concentrated effort to disengage. But with practice, I'd learned to throw the switch much more quickly; so now, within a few minutes, I sat up and started to think.

What had Woods meant about my boss and me making a fool of him once before? Wait a minute—my first impression of the detective had been that he seemed familiar, and I knew that a lot of municipal employees had been among our clients. Now that I had a chance to gather my wits and really consider it, I was convinced I had seen Woods sitting in the courtroom when I testified at my boss's trial.

Which suggested that Woods was one of the thousands who had lost money with Stramp Investments. And no doubt he, like everyone else, believed that I had been in on the scheme. *Shit!* He intended to move heaven and earth to prove I had murdered Joelle, if for no other reason than revenge.

# CHAPTER 2

My mind raced as I finished up the basket I had been working on when Woods arrived. What should I do? I couldn't face being forced into the limelight again. When the news came out that Ronald Stramp was a swindler, and his investment firm nothing but a Ponzi scheme, I had been arrested—briefly—and come under intense scrutiny by the FBI, the federal regulators, the media, and, worst of all, the people in my hometown.

It didn't matter that I had quit my job at Stramp Investments months before the fraud was revealed; I could see in my fellow Shadow Benders' eyes that they were thinking the apple hadn't fallen far from the tree. That like my father, I was a criminal, too.

Eventually, when I was never brought to trial, the stalkerazzi disappeared, and the furor over my involvement in the Stramp scandal faded away. Since then, I had worked hard to keep my head down and blend in to the community I loved. But another brush with the law and I'd be the town freak forever.

Despite my affection for Shadow Bend, the thought of the whispering and gossip in town if I was accused of murdering Joelle Ayers made me want to move to Bora Bora, or Timbuktu, or even New York City—a place I considered about as inviting as Afghanistan. Except I could never do that to my grandmother. The geriatric specialist we were working with had told me that the familiarity of her hometown would be a huge plus in keeping Birdie independent and functioning for a long, long time. He had warned that although Gran was doing well, with only minimal cognitive impairment, any major changes in her life might accelerate her deterioration.

Chewing on the end of my ponytail, I made a decision. It was time to consult with my lifelong pals Boone St. Onge and Poppy Kincaid. Not only were they the only ones I trusted, but Boone was my attorney, and Poppy owned Gossip Central, the most popular watering hole in the county.

I had already texted Boone the all clear once Woods left the store, and now I phoned him and Poppy to arrange a get-together. We agreed to meet at Poppy's bar after work. It was closed on Mondays, so we'd have the two things we needed—privacy and booze. Lots of booze.

The prospect of sharing my problems with friends, and the promise of a frozen margarita the size of a goldfish bowl, got me through the rest of the day. But if I had to pull up my big-girl panties one more time to deal with something that wasn't my fault, I was afraid the elastic would break and someone would get an unauthorized look at my derrière.

At exactly six p.m., after helping Tammy Harper carry her son's birthday basket to her minivan, I locked up Devereaux's and hopped into my sapphire black Z4. I loved that car; it was one of the few vestiges of my old life that I had held on to, rationalizing that if I sold it, I'd never get what it was worth. Plus, I knew that chances were mighty slim that I would own a vehicle like it ever again.

Gossip Central was located just outside the city limits, which was best for all concerned, since Poppy's father was the chief of the Shadow Bend police force. I tore down the blacktop toward the bar, Rihanna's newest hit blaring from my radio as I passed weathered farmhouses and snow-covered fields. Geese formed a black arrow in the cobalt sky, and a goat stuck his head out between the fence rails, staring at me as I zoomed by. I waved at the inquisitive animal, loving the peacefulness of the deserted countryside and relishing the lack of traffic and congestion that I'd faced every day when I commuted to Kansas City.

The road had been cleared after last night's snowstorm, but I kept an eye out for ice patches and suicidal deer. By the time I turned into the bar's parking lot, the wind had picked up and the sign over the entrance swung on its chains, emitting a bansheelike howl.

Huddled in my leather trench coat and wishing I could afford to replace it with something more practical, I prepared to face the cold. The coat had been ideal when I bought it two years ago in my prior life, but it sadly lacked the warmth needed for the rural Midwest.

After wrapping my wool scarf tightly around my throat, I sprang out of the Z4 and ran up the steps. Poppy was waiting for me and swung the door wide, relocking it as soon as I was inside. With her cobweb of silvery blond hair, amethyst eyes, and delicate build, she had many men believing she was an angel. They often paid dearly for that mistake, quickly discovering that the only angelic title she was likely to claim was "fallen."

"Boone's in number five," Poppy informed me. "I'll grab us some drinks and meet you there."

Gossip Central had started life as a cattle barn, and Poppy had played on that theme. The center area contained the stage, dance floor, and bar, while the hayloft could be rented for private parties. She'd converted the stalls into secluded niches with comfortable seating and themed decorations. Secluded, that is, except for the concealed listening devices.

Poppy liked to know what was being said in her bar. She never shared the information with anyone except occasionally Boone and me, but she enjoyed the power. Poppy had serious control issues—a gift from a father who made a Marine gunnery sergeant seem like a warm, cuddly teddy bear.

Boone was seated on a brown leather love seat in our favorite alcove, the one we'd nicknamed the Stable. He greeted me with a wide smile, his teeth strikingly white against his tanned face. He claimed that his skin was naturally that color, but both Poppy and I knew about the clandestine tanning bed in his back bedroom.

Which was only fair, since he knew all our deep, dark secrets. My biggest one was a tiny shooting star tattoo that I had gotten during a college spring break trip to Mexico, and Poppy's was how she had gotten the financing for the bar.

After shedding my coat, I plopped down beside Boone, and he snatched me up in a swift hug. Before letting go, he asked, "You okay, Dev?"

I shook my head, knowing I didn't have to pretend with him. "Not really."

"You didn't tell us much when you called." Poppy placed three glass mugs on the wood-and-wrought-iron feed box that served as a coffee table, then dropped into one of the pair of saddle-stitched club chairs facing us. Her fanny hadn't even touched the leather seat when she demanded, "What's up?"

"It's hard to know where to start." I grabbed my mug and took a healthy gulp. I had been craving tequila, but an Irish coffee would do, at least for the first round. The hot liquid laced with smooth whiskey slid down my throat, warming and relaxing me for the first time since Detective Woods had barged into my store.

Boone barely allowed me to swallow before ordering, "Just tell us everything!"

"You know the text I sent about police harassment?"

"Yes." Boone's hazel eyes crinkled. "To be perfectly honest, until you called and explained, I wondered if it was a joke. It almost sounded like the plot of one of those trashy romances Poppy reads on the sly."

"They are not trashy," Poppy protested.

I rolled my eyes. I could understand Boone's mystification regarding Poppy's choice of reading material. After all, there was a lot of irony in the self-professed town bad girl devouring sappy love stories. But what Boone didn't realize was that Poppy liked these books because she knew exactly how they would end. Literature often didn't have any kind of definitive conclusion, and that was too much like real life for Poppy.

"You just don't like them because they have a happily-ever-after ending," Poppy accused, crossing her arms.

"Which is totally unrealistic," Boone sneered. "Name three couples any of us know personally who have been married for more than five years and are still in love."

*Hmm.* That was a toughie. Certainly no one in my immediate family. My mom was on husband number four, or maybe five. I'd lost track. Since I heard from her barely once a year, the only way I ever figured out she had divorced and remarried again was when her last name changed on the return address of her annual Christmas card.

Poppy's parents had celebrated their thirty-fifth anniversary last June, but it would be hard to claim that Mr. and Mrs. Kincaid were still in love, especially since he seemed to spend every waking moment at the police station.

Then there was Boone, whose folks hadn't spoken to each other since he was five. Oh, they were still married and still lived in the same house, but they communicated only through notes. The invention of e-mail had been a real blessing for them, not to mention saving a lot of trees.

When neither Poppy nor I could meet Boone's challenge, she said, "Okay. Maybe romances aren't that realistic, but neither are the suspense thrillers you read. How many serial killers can there be who decapitate their victims and screw their corpses?"

"Uh, guys." Before Poppy and Boone got into an all-out literary debate—all three of us were avid readers, but with extremely different tastes—I intervened. "Could we discuss my problem before I'm too drunk to care?" To prove my point I chugged the remainder of my drink.

"Sorry." Poppy and Boone apologized in unison.

"Okay, then." I took a deep breath and told them everything, recapping what I had said on the phone and fleshing out the details.

"How does Woods know the fingerprints on the murder weapons are yours?" Poppy asked.

"The cops fingerprinted me when I was arrested after my old boss's Ponzi scheme came to light." My heartbeat still skittered into high gear when I thought about that time. "And even though Boone bailed me out within a few hours and the charges were eventually dropped, my prints are still in the system."

"That's certainly not fair," Poppy huffed. "They shouldn't keep your prints if you're innocent."

"Honey, you have no idea how much data the government has on all of us." Boone wrinkled his nose. "And they never willingly get rid of any of it."

Boone was a bit of a conspiracy nut, and I knew I had to stop him before he started in on JFK's real killer, and the true story behind the most recent stock market crash, so I asked, "How much trouble am I in?" Since he was the lawyer in our group, his opinion carried the most weight.

"It's hard to say." Boone pushed a swath of tawny gold hair off his forehead. "Most of my practice is in real estate and divorce, not criminal law."

I cringed. Boone messing up his perfectly styled tresses was never a good sign.

"Depending on how big a jones this Detective Woods has for you, he could make your life miserable." Boone frowned, then used his thumb to smooth the line between his brows. "You probably wouldn't be convicted, but then again, juries are a crapshoot, and with your past . . ."

He didn't have to draw me a picture. A jailbird father and a crooked boss wouldn't win me any sympathy or earn me much benefit of the doubt. "Damn it all to hell!" The Irish coffee threatened to come back up. That was not the answer I wanted to hear.

"Do you think Woods would go as far as planting evidence?" Poppy asked.

"Maybe." I shrugged. "When I was employed at Stramp Investments, I worked with people so shady, their code of ethics and a list of the seven deadly sins were identical, and they didn't scare me half as much as Woods does." I rested my chin on my fist. "What am I going to do?"

"I have one idea." Boone whipped out his cell and put it on speaker. "Maybe if I, as your lawyer, lodge a complaint that Woods has a conflict of interest regarding you, another detective will be assigned to the case. I'll also mention that he sent his partner away when he interviewed you."

Poppy and I listened intently as Boone spoke to Woods's superior officer. Boone's argument was persuasive, and my hopes soared, until I heard the lieutenant say, "Thank you for your concern, Mr. St. Onge, but I assure you Detective Woods would never indulge in a personal vendetta. I'm sure Ms. Sinclair misunderstood him. And partners often split up to conduct interviews."

After Boone hung up, the three of us sat in frustrated silence until Poppy jumped up and said, "Time for another drink." She headed to the bar. "Then we'll figure out who the real murderer is."

Two margaritas later, I was feeling slightly better, though we hadn't made much progress in figuring out who the killer was. Both Boone and Poppy were eager to try their hand at investigating, if only they could agree on who got to be Nancy Drew.

"Hey, guys," I piped up, interrupting their bickering, "could we get serious about this? My neck's on the line here."

"Geesh!" Boone complained. "You're no fun."

Poppy saw the unhappy look on my face and said, "What we really need to do is come up with some better suspects than you. Ones that detective can't ignore."

"It's always the significant other." Boone's grin was wolfish. "Which means Noah Underwood did it."

The rivalry between Boone and Noah had started when Noah was elected class president in sixth grade. It had continued throughout high school and into their adult lives. When Noah and I were dating, he and Boone pretended to get along. But the minute Noah betrayed me, Boone's true feelings reemerged. From then on, he never bothered to hide his contempt for the good doctor.

Shoving aside the big lump of regret that seemed to form in my stomach whenever my ex-boyfriend's name came up, I tried to focus on the Noah of today: the thirty-year-old successful physician whom the rest of the town adored.

Including Poppy apparently, since she immediately leapt to his defense. "Noah wouldn't murder anyone." She shook her head. "From what I saw when Joelle came in here, she was a scum-sucking slut, but she did get Noah to come out of his shell."

"Out of his shell?" I snorted. "What is he, a man or a mollusk?"

"You know, even though he dated, he was never the same after you two broke up." Poppy's voice sounded suspiciously affectionate. "Of course, neither were you."

"*We* did not break up." Poppy's soft spot for the doctor was beginning to annoy me. "*He* dumped me during the worst time of my life. And I wasn't the same because my dad was in prison and my mom ran away, not because Noah dropped me like a rancid doggie bag rather than be sullied by my family's disgrace."

"Still." Poppy's expression was stubborn. "That doesn't make him a murderer."

"Then give me some other choices," I said in as

even a tone as I could muster, majorly disappointed in my BFF.

"And we're not taking him off the list." Boone dramatically produced a slim gold pen and wrote Noah's name on a cocktail napkin.

"How about those friends of Joelle's?" Poppy suggested. "When she and Noah became engaged, they were mad enough to spit nails."

"That's right. The Country Club Cougars." Boone dissolved into what could only be described as a fit of giggles. He had coined that nickname for the ladies who hung out at the country club and were on the prowl for husbands. He called their younger counterparts the Country Club Kittens.

"Boone," I admonished. "Focus."

He sobered and said, "I was here the night Poppy's talking about, and I thought the Cougars were going to snatch Joelle bald when she showed off that five-carat diamond engagement ring."

"Yeah." Poppy nodded. "You have to watch women like that. They're mean because they're hungry. The only calories they consume are in their martinis."

I chuckled. It had taken me years to become comfortable with my curvier-than-acceptable figure, but I was no longer jealous of the size double zeros Poppy was talking about—at least not very often.

"Put that skanky Anya Hamilton on your list,"

Poppy ordered. "She and Joelle were supposed to be besties, but the minute Joelle got that Jaguar from Noah as an engagement gift Anya started trash-talking her like they were both competing for the same beauty pageant crown."

Boone inked the words *Anya Hamilton* on his napkin, then added *Nadine Underwood*. "And we can't forget dear old Mama. I heard she just about busted a gusset when her little sonny boy brought Joelle home for Christmas dinner and proposed in front of everyone."

"My mom's in the same prayer circle as Mrs. Underwood," Poppy said with a snicker. "And she said Mrs. U had a mock wedding invitation made up that said: 'You are regretfully invited to the wedding of my son, the doctor, to some scheming, lying floozy. My heart attack is scheduled for 7 p.m., Saturday, June 21st. Hopefully the divorce will take place Sunday, June 22nd.' Mom said she passed them out at last month's meeting."

"Oh, my God!" I squealed. "I wonder if she's sorry now that she objected to Noah dating me."

"Nope." Boone shook his head. "She wants her sweetums all to herself. She'd hate anyone he married."

"You know," Poppy said, tapping a fingernail against her lips, "we're making this all about Noah, but there was at least one guy who wanted Joelle for himself."

"Geoffrey Eggers," Boone said. "Did you hear about the huge scene he caused at the New Year's Eve ball?"

Poppy nodded, but I shook my head and asked, "What did our beloved mayor do?"

"His Honor got drunk and challenged Noah to a duel," Boone informed me, nearly wiggling with glee.

"How did I miss that juicy bit of news?" I really had to get out more. "Why didn't you two tell me about it?"

Poppy and Boone looked at each other uncomfortably until Boone reached over and patted my knee. "We know you hate it when we bring up Dr. Noah Dull."

"That's not true." It was my turn to look sheepish. I hadn't realized I was that obvious about my feelings. "I don't care if we talk about him."

"Liar." Poppy leaned forward and punched me lightly on the arm, then turned her attention back to the original topic. "Anyway, what if Geoffrey decided that if he couldn't have Joelle for himself, he'd kill her and make it look like Noah did it?"

"If that was his plan, he did a piss-poor job of it." I blew a curl that had escaped my ponytail out of my eyes. "Which actually lends credibility to your theory, since he's done a rotten job of everything he's tried since becoming mayor thirteen years ago."

"Right." Boone turned up his nose. "He could barely run the bank back then. He should have left running the town to someone else."

"You know, he was in here not long ago telling me how depressed he was." Poppy drummed her long red nails on her black-leather-clad knee.

"Why was he telling you?" I didn't think they were that friendly.

"He wanted me to give him something to make him feel better," Poppy explained. "You know, a bartender is just a pharmacist with a limited inventory."

Boone laughed. "You are so bad."

"Hey." Poppy shrugged. "I tried being good once, but I got bored."

After we all became serious again, I said, "But isn't His Honor way too old for Joelle? He's about the same age as our fathers."

"True," Poppy sneered. "But Joelle wasn't as young as she claimed to be. She's at least forty."

"Really?" I thought back to that day when the willowy brunette had sashayed through the door of my shop to order the basket for Noah. Her high, exotic cheekbones, delicate features, and thick dark hair that hung in long, graceful curves over her shoulders had suggested a woman hovering on the brink of thirty. "How do you know that?"

"Her hands." Poppy demonstrated by holding out her own graceful hands, palms down. "See, mine are smooth and unblemished, but around forty age spots start to pop up and wrinkles appear. Women can use makeup, dye their hair, and have plastic surgery for everything else, but the back of their hands will give them away every time."

"Hmm." I raised a brow. "You'd think a physician would notice that."

"Not when those hands are squeezing your balls," Boone scoffed.

"Yep," Poppy agreed. "Talented fingers make men blind to a lot of things."

Not wanting to picture Joelle and Noah in those circumstances, I quickly changed the subject. "So, do you really think if we give Detective Woods these other suspects he'll leave me alone?"

"Probably not." Boone sucked on the end of his pen. "There's got to be something more we can do to get his attention off you."

"Well." Poppy got up and blew an imaginary speck of dust from a bridle hanging on the plank wall. "You did say that Woods accused you of still being in love with Noah, which was why he claimed you killed Joelle."

"Yes." I recognized the look in my friend's eye and braced myself for the bomb she was about to drop. "He seemed to think I quit my job so I could fulfill my lifelong goal of marrying Noah."

"So, if you're seen around town all hot and heavy with someone else—*pfft*." Poppy snapped her fingers. "His motive for you is gone."

"There's only one flaw in that plan." My shoulders sagged. "How to find a guy to date. There aren't exactly a mob of them knocking at my door."

"She's right," Boone said to Poppy, then poked me in the shoulder. "When's the last time you went out with someone?"

"Before I bought the store and Gran started needing more attention." I scowled at him. He knew perfectly well it had been over a year. "There just aren't many single guys around here. At least not any I'd have anything in common with."

"Forget in common," Poppy ordered. "We're not looking for your soul mate. Just someone hot that you can do the horizontal tango with for a month or so to show that detective you aren't still mooning over Noah."

"Fine." I squirmed. "But there's still the little matter of finding someone who is willing to date me." Boone opened his mouth, but I held up my palm to him. "Let's face it—if a guy is just out for a good time, I don't exactly look like a Playboy bunny."

"No," Poppy agreed, a little too quickly for my taste. "But if you'd fix yourself up a little you wouldn't have any trouble getting asked out."

She walked over and stood in front of me. "When's the last time you wore makeup?"

"The day I quit my job," I mumbled.

"You have beautiful hair." Poppy leaned forward and touched my ponytail. "A lot of women pay big bucks to get this cinnamon gold color you have naturally, but you scrape it back into a ponytail instead of showing it off."

Not wanting to sound like I was trying out for the Poor Pitiful Me contest, I didn't mention the reason for my ponytail. Having my hair cut by someone who knew how to handle the thickness and the curls was another luxury I'd had to forgo once I gave up the big bucks of the financial industry.

Boone turned toward me. "Not to mention your gorgeous eyes. Do you realize people wear aquamarine contacts so their eyes will look like yours? But you do nothing to emphasize them."

"All right already." They were tag-teaming me and I was beginning to get mad. "I get it. I'll fix myself up a little." *Geez.* You would think they'd never seen me looking good.

As if reading my mind, Boone tilted his head. "You know, the last time I saw you wear anything but a business suit or jeans was our junior year of high school at the Valentine's Day dance."

"I have worn dresses and nice clothes since then. You just weren't present at the time."

"Boone's right," Poppy disagreed. "That dance

40

was the week before you and Noah split up." She bit her lip. "Maybe the detective is right about your feelings for Noah."

"Don't be silly." I cleared my throat—it was hard to talk around the lump that was stuck there. "How many times do I have to tell you that was over a long time ago?"

"Was it?" Poppy's expression was sympathetic as she added softly, "You know, unrequited love is painful, not romantic."

Before I could respond to her pronouncement, my cell started playing "Sunrise, Sunset." I snatched it from my pocket and flipped it open. As I listened, I jumped up and shrugged into my coat.

Dashing out of the alcove with Boone and Poppy at my heels, I said into the phone, "I'm on my way. Thanks."

"What's wrong?" Poppy demanded.

I paused half in and half out of the front door. "Your dad just arrested my grandmother."

# CHAPTER 3

With my little black sports car in the lead, Poppy's ginormous silver Hummer hugging my bumper, and Boone's Mercedes sedan bringing up the rear, we looked like some kind of peculiar parade heading into town.

Considering that my father was in prison for causing a fatal accident while driving under the influence, I was worried that none of us should be behind the wheel, so I kept my Z4 at a steady thirty-five miles per hour rather than my normal seventy.

If I hadn't needed to get to my grandmother right away, I would have eaten something and waited several hours before driving, but there was no way I would leave her in jail for that long. And Poppy and Boone had refused to stay behind at the bar, despite my assurances that I could handle springing Gran on my own.

At least Boone had a legitimate reason to accompany me; Birdie might need a lawyer. I suspected, however, that Poppy was along for the ride more because she never missed an opportunity to pick a fight with her father than because of her friendship with me—especially since stirring up Chief Kincaid was *so* not the way to persuade him to release my grandmother.

The police station's location between the hardware store and the dry cleaners on Shadow Bend's main street often made parking a problem. But seeing as it was long past normal business hours, all five spaces in front were free, and I took the one nearest the entrance. Poppy and Boone pulled in on either side of me, a little like the president and his Secret Service escorts.

Happy as I was that we had arrived safely, I

dreaded going inside. The square cinder-block building reminded me of a mini prison, and the newly installed bars and bulletproof glass on the front windows didn't help matters.

My stomach churned as I pushed the door open. What on earth had my grandmother done to get arrested? She'd been responding so well to the medication the geriatrician had given her, and he had assured me that since the onset of her dementia had been noticed unusually early, there was every reason to be optimistic.

Gran had been fine when I left home that morning, and she hadn't had any plans to leave the house, so what had happened? The woman who had found her cell phone and used it to call me had said that Chief Kincaid had taken Gran away in his squad car, but she didn't know why.

Now, despite the doctor's assurances to the contrary, I wondered if Gran needed a caretaker. If she did, where would I find the money for one? I had sunk everything I had into Devereaux's Dime Store and Gift Baskets, and in today's economy, the few possessions I had kept wouldn't bring enough cash to make much of a difference. Not many people were buying fancy cars, leather coats, or expensive jeans and designer blouses anymore.

Eldridge Kincaid was in the lobby when I walked in. There wasn't a visible wrinkle in his highly starched khaki uniform and his gray buzz cut stood at attention, making me conscious of my own rumpled appearance. His expression was neutral until Poppy crowded in behind Boone and me. Then something flickered in his steel blue eyes, but it was gone before I could interpret it.

"Where's my grandmother?" I demanded.

He was silent and unmoving. Kind of like an Easter Island statue but less responsive.

Impatient with his power games, I snapped, "Don't you have anything better to do than harass little old ladies?"

His brows rose into his hairline and he barked, "You will respect the uniform."

"Stuff it, Dad." Poppy pushed past me. "What did Mrs. Sinclair do, jaywalk?"

Before Poppy could make things worse, I quickly reeled in my own resentment and said, "Sorry, Chief." I knew better than to let my feelings get the best of me, but the stress of the day had left my emotions raw. "We're just concerned about Birdie. No disrespect meant."

Chief Kincaid huffed, but pointed to me and said, "You and I will talk in my office." He motioned to Boone and Poppy. "They will wait in Reception."

"You can't push us around like that. We—"

"Sir." Boone quickly cut Poppy off. "I'm Mrs. Sinclair's attorney and therefore have a right to be present when she's questioned."

"Mrs. Sinclair did not invoke that privilege." The chief turned his back and started up the short flight of cement stairs that led to the rest of the station. He didn't turn his head when he asked, "Do you want to speak to me or not?"

"She doesn't—"

"Yes." It was my turn to cut Poppy off. I dashed up the steps, pausing briefly at the top to say to Boone and Poppy, "I'll come get you if I need you."

Chief Kincaid double-timed through the waiting room and held open the door to his office, shutting it firmly behind me once I was inside. He settled into the seat behind the desk before nodding me into a chair facing him.

Silently he straightened the immaculate leather blotter, lined the telephone up with the edge, and buffed out a fingerprint marring the shiny brass surface of his nameplate. Finally he looked up and said, "The debt you have to the people who took care of you is nothing compared to the responsibility you have to the people you want to take care of."

I wasn't sure what he meant. Was he referring to his daughter or my grandmother? Either way, I nodded my agreement. He was the type of man it was best not to interrupt. You had to listen to what he wanted to say and never offer a differing opinion until after he gave you the information you needed.

"You can pay back the people who took care of you," he continued, "but the ones you want to keep safe will be your concern until one of you dies."

"Right." He was getting up a head of philosophical steam, and I tried to keep up. "And sometimes those two are the same people, like my grandmother. She took care of me when my parents abandoned me, and now I need to keep her safe."

"Absolutely." He smiled as if I had said something clever, then pointed a finger at me. "At present you are not doing a very good job."

"Why?" I felt so tightly coiled, I ached. "What happened to her?"

He took a small notebook from his breast pocket and flipped it open, then read, " 'At twenty hundred hours a citizen called nine-one-one and reported that an elderly woman was wandering around White Eagle trailer park wearing a purple wool coat and yellow rubber boots, asking for a cigarette.' "

"Oh, my God!" Had Gran lost thirteen years of her memory? She'd quit smoking the day she took me in and became my guardian. "Is she okay?"

Ignoring my question, he continued: " 'From the description, I suspected it was Mrs. Sinclair, so instead of sending the officer on duty, I went out personally. She appeared physically unharmed but was overwrought, so I took her into custody and called her granddaughter's store and home. No one answered at either location.'"

"I was at Gossip Central," I mumbled, feeling guilty for having gone there rather than straight home as I usually did. "Why didn't you call my cell?"

"I was in the process of locating the number when you arrived."

"Oh." I didn't need to ask why he hadn't contacted his daughter for my cell phone number. He hadn't spoken directly to Poppy in two years. "So, can I take Gran home? She didn't break any law or anything, did she?"

"No, she didn't break any laws. And yes, you may take your grandmother home." He stared at me. "But this can't happen again."

"Of course not." I stood up. "I'm totally shocked by her behavior. She's been doing so well. She just saw the geriatric specialist a couple of weeks ago."

Before I could take a step toward the door, he said, "Maybe one of those detectives from Kansas City who talked to her this afternoon threw her off balance."

"What?" My legs started to buckle and I sank back into the chair before I fell. "How did you— Did he—I mean—" I stammered to a halt, not sure what I wanted to ask.

"Professional courtesy. They stopped by to tell me about the murder and to notify me that they'd be questioning some people in my jurisdiction. No, I did not share that information with any of my staff."

"Oh. Good." I took a calming breath before asking, "Did they say who they were going to interview?"

"Yes." Chief Kincaid gave a slight nod of his head. "Woods was planning to speak to you and your grandmother, and his partner was going to handle Ms. Ayers's friends."

"Joelle only hung around with newcomers, right?" I felt a tiny flicker of relief. "No one in town?"

"To the best of my knowledge, they were only talking to the country club crowd." Chief Kincaid looked me in the eye. "I assured Woods and his partner that that bunch didn't mingle with the native Shadow Benders."

"So there's a good chance the KC cops' interest in me won't hit the local grapevine?"

"Yep. Townies don't gossip with the country clubbers." Chief Kincaid leaned forward, a concerned expression softening his normally severe gaze. "Look. You've always been a good friend to my daughter, and I'm fully cognizant of how many predicaments you've rescued her from. I also know that you've had a rough time, what with your parents' and your ex-boss's actions, so I'll give you a piece of advice, off the record."

"Uh." I clutched my purse to my midriff,

48

almost more scared of this kinder, gentler Eldridge Kincaid than of the usual forbidding, harsh one. "Okay."

"Hire a private investigator." He said the last two words as if they tasted like dog poop.

"I don't have that kind of money, and—"

Eldridge cut me off. "I gave this same advice to your father and he ignored me. I knew he hadn't embezzled money from the bank, but old Chief Moody said it was a federal matter and ordered me to stay out of it. Then when your dad T-boned that car and tested a blood alcohol level of one-point-nine . . . There was nothing more I could do. Especially once they found those pills in the glove compartment."

"Oh." Stunned, I collapsed back in my chair. I was aware that my father and the chief had been pals back then, but no one except my grandmother had ever said they thought my dad was innocent. My father had never been convicted of the embezzlement charge, but everyone assumed he was as guilty of that crime as he had been of killing that poor girl whose car he crashed into when he was drunk. It hadn't helped his claim of innocence when the prosecutor argued that he was trying to sneak out of town at the time of the accident.

"Funny thing, though." The chief's voice roused me from my daze. "Kern was well known for his antidrug stance, plus we were friends since kindergarten and I never saw him drink more than a couple of beers."

"That's because he was framed," announced a voice from the doorway.

Neither one of us had noticed the office door opening, but standing on the threshold, looking like a pissed-off Pekinese, was my grandmother, Birdie Sinclair. I wondered how long she'd been there and how much she'd overheard.

"Hi, Gran." I had listened to her theory of my father's innocence many times in the past thirteen years and was in no mood to rehash it yet again. "Let's get you home. Then we can talk about Dad."

"In a minute." She spared me a brief glance before marching over to the chief, her pale blue eyes sparking with anger. "First I need to clear something up here." Slapping his desktop for emphasis, Birdie demanded, "Eldridge Kincaid, since when is it a crime to ask someone to loan you a cigarette?"

"Now, Mrs. Sinclair, you know I never arrested you." His tone was placating, as if he were speaking to someone not in her right mind. "I just took you into custody so you'd be safe until I could locate your granddaughter."

"Sweet Jesus! I was perfectly fine until you showed up." Birdie glared at him. "With your lights flashing and your siren blaring loud enough to wake the dead."

"But, Gran, what were you doing at the trailer park?" I asked.

"After that idiot detective from the city all but accused you of murdering that trashy Joelle Ayers, I needed a cigarette." For the first time Birdie looked a little shamefaced. "Yeah, I know you thought I quit smoking a long time ago, but every once in a while I still have a couple of puffs."

"So, why go all the way to White Eagle?" Our house was across town from the trailer park. "Why not just get a pack from a store or a gas station nearby?"

"I couldn't find my purse," Birdie muttered.

"You could have called me and asked me to drop off some money for you. You wouldn't have had to tell me what it was for."

"I didn't want you marking it down in that, that . . . uh . . ."

"Journal," I supplied. The doctor had said it was best to supply the word she couldn't recall, rather than let her become stressed.

"Right. That tattletale list the doctor told you to keep." She glowered at me. "Just because I misplaced my purse or can't come up with a word once in a while doesn't mean I'm senile."

"Of course not." *Shoot!* I hadn't meant to make her feel like I was spying on her. "So, you got in the Land Yacht and drove across town?" I had nicknamed Gran's Buick Park Avenue the Land

Yacht when I was a teenager, and the name had remained with us through the years, as had the car.

"My friend Frieda smokes, and I knew she'd be home since that stupid dance program she never misses was on TV." Gran flipped her long gray braid over her shoulder with the defiant swagger that only a teenage girl or a ticked-off senior citizen can properly master. "Everything would have been fine, but Frieda never told me she was moving her trailer to a better location. The spot next to the laundry room opened up last month and she finally got her no-account son to come and haul it over there for her."

"So you were looking for Frieda to borrow a cigarette because the detective accused me of murdering Joelle?" I wanted to make sure I had the evening's events straight.

"Right. Everything was under control." Gran's face folded up into an accordion of wrinkles. The remnants of the deep summer tan she'd gotten working in the back garden made her look like a golden raisin. "Until his majesty here swooped in and grabbed me. That's when it all went to hell in a handbasket."

Which was about as mind-numbing an understatement as I had ever heard.

Gran and I tried for another half hour to persuade Chief Kincaid that she was rational and I wasn't a neglectful granddaughter, but there was no changing his mind. Then we spent another fifteen minutes filling in Boone and Poppy on Gran's adventures.

In his role as Gran's attorney, Boone was satisfied with the outcome, but Poppy was convinced that her father was an incarnation of Gonghis Khan intent on conquering Shadow Bend, one senior citizen at a time.

Since Gran insisted that I take her to the trailer park to pick up the Land Yacht and her phone before we could go home, it was well past eleven o'clock when I followed her down the long driveway to our house. We lived on the edge of town, on the ten remaining acres of the property my ancestors had settled in the 1860s.

Due to premature deaths, several generations of only children, and entire families packing up and moving away, Gran and I were the last Sinclairs in Shadow Bend. When my grandfather died fifteen years ago and my father declined to become a farmer, Gran had begun selling off the land surrounding the old homestead to pay taxes and support herself. I cringed every time another piece of my heritage vanished, which is why I cherished the few acres we had left.

It was too dark to see the duck pond I picnicked alongside in the summer, or the small apple orchard whose fruit I gathered in the fall for Gran's famous pies, but as we drove through the shadow of the white fir and blue spruce lining either side of the lane, I felt myself relax. Gran and this place had been my only refuge after my father went to prison and my mother walked out on me.

A pool of artificial brightness created by the halogen light mounted on the garage roof greeted us as we stopped in front of the house. Like city streetlights, it turned on at dusk and off at sunrise, providing us with an oasis of illumination when we came home after dark.

Gran hopped out of her Buick, moving as if she were seven years old rather than over seventy. The evening's activities seemed to have energized her while they'd sucked me dry. By the time I got inside and removed my coat, Gran had already turned on all the lamps and was in the kitchen filling the copper teakettle.

I got down the delicate china cups and saucers adorned with violets and wisps of curling ivy, then sat at the old wooden table and waited. Gran made tea only when there was something serious she wanted to discuss with me. Generally, she was more of a Jack Daniel's type of gal.

As she fussed with the tea leaves and arranged cookies on a plate, I looked around. There was nothing fancy or new in the room, but everything reminded me of the home Gran had given me as an abandoned teenager. It was here at this table, drinking from these cups, that she had broken all the bad news since we'd lived together.

After settling into her chair, Gran said, "Are you going to take Eldridge's advice?"

"About what?"

"Hiring a private detective." Gran reached down and swooped up Banshee, her ancient Siamese cat.

I would have pulled back a bloody stump if I tried that trick. Gran was the only one the feline allowed such liberties. He shot me a malevolent stare and settled on her lap.

"No. Of course not." She had surprised me; I'd thought she meant getting someone to take care of her. "Everything will turn out fine. I'm innocent."

"So was my poor Kern, and look what happened to him." She broke an Oreo in half as if it were someone's neck.

"Maybe of the embezzlement." After all, none of the money he supposedly stole had ever surfaced. "But there's no getting around the fact that he killed a girl while driving drunk, or that he had a bottle of OxyContin in his car."

"That wasn't his fault." Gran crossed her arms. "Kern said that he had no memory of drinking or even getting behind the wheel. The last thing he recalled was meeting with his boss at the bank."

"Gran." I took a quick sip of tea and burned my tongue. "That still doesn't explain the alcohol in his blood or the pills."

It hurt me to point out the impossibility of my

father's innocence. Prior to his arrest, I had been a daddy's girl, convinced he could do no wrong. When he was first accused, I didn't know what to think. But once reality smacked me in the face and I realized how he had betrayed everyone who loved him, I had turned my back on him. The pain of what he had done and the consequences of his actions had been too much to bear.

"There must have been a mix-up at the lab. Kern probably had a heart attack from all the stress he was under, which is why he lost control of the car." Gran thunked her cup into her saucer. "And anyone could have planted those pills. He never locked his car."

"But—"

"Sweet Jesus!" Gran interrupted me. "He was tried and convicted in less than six months. Who knew that small counties like ours had such speedy trials?" She wiped a tear from her cheek. "We should have hired a PI back then, but your grandfather had just passed away the year before and I was having a hard time with decisions. I'm not making the same mistake twice. We're hiring one for you first thing tomorrow."

"We just don't have the money," I explained as gently as I could. "Everything I have is invested in the store."

She frowned. "You never said you were having trouble meeting expenses."

"That's because I'm not." Trying to lighten the mood, I deadpanned, "It isn't hard to meet expenses when they're everywhere."

Gran ignored my feeble attempt at humor. "I'll sell the house and the rest of the land if I have to." She swallowed hard and blinked away tears. "I can't lose you, too."

"You will not sell your home." I got up and hugged her. "I promise I'll be fine. Boone and Poppy are going to help me. We'll find a better suspect for Detective Woods and he'll have to leave me alone."

Gran didn't look convinced. Then again, neither was I.

# CHAPTER 4

It had been an awful night, and so far the morning wasn't shaping up to be much better. I had slept through my alarm, spilled coffee down the front of my last clean Devereaux's Dime Store sweatshirt, and slipped on the ice running to my car. If it hadn't been for the fact that I couldn't afford to lose the income, I would have played hooky and gone back to bed. That was the problem with being the boss—no sick days.

Regardless of how bad a mood I might be in, the minute I walked into my shop, its old-fashioned charm immediately enveloped my senses and made me smile. I had always loved this store. When I was a kid, my mom brought me to the soda fountain for peppermint stick ice cream after getting a shot at the doctor's, Dad took me to the candy counter every Sunday for Bonomo Turkish Taffy, and Gran let me tag along whenever she went to buy a bottle of Evening in Paris—her favorite perfume.

Which is why when I heard that the Thornbee sisters, age ninety-one, were selling the five-and-dime, I immediately put in an offer. The twins' grandfather had built the shop when Shadow Bend was no more than a stagecoach stop, and the thought of the business being turned into a Rite Aid or a CVS had galvanized me into action.

While I stood thinking about the store, Hannah Freeman arrived. A senior at the local high school, Hannah worked for me three mornings a week as part of her vocational ed program. Once she and I turned on all the lights, the place began to fill with the first customers of the day.

Their excited voices created a cheerful hubbub that wasn't muted by any newfangled acoustical tile or cork matting. Instead, the sound of people socializing with their neighbors echoed off the old tin ceiling and hardwood floors. Although I had doubled the interior space, installed Wi-Fi, and added the basket business, I had tried to keep the character of the original variety store intact.

Tuesdays, the Quilting Queens and the Scrapbooking Scalawags met here. I gladly provided them with worktables—square footage was cheap in Shadow Bend—and gratefully reaped the benefit of their purchases. Not only did they buy the materials for their projects from me, but they also bought refreshments and any other odds and ends that caught their eye.

I greeted the members of both groups, then walked through the aisles checking that the wooden shelves were fully stocked and that the other customers had everything they needed. After making the rounds, I took over behind the old brass cash register, allowing Hannah to handle the soda fountain and candy case.

It both surprised and delighted me that no one mentioned Joelle's murder or my visit from the Kansas City detective. Chief Kincaid had assured me that Woods and his partner had talked only to Gran, the country clubbers, and me, and if that was truly the case, there was a chance—albeit a slim one—that I could keep my involvement quiet.

After all, Joelle wasn't a native, and she had spent much of her time with the new people, those who had moved to our little community from the city and kept their distance from the locals. So, possibly, since Joelle *was* an outsider, and the born-and-bred Shadow Benders didn't mix much with the commuters, my involvement could fly under the town's radar.

As I offered up a prayer that I would avoid becoming grist for the rumor mill, I could only hope that the fact I hadn't attended church in twelve years didn't mean God had stopped listening to me.

What with the brisk morning business and the lack of gossip, I was feeling a lot better by the time Hannah left to attend her afternoon classes. The hours after lunch and before school let out were usually slow. A lot of days I didn't see a single shopper from one to three. Which was fine with me, because that was when I generally worked on my basket orders. But today, before I got started on Sister Mary Catherine's Silver Jubilee Extravaganza, I decided to treat myself.

The evidence of my fluffy figure to the contrary, I usually stuck to a sensible diet—or at least tried to—but the past twenty-four hours had been hell and I needed the comfort of something decadent. Furthermore, I knew exactly what I wanted—a double-thick dark chocolate milk shake with extra whipped cream and two cherries on top.

Anticipating the first sweet swallow, I searched for a straw. Where had Hannah hidden them? The teenager was a good worker, but her idea of logical storage and mine didn't always mesh. Finally I gave up, grabbed the glass, and took a huge gulp.

As I was relishing the taste of the rich chocolate

and the smooth sensation of the silky ice cream sliding down my throat, the sleigh bells above the entrance jingled and an incredibly gorgeous man strode in. He was at least six-four, with the type of powerful, well-muscled body produced by hard work rather than hours in a gym.

A shiver ran down my spine, and a flash of heat swept through my body. His arresting good looks totally captured my attention. Where had this guy been hiding all my life? Not in Shadow Bend, that was for sure.

He stopped just inside the door and did a swift recon of the store. Spotting me behind the soda fountain, he took in the huge milk shake I still held and his sapphire blue eyes twinkled. His lips twitched when his gaze reached the whipped-cream mustache above my mouth.

*Great!* A hot man finally crosses my path and I look like a greedy six-year-old. I hastily put down the glass, grabbed a napkin, and wiped away the evidence of my immaturity, wishing for the first time in ages that I had bothered to put on makeup, done my hair, and worn something other than an oversized sweatshirt and jeans.

As he moved toward me, I noticed that his face was lean and chiseled and that his bronzed skin pulled taut over the elegant ridge of his cheekbones. The strong column of his throat rose from the collar of his shearling jacket, and faded Levi's molded the muscles of his thighs.

He was the kind of man who would look good wearing anything or, even better, nothing at all. It was a testament to my sadly lacking love life that I was thinking entirely inappropriate thoughts about a perfect stranger the day after I'd been accused of murder.

Not wanting to consider what that said about my character, I made an effort to regain my poise and asked, "May I help you?"

"Are you Devereaux Sinclair?"

"I am." I sincerely hoped this would not turn into a déjà vu of yesterday. "And you are . . . ?"

He held out a large, calloused hand. "Jake Del Vecchio. Tony is my granduncle."

The Del Vecchios had arrived in Shadow Bend around the same time the Sinclairs had. Our properties shared a border, and Tony had purchased all the land we had sold off. Although Tony ran one of the largest and most successful cattle ranches in the state, he was getting up there in years. I'd heard that a relative had come to help him out, but I hadn't come across the guy until now.

"Nice to meet you." I leaned forward to shake Jake's hand. The touch of his palm against mine sent another shiver through me, and my pulse began to pound. I had to suck in a much-needed breath before I could ask, "How's your uncle?"

"Uh." He swallowed hard. "Fine."

We stared at each other, and for a nanosecond,

I could actually see the sexual awareness zinging between us. Then a shutter seemed to come down over his eyes, he released my hand, and whatever had been there was gone.

"I haven't seen Tony in quite a while." Tony might be our nearest neighbor, but he had never socialized with us. I had frequently wondered why. "He doesn't seem to leave the ranch very often."

"Yeah." Jake's tone indicated he was back in control. "He's always been like that, even before Aunt Sabina passed away a few years ago. A lot of times when I came to stay with them, we'd only go into town once or twice the whole summer."

"Did we ever meet?" I asked, sure that I would have remembered him but thinking it would have been odd if we hadn't.

"A few times, when Aunt Sabina took me with her to the grocery store." Jake grinned. "Guess I didn't make much of an impression."

"Sorry about that." I shrugged. "You know how it is in a small town. The cliques are formed in preschool, and it's hard for new kids to join in, especially if they're stuck out in the country."

"I never considered myself stuck. I loved working the ranch with Uncle Tony and being fussed over by Aunt Sabina, but I know what you mean."

We smiled at each other in mutual understanding until I asked, "Is there something I can do for you?"

"I hear you might be in some hot water." Jake raised a questioning brow. "Tony asked me to try and help you."

"Help me?" Tony wasn't exactly a regular on the grapevine. How could he have heard about my problem so fast? "With what?" I crossed my fingers, hoping that this was about something other than me being a suspect in Joelle's death.

"Your situation." Jake took a seat on the middle stool across the counter from me and unbuttoned his coat. "Tony said you're the prime suspect in the murder of a local woman."

My heart sank. If that cat was out of the bag, it would claw my reputation to shreds by dark.

"I take it you're not guilty?" His tone was quizzical.

"Of course not," I responded automatically, then got back to what I considered the most important question. "Who told Tony that I was under investigation?"

"It's a long story." Jake took off his Stetson and ran his fingers through his coal black hair, making me itch to do the same.

He was the type who made even shy women want to get naked with him—and I had never been accused of being shy. I was completely ambushed by the intense attraction I felt for this guy. No one else had ever made my knees go weak or produced such a kaleidoscope of sensual images flashing through my mind.

*Oops!* I must have been silent too long, because now he was looking at me strangely, and I quickly said, "Go on." What had we been talking about? Oh, yeah, me being a killer. *Duh.* I couldn't believe that a guy, even one as attractive as Jake, was distracting me from the fact that a revenge-crazed cop was trying to send me to prison for something I didn't do.

"Your grandmother called Tony and told him all about that KC detective who was nosing around yesterday."

"Fu— I mean, shoot!" I came out from behind the counter and took the stool next to him. "Why would she do that?" As far as I knew, Gran and Tony had a neighborly but not close relationship. She'd never asked him for help before, so why had she turned to him now?

"You don't know?"

"Know what?" I absentmindedly ate one of the cherries from my shake.

"Well." Jake snagged the second cherry and popped it into his mouth. I watched as he chewed and swallowed. "After Tony took your grandmother's call, he told me that he and Birdie were an item back in the day, which is why he wanted me to help you."

"You're kidding me. What happened between them?" *Please, please, please don't let Tony Del*

*Vecchio be my real grandfather,* I begged silently. I so didn't want to be related to Jake.

"According to Tony, he and your grandmother dated when they were teenagers, but since he's a couple years older than Birdie and she wouldn't marry him until she graduated, after he finished high school he enlisted in the Marines."

"What happened?"

"Near the end of the Korean War, Tony was reported MIA and Birdie married someone else."

"Oh." That explained why Tony and Birdie had kept their distance all these years.

"Yep." Jake's tone was neutral, but I could see the disapproval in his expression.

"What? You think she should have waited for him even though there was no way to know if he was alive?" I didn't think either of us should judge Gran without knowing all the facts.

"She got married three months after hearing that Tony was missing in action." Jake shrugged. "Seems like she could have hung in there a little longer than that."

"Well, since Gran felt she could confide in Tony about my problem, and he asked you to help me, I guess he doesn't hold a grudge," I pointed out. "Maybe you should follow his example."

"I doubt anyone really gets over being betrayed." His glare burned through me.

"Nevertheless, we don't know the whole story, so there's no use discussing it."

Jake seemed a lot angrier than the situation warranted, and I was trying to figure out why when suddenly his heated expression cleared and he said, "You're right."

"I am?" I gave myself a mental shake. Why was I acting like a ditzy blonde from a bad chick flick? "I mean, of course I am."

"The last thing I want to do is fight with you." He gave me a lazy smile that had no doubt obliterated the defenses of many otherwise sensible women in his past. "Although I bet making up would be fun."

"Oh." That pickup line might have sounded cheesy if another guy had said it, but from Jake, it made my mouth go dry. Forcing myself to focus, I said, "Okay, now I know how Tony found out, but what makes him think you can help me?"

I was gearing up to be angry with Gran and Tony for assuming I needed a man to save me, but for the first time since entering my store, Jake's air of utter confidence faltered. He got up, moving stiffly, and I noticed the taut, controlled lines of his face that indicated that he was in some kind of pain.

Before I could ask him about it, he said, "I'm a deputy U.S. Marshal."

"Are you taking a leave to help your uncle on the ranch?" Okay. That explained why Birdie had asked for Tony's help now but hadn't when my father was arrested. Considering that Jake would only have been in his late teens, he wouldn't have been a Marshal back then.

"No. Eighteen months ago my leg was injured in the line of duty. Now that I've finished all the surgeries and physical therapy, I'm on leave until the docs decide whether I'm fit for service."

"I'm so sorry to hear that." The idea of Jake being wounded made me cringe. "How did you get hurt?"

"I'd rather not talk about it." He paced between the soda fountain and the candy case, stopping directly in front of me. "Let's just say it was my own stupid fault."

"Okay." I didn't press him. Whatever had happened must have been traumatic both physically and emotionally.

"One other thing before you accept my help." He eased back onto the stool next to me. "Being around me might be dangerous."

"Why?" Was he talking about the chemistry zipping between us like an exposed electrical wire?

"A bad guy I helped convict was recently paroled and might be coming after me."

"Then what are you doing in Shadow Bend?" The thought of him being hurt or killed tore at my insides. "Shouldn't you be in witness protection or something?"

"Marshals don't go into witness protection;

they provide witness protection." He grinned. "Besides, the scumbag is too stupid to figure out how to find me. He's probably already in Mexico."

"Then he isn't exactly a Moriarty clone?" I tested Jake's knowledge of the greatest criminal mastermind ever.

"No, but I'm a pretty decent Sherlock Holmes, so how about I poke around and see if I can't find out who killed your ex-boyfriend's fiancée?"

"Noah isn't really my ex-boyfriend." I truly wished Gran hadn't included that part in her report to Jake's uncle. "We dated in high school for a little while—that's all." I hoped Gran hadn't told Tony the whole sordid tale.

"Sure." Jake's expression was hard to read. "I understand he dumped you when your father went to prison."

"You know small towns—" I tried for a little damage control. "It's not what really happened that counts. It's what makes the best story."

"Right." Jake drummed his fingers on the counter.

I stared at his left hand, ridiculously pleased to see that there was no wedding ring. Not that the absence of a piece of jewelry proved he was single, but at least there was still the possibility he was unattached.

"So, how about letting me investigate?" he asked.

My first inclination was to turn him down. I

wasn't used to people wanting to help me, and it felt weird putting my trust in a stranger—even if he was better-looking than most of today's movie stars. Then again, I wasn't in a position to refuse any assistance. If I was sent to jail, Gran would have no one.

"Okay. Here's what my friends and I have come up with so far." I filled him in on the information Boone and Poppy had given me, finishing with, "I've been thinking. It seems to me Poppy can probably get the most out of the mayor since he's a letch and she's gorgeous. My other friend is good with mothers, so he should chat up Mrs. Underwood. That leaves Joelle's friend Anya Hamilton, and I'm betting she would be putty in your hands."

"Are you saying you think I'm attractive?"

I blushed and quickly retorted, "You're a male with all your own teeth and hair. I understand that's enough for the Country Club Cougars."

"Ouch." He touched his chest. "That hurts."

"I doubt a big bad U.S. Marshal like you can be wounded by mere words."

"That all depends on who says them." He seemed to be looking inward for a moment, then straightened and got back to business. "This afternoon I'll do some digging into both the victim's and the suspects' backgrounds and speak to this Anya woman. Any idea where I can find her?"

"Let me make a call." I found myself studying his profile as I spoke to Poppy. Once I assured her that I'd fill her in later, she told me that Anya would most likely be at the country club, since her group played Bunco there every Tuesday afternoon from two until four.

After I described Anya and shared her probable location with Jake, he wrinkled his brow and asked, "What on God's green earth is Bunco?"

I explained about the dice game.

"Okay." He twitched his shoulders. "I'll aim for the end of their party so I can talk to her alone."

"Great." His massive self-confidence made me feel almost optimistic. "And I'll give my friends their assignments."

"Good." He put on his hat and stood. "I'll call you tonight with anything I find out."

I got up, too. "Excellent." We both started toward the door.

We were passing a wire rack of paperback novels when he said, "You and I should talk to Dr. Underwood together."

His words made me feel as if someone had slammed me into a concrete barrier. I hadn't spoken to Noah in years. In fact, I had spent an embarrassing amount of energy avoiding him. The thought of now confronting him made me stumble over my own feet, and I grasped the book rack for support. At the same time that Jake tried to steady me, the shelves spun me around and

71

crashed me into his chest. He automatically put both arms around my waist, pulling me closer.

*Great!* I had always made fun of the heroines in Poppy's romance novels for conveniently "falling" into the hero's arms, and I had just done the same thing.

But when our hips locked together like Lego blocks, I forgot all about what a cliché the whole scene was, and groaned. It had been ages since I'd had anything pressed against that part of me except me, and it felt darn good.

"Are you all right?" His voice washed over me like molten sin.

My breath snagged in my throat, and all I could do was nod.

"Good." His whisper was ragged.

I could feel his lips not quite touching my ear and his uneven heartbeats against my chest. The slight citrus scent of his aftershave was intoxicating. There was an undeniable attraction between us, and while I knew I should step back out of his embrace, I couldn't make myself move.

What had gotten into me? I didn't know this man from Adam, and at the rate we were going we would end up having sex right here, right now—the unlocked door and OPEN sign in the window an invitation for anyone to walk in and catch us in the act.

What was I getting myself into? More to the point, did I care?

# CHAPTER 5

I wasn't sure if I was grateful or disappointed that Boone chose that exact moment to arrive. Either way it stopped me from seeing just how spick-and-span my cleaning service kept the store's hardwood floor.

Boone's cheerful tenor preceded him over the threshold. "Dev, I just had a perfectly marvelous idea and couldn't wait another minute to tell you. Why aren't you answering your cell ph—?" His words stuttered to a standstill as his gaze fastened on Jake.

At the first sound of the sleigh bells, Jake had released me and taken a discreet step away. Now he touched the rim of his Stetson and said, "I'll call you tonight."

As Jake sauntered out the door, Boone demanded, "Who was that?" Without waiting for my answer, he leered. "It sure didn't take you long to find some arm candy to convince that cop you aren't still hung up on Dr. Dud."

*Uh-oh!* Boone was staring at me, a smirk on his handsome face. When I'd accepted Jake's offer to help, it hadn't dawned on me that my friends would tap him to play the part of my Romeo in their scheme.

*Crap!* I knew if I didn't say something to stop

him, Boone would be booking Jake and me a hotel room and posting about us on Facebook. My mind raced, searching for something that would distract him, but I couldn't get my brain out of neutral, so no great idea came to me.

"Dev?" Boone poked me in the shoulder. "What's wrong with you?"

"Nothing." My voice came out funny, sort of strained and scratchy. "I'm fine."

"So, enlighten me about the cowboy cutie that just exited stage right." Boone waited expectantly.

I cleared my throat. "That was Jake Del Vecchio, Tony Del Vecchio's grandnephew. He's working on his uncle's ranch while on leave from his job as a U.S. Marshal."

"I heard a relative was staying with Tony." Boone unbuttoned his camel hair topcoat. "But since the old guy doesn't socialize, no one had any details."

"Jake's going to help us find out who killed Joelle." Hoping to distract Boone from Jake, I continued. "But we can talk about that later. What's your great idea?"

"Dev, Dev, Dev, Dev, Dev." Boone gave an elegant snort. "How long have we known each other? Oh, yeah. Since our paste-eating days in kindergarten. Do you really think you can drop a bombshell like that and then change the subject?" He shook his head. "Seriously, girl?"

"It was worth a try." I led Boone over to the

soda fountain. "Do you want coffee or something?" My milk shake had long since melted into an unappetizing sludge. Jake's appearance had switched off one appetite; too bad it had turned on another one.

"No." Boone perched on a stool. "What I want is for you tell me everything."

"Fair enough." I sat next to him. "It turns out that Gran and Tony had a thing when they were teenagers, so she called him for help with my problem." I held up my hand to stop Boone from interrupting. "They dated, but he ended up joining the Marines, went MIA in Korea, and she married my grandfather instead."

"Funny I never heard anything about that before." Boone pursed his lips. "You'd think someone around here would have mentioned it."

"Why? I don't think it was any big secret, just ancient history." I got up and emptied the contents of the milk shake glass in the sink. "I know people like to gossip about high school sweethearts, and keep an eagle eye out for rekindled romances, but even Shadow Benders draw the line at relationships that happened sixty years ago."

"Too bad your teenage romance was a lot more recent, because just this morning one of my clients mentioned how nice it would be if you and the good doctor got back together, especially now that Joelle is dead." Boone's smile was snarky. "Seems that during her last visit to Dr. Dreadful, he mentioned how glad he was you bought the dime store."

"I know you can't reveal your client's name, but I hope you told her that I haven't had any feelings for Noah Underwood in over a decade." I was an excellent liar. Another skill I had picked up during my years in the investment business. "Now, can we get back to what we're going to do to keep me out of prison?"

"Sure. Let's go back to Jake."

"Why?" *Shoot!* In my hurry to change the subject from Noah, I had forgotten we'd been discussing Jake. "I already told you Gran called Tony this morning all upset about Detective Woods accusing me of murder, and Tony offered Jake's help."

"As a Marshal?" Boone's expression was playful. "Or as your lover?"

"Don't even go there." I concentrated on drying the glass I had just washed, but made just enough eye contact to show him I meant business. "Nothing like that is going to happen." Sure, Jake and I had chemistry, but now that I was aware of his effect on my libido, I'd be able to keep myself under control. At least that was the plan.

"So what's he doing that requires him to call you tonight?" Boone said, watching me over tented fingers.

I wiped down the marble counter. "Having a chat with Anya Hamilton this afternoon."

"Well, I hope he has your cell number." Boone's voice held a hint of satisfaction and he smiled widely. "Because you won't be home tonight."

"Why not?" I didn't like his tone or his grin. "Where will I be?"

"With me." Boone was nearly quivering with excitement. "We're going to a fund-raiser tonight. One put on by the CDM to save the Lee Mansion."

"Why would I want to do that?" CDM stood for the Confederacy Daughters of Missouri, and the Lee Mansion, which was supposed to have been owned by a distant relation of Robert E. Lee, was their latest cause.

"Because Dr. Dishonorable's mommy is the president of the CDM."

"Tell me something I don't know." I made a scornful noise in the back of my throat. "Nadine's been president since gravel was a rock."

"Yes, she has." Boone's tone was impatient. "Which is why it's the perfect way to guarantee that we nonchalantly run into her. Once we have her cornered, we can question her about Joelle's death."

"You're right about it being best to make it seem like a casual meeting, but I think you should go alone and talk to her." The last thing I wanted to do was spend an evening at an event with Nadine Underwood. No—correction. The absolutely last thing I wanted to do was go with Jake to talk to her son, Noah. "She hates me, so she'll be more willing to chat with you if you're by yourself."

"Of course, I thought of that." Boone rolled his eyes at my obtuseness. "The reason you need to come with me is so we can play good cop, bad cop."

"And I'm the bad cop, right?"

"Duh."

I opened my mouth to argue, but closed it without speaking. Trying to resist Boone once he had made up his mind was both exhausting and futile. Instead I asked, "What time are you picking me up?"

"Quarter to seven. And wear an expensive dress."

After Boone left I called Poppy back and gave her the lowdown on the newest member of our Scooby Doo detective team. Now all we needed was a Great Dane, and we'd have the whole cast of characters.

# CHAPTER 6

Jake walked the three blocks to where he had parked his truck, replaying what had just happened. His uncle hadn't mentioned how pretty Birdie's granddaughter was or the strange mix of strength and vulnerability she possessed. Devereaux Sinclair wasn't what he had expected, and he hated being caught by surprise.

He winced as he climbed into the pickup's cab. His leg seemed to bother him more when the weather turned cold and windy. The physical therapist had said he'd always have a certain degree of soreness, but it was impossible to tell at this stage of his healing whether the pain would be a twinge once in a while or so debilitating that he'd never be able to pass the U.S. Marshal reinstatement physical.

Ignoring his discomfort, and his uncertain future, Jake put the truck in gear and headed toward Brewfully Yours. The local coffee café had Wi-Fi, and he needed to get online. His uncle Tony's ancient computer was connected via dialup, and downloading information from that antique took longer than Jake's patience could handle.

It was only a little past two o'clock, so he had a couple of hours before he needed to head out to the country club, and he intended to use the time reaching out to a few of his colleagues about Joelle Ayers. He also planned to do some research of his own on Miss Devereaux Sinclair.

Tony had filled him in on her previous employer's trouble with the law, but Jake wanted to make damn sure she was as innocent of any wrongdoing as his uncle thought she was. All he needed was to hook up with another con artist. The last one had left him bleeding on the side of the road, and he hadn't even felt any attraction for her. He'd just been trying to do the right thing.

As he passed the dime store, Jake glanced in the big plate-glass window and saw Devereaux talking to the fellow who had burst in on them. Was he her boyfriend? She was avoiding eye contact with him, staring over the guy's shoulder while she twisted the end of her ponytail. Something about the conversation was making her uncomfortable. Was the guy questioning her about him?

Jake felt an unwelcome surge of desire as he scrutinized her. His instincts told him that she was trouble, but his body didn't care. Even dressed in old jeans and a baggy sweatshirt, she couldn't hide her curves. The aloof expression on her face seemed at odds with her body's softness. Softness a man could sink into and lose himself in.

His attraction to her annoyed him. He shook his head. What was he thinking? One thing he'd learned early in his career in law enforcement was to maintain his distance from the good-looking females involved in a case. Too many foolish women imagined they were in love with the image of a U.S. Marshal, but once they were faced with the reality, they ran the other way. And if they didn't, they wanted something from him—usually something illegal.

Still, as he entered the café, the memory of Devereaux's sea green eyes interfered with his breathing, and for a crazy moment he wanted to get in his truck, drive back to her store, and see if her eyes really were that color.

A strong cup of coffee and some quality time focusing on his laptop helped take his mind off Devereaux, and the next thing he knew it was three thirty. Grabbing his coat and computer, he hurried to his pickup and headed to the country club. A few miles out of town, he turned between two enormous brick columns and drove past the snow-covered golf course. The clubhouse was an ultramodern design with lots of angles and an impressive entrance consisting of mahogany double doors and overhead windows that appeared to hang unsupported over the steps.

When Jake stepped inside the foyer, an elegantly dressed woman looked up from the reception desk. "May I help you?"

"I'm picking up a friend," he lied smoothly. "She's playing Bunco."

"Last door on your left." The woman dimpled up at him. "If she's not ready to go yet, feel free to come back and keep me company."

"Thanks." He touched the brim of his Stetson and followed her directions.

Stopping just outside the party room, Jake peered through the half-open door. He was in luck. The game must have just ended because the women were gathering their purses and coats and exchanging air kisses.

It wasn't hard to spot Anya Hamilton. Devereaux had described her as willowy, with straight sable hair to her waist, hazel eyes, and painstakingly stylish clothes. Jake wasn't sure what color sable was, but the brunette Barbie with crow's-feet had to be her. He was a little surprised to see the laugh lines. Women like Anya Hamilton didn't tolerate wrinkles. He shrugged. Maybe she'd been snowed in on the day of her last Botox appointment.

Anya and another dark-haired woman were among the last to exit. As the others passed them, a petite blonde paused and said, "I know how devastated you must be, darlings. You two and Joelle were like triplets. Call me anytime you need to talk."

Jake took in Anya and her companion, wondering whether to try to speak to them both.

Devereaux hadn't mentioned the other woman, but maybe she wasn't aware of Joelle's additional "sister."

Anya and her friend were bringing up the rear of the group when Jake effortlessly cut them from the herd. He patted the tiny canine poking out of Anya's oversized purse and asked, "What's this little guy's name?"

She giggled. *"Her* name is Bonbon."

"My bad. I guess the pink bow and jacket should have tipped me off." Jake flashed a repentant grin. "Can I buy you two a drink to apologize?"

Anya looked him up and down appreciatively, then said, "I'm available, but Gwen has an appointment. Don't you, darling?"

Gwen narrowed her eyes, but said, "Yes." She excused herself and walked away. Throwing Jake a flirty smile over her shoulder, she added, "Maybe next time."

Jake took Anya's elbow and guided her toward the bar he had passed in his search for the Bunco room. It was empty, and as they entered, the bartender quickly fumbled with the remote, shutting off the TV.

Once they had ordered and were settled in a booth by the window, Jake said, "I overheard your friends mention that someone had died."

"Yes." Anya's expression saddened. "My BFF was murdered last Saturday night."

"Murdered?" Jake forced surprise into his voice. "Around here?"

"In Kansas City."

"Oh." Jake paused as the bartender served their drinks. "Was she mugged?"

"No." Anya touched a manicured hand to the back of her hair.

Jake noted Anya's gesture and recognized it was calculated to make him think she was uncomfortable with what she was about to say, when in fact her eyes glowed with titillation.

"It was a sex crime."

"Really?"

"Yes." Anya's voice held a note of excitement. "My friends and I think the killer was her fiancé's ex-girlfriend. Everyone says she was horribly jealous when Joelle and Noah got engaged."

"Interesting." Jake took a swig of beer to hide his annoyance that Anya and her crowd were already lining Devereaux up to take the rap for Joelle's murder. "Did the guy break up with his ex in order to date your friend? I mean, being dumped would definitely give that woman a possible motive to kill her."

"Well . . ." Anya sipped her apple martini. "Not exactly. But still."

Jake made a noncommittal sound implying agreement, then asked, "So you and Joelle were best friends?" He put his bottle of Corona on a coaster. "Did you go to school together?"

"No." Anya wrinkled her nose. "Joelle only moved here last summer, but the minute we met, we just clicked and became immediate besties."

"Did you have a lot in common?" Jake took her hand. "Was she as beautiful as you are?"

"Well, I've been told I'm prettier." Anya's tongue traced her lips. "But we did like the same things—Chihuahuas, the same fashion designers, the same kinds of cars, and—"

"The same men?" Jake interrupted.

"The same type."

"What type is that?"

"It depends." Anya petted Jake's arm with her free hand. "For fun, the ones that look like you."

"And otherwise?"

"The ones like him." Anya nodded toward a man who had just taken a seat at the bar. The guy resembled an expensively dressed koala bear, with twin tufts of hair on either side of his head, a wispy white beard that ran from ear to ear, and a paunch the size of a watermelon.

"Isn't he a little short for you?"

"Not when you stand him on his money."

"Ah." Jake chuckled, not at all shocked by what Anya and Joelle felt was important in selecting a husband. "Which type was Joelle's fiancé?"

"Noah is a rare guy." Anya licked her lips again. "He's hot *and* rich."

"So then you and Joelle were both interested in

this Noah character?" Jake flashed her a mock scowl, released her hand, and grabbed his beer. "Should I be jealous?"

"Well"—Anya fluttered her lashes—"that depends. What do you do for a living?"

"Right now I'm working on a cattle ranch." Jake winked. "After that, who knows?"

"Yeah." Anya sighed. "That's what I thought. Hunky guys are almost always underemployed."

"Except for Noah?"

She nodded. "He's a doctor."

"I guess that means I don't have a chance." Jake gave her a mock scowl. "Since you'd probably like to be Mrs. Doctor Noah?"

"Maybe. Successful men in this town are at a premium, so now that Joelle is gone . . ." She trailed off, then seemed to catch herself, and her tone became defensive. "But never when she was alive. That wouldn't be nice or honest."

"And I'm sure you're always nice." Jake grinned, then asked, "How about Joelle? Was she always nice and honest?"

"As if." Anya adjusted the diamond tennis bracelet on her wrist. "You didn't want to cross her. And she was real secretive."

"In what way?"

"For one thing, she never wanted anyone in her condo, while the rest of us girls always showed each other our inner souls."

"Inner souls?"

"Our closets." Anya gave a high-pitched laugh and whapped Jake on the biceps with the back of her hand. "Silly boy. Did you think we belonged to a cult?"

Jake forced a chuckle. "So you were never inside Joelle's place?"

"She never invited me or Gwen—Gwen is my other best friend, the one who didn't have time to join us."

"I see." Jake noticed that Anya had avoided a direct answer, but he didn't press her. Instead he asked, "Can you think of anyone who would want to kill Joelle, besides her fiancé's ex? Does someone gain a lot of money from her death, or did anyone hold her responsible for something bad that happened to them?"

"Hey." Anya narrowed her eyes. "Why are you asking me all these questions about Joelle and the murder?"

"No reason." Jake twitched his shoulders. "What would you like to talk about, darlin'?"

"Hooking up later on?"

"I'm sure that could be arranged." Jake stalled, considering whether it would be worthwhile to romance Anya any further. She was clearly growing suspicious or bored or both with the topic of Joelle, and he had only one more question, so he asked bluntly, "Where were you Saturday night?"

"It was Valentine's Day weekend, wasn't it?"

Anya's tone was playful, but her expression was hard to read. "Where do you think I was?"

Jake shrugged.

"With a man, of course." Anya reached in her purse and reapplied her lip gloss. "That's where I am every Saturday night. You could have been the lucky guy this Saturday night, but I have a feeling that's not what you were looking for after all."

# CHAPTER 7

Sweet Jesus!" Gran stared at me with equal measures of incredulity and concern. "You're going to a CDM party?"

"Yes." I continued to flick hangers back and forth in my closet. "Boone and I are going to gang up on Nadine Underwood and force her to tell us everything she knows about Joelle Ayers."

"But you swore you'd never have anything to do with that, that . . . uh . . ."

"Crowd?"

Gran nodded, smoothing her psychedelic print culottes. Her fashion sense was eclectic—one day she might dress like Jackie Kennedy, the next like a hippie love child. "So why are you going?"

"I was sixteen and the board had just told me I couldn't attend the Initiate Ball because they didn't want a murderer's daughter as a member."

Besides pressuring her son to break up with me, Nadine had made sure that I was ostracized by all the social groups of which I would have normally been a part.

"You were devastated." Gran tilted her head, then quickly straightened it, the gesture that had earned her the name Birdie.

"Yep." It was hard to deny the truth. "But I'm not supporting them in any way, shape, or form. I'm using a free ticket. I'll eat their food, drink their booze, and ruffle Nadine's feathers a little. Sounds like the perfect evening to me."

"In that case, go to it and don't take any prisoners."

"That's the plan."

"So what did you think of Tony's grand-nephew?" Gran's tone was casual, but I detected a matchmaking gleam in her eye.

"He seems competent." I kept my voice indifferent. "His law enforcement contacts should be useful."

"True." She pursed her lips. "What does he look like? I remember thinking he was handsome the few times I saw him in town with Tony when he was a teenager. But that's been a while."

"I didn't really notice." I cringed at my bald-faced lie and waited for the lightning bolt from heaven to strike me dead for fibbing to my grandma.

"Oh." She shot me a disbelieving look before

89

heading back to her TV program. Banshee followed at her heels, releasing a cloud of noxious gas just before he exited my room.

Once she was gone, I hurried into the bathroom, clutching the plain brown paper bag I had brought home with me. Reassuring myself that I wasn't doing this just because Jake had phoned to say he'd drop by when I got home from the CDM party, I opened the cold wax kit.

I admit it had been a long time since I'd shaved. Poppy's shih tzu had less hair on his legs than I did on mine. But, come on, why bother if all you wear is jeans and no one sees you naked?

The instructions recommended rubbing the strips together in your hand to soften them, but being the overachiever I am, I thought using my hair dryer to melt the wax would be a better plan. And it was, if you think applying 2,500-degree molten lava to your inner thigh is a good idea.

Okay, that was a bit more painful than I'd expected, but it really worked. My skin was baby smooth. Once I had denuded the rest of my lower extremities, I moved north. Shimmying out of my underwear, I drop-kicked them into the hamper and put my foot on the closed toilet lid.

Selecting an extra long strip, I heated it up, placed it along my bikini line, and continued south. *Hmm.* Was this really necessary? Before I could talk myself out of it, I yanked.

It was a good thing I had Pink blaring from the

iPod speakers so Gran couldn't hear me scream, because everything went red, literally. Although my vision was affected for only a couple of seconds, I was pretty sure my flesh would be crimson until Easter.

Practicing what my yoga teacher had taught me before I couldn't afford to take the class anymore, I managed to breathe through the pain. Then I realized I had to do the other side. Now I remembered why I didn't date.

Since I had stopped working in the city, it usually took me ten minutes, sometimes less, to dress in the morning. Not tonight. I seemed to have forgotten how to put on not only pantyhose but also mascara. Three pair of ruined hose and a couple of eye stabs later, I was good to go. Except for my hair.

It's long, thick, and naturally curly, which sounds good in theory but really means it's hard to style. Keeping an eye on the clock, I wrestled with the flatiron until I heard the doorbell.

"Wow!" Boone's eyes widened when I answered the door. "You clean up nice."

"Gee, thanks."

"You should do it more often."

"Gee, thanks." I tugged at the lace-edged sweetheart neckline of my black silk dress. "Can we just get this over with?"

"What's your hurry?" Boone helped me on with my coat. "Got a hot date afterward?"

"How did you know?" I pushed him out over the threshold, herded him toward his car, and got in. "Brad Pitt is coming over at midnight. He's dumping Angelina for me."

"That's quite an imagination you have there." Boone snickered, then turned the big Mercedes around and headed down the lane toward the main road.

The Lee estate was on the other side of town from my family's property. While Boone drove, he and I discussed what was new in town. Along with the St. Onges and the Underwoods, the Sinclairs had been among the five founding families of Shadow Bend. Although I was a little ambivalent about some of its citizens, I loved all the parts of my town. From Marie's Unique Boutique to the Clementine auction house, and from the John Deere dealership to the pawnshop, it was my home. But I had to admit I was excited to hear that a Chinese restaurant had opened. Until now, the only culinary adventure available to us had been the pulled-pork wagon parked out at the Votta greenhouse.

When we arrived at our destination, we found the outside of the mansion lit up like a movie set. And although the place clearly needed a lot of renovation, the sweeping steps, white columns, and wide porch made an impressive sight. A valet helped me out of the car and handed me over to Boone. I wondered if both men really thought I was incapable of exiting a vehicle and walking into a building without assistance.

As we entered the grand foyer, we found the head honchettes of the CDM arranged at the foot of the curving staircase greeting their guests. After we surrendered our coats to the maid standing near the entrance, Boone steered me away from the receiving line and into the huge ballroom.

"I thought we wanted to talk to Nadine." I tried to turn back, but his hand gripped my arm. "She was right there. Didn't you see her?"

"Patience, darling." Boone smiled at the white-gloved waiter offering us a selection of drinks. "Enjoy the hospitality."

I looked around at the expensive liquor being poured and the costly hors d'oeuvres being passed, and felt slightly nauseated. Considering that most of the citizens of Shadow Bend were struggling to survive the dip in the economy, this overindulgence seemed obscene. Not to mention a bit hypocritical.

Motioning to the excess, I hissed in Boone's ear, "Isn't the purpose of the evening supposed to be to raise money, not spend it?"

Without moving his lips, he said, "You have to take events like this with a grain of salt." Nodding and smiling at the crowd, he added, "And I've found adding a slice of lime and shot of tequila helps as well."

In my previous life, when I had routinely

93

attended similar fund-raisers, I often wondered why the committee didn't just give the charity the cash they spent on the elaborate parties instead of soliciting donations. My only guess was if they did that, they wouldn't be able to display their generosity in such a public manner.

"When are we going to talk to Nadine?" I tugged on Boone's jacket sleeve. "I just want to get this over with and leave."

"We need to catch her alone." Boone selected a martini from the server's silver tray.

"Oh." I took a cosmopolitan, allowing the man finally to move on. "Any idea how we do that?"

"Mingle." Boone headed toward a cluster of thirtysomething professionals I recognized from around town. "And once everyone arrives, keep an eye out for Nadine."

"That should be pretty easy." I followed after him. "You know milady will make a grand entrance into the ballroom once she's through with the receiving line."

As we traveled from group to group, I was surprised that Joelle's murder was not a more prominent topic of conversation. After all, she'd been engaged to the son of the CDM's president. Granted, a few people mentioned Noah's absence due to her death, but no one pursued the matter or seemed all that broken up about her demise.

An endless supply of servers wove their way through the crowd with silver trays laden with exotic goodies, and I had just stuffed a caviar blini into my mouth when Nadine flounced into the room. She wore a stunning gray chiffon gown edged in crystal beading and delicate platinum satin sandals with heels higher than I would have ever dared attempt.

Everyone hushed as she took a microphone and tapped it for attention. "Welcome to the Lee Mansion, a glorious reminder of our past that must be preserved at all costs."

Her gaze swept the assemblage, and Boone moved so that I was out of her sightline. He kept a wary eye on our hostess and dropped his voice. "I'm going to persuade Nadine to accompany me to the parlor for a private chat. Give me five minutes, then burst in."

"Gotcha."

A few moments later she finished her speech and Boone glided up to her. I watched Nadine's lashes flutter and heard her trilling laughter as he kissed her hand. Considering that Boone was my age and she was in her early seventies—she had been over forty when she finally produced an Underwood heir—I found her behavior a bit disconcerting. Then again, no one would look twice if an older man flirted with a woman thirty years his junior, so I tried not to judge her too harshly.

Intercepting a passing waiter, I grabbed another cosmo and used the time Boone had told me to wait to gulp it down. After checking my watch, and with the liquid courage burning through my veins, I marched out of the ballroom and headed toward the parlor.

The antique furniture was in desperate need of refurbishing, but the graceful lines and perfect proportions were a reminder of how spectacular the pieces had been in their heyday. Which, in a way, was also true of Nadine. She had been a beauty, but years of sun worship and bitterness had taken their toll.

Boone and Nadine were seated on a divan placed at a right angle from the open archway. As I hesitated, I saw her clawlike hand pat Boone's knee while the pleats of skin on her face rearranged themselves as she talked.

Taking a deep breath and straightening my spine, I swooped into the room. I hadn't spoken to Nadine since the day she told me I was no longer eligible to become a CDM member. Since we traveled in completely different circles, avoiding her had been easy. Avoiding Noah had been a bit trickier, but it's amazing what you can accomplish if you really set your mind to it.

Nadine's face registered shock when she recognized me, but it took her only a split second to get her expression back under control. "Devereaux, my dear, what a surprise. I don't recall seeing your name on the guest list." Her voice oozed condescension.

"Boone brought me." I casually seated myself

in a rickety Sheraton chair with tattered cross-stitched Victorian floral upholstery, hoping it wouldn't collapse under me. "I wanted to talk to you about Joelle Ayers's murder."

Nadine ignored me and pouted at Boone. "Surely you knew how awkward Devereaux's presence would be for me."

"I'm sorry, my dear." His contrite smile had a steel edge. "But surely you know how difficult it is for me to turn down a damsel in distress."

"Of course." Nadine's voice was thick with disgust. "And Miss Devereaux here is so-o-o-o-o good at manipulating innocent young men."

Seriously? I clenched my jaw, but managed to keep my tone civil. "Just answer a couple of questions and I'll leave quietly."

"And if I don't give in to your demands?" Her eyes flashed in outrage.

"Then I create a scene." I knew she dreaded that above almost anything else—except maybe me, or any other woman, marrying her son. "There are a lot of people out there who would love to tell the story of me accusing you of misusing CDM funds. In fact, I'm pretty sure I saw the society editor from the paper."

"But that's a lie," Nadine yelped.

"And your point is?" I enjoyed how astonished she seemed that someone would fib about her. She did it to others quite frequently.

Nadine looked to Boone. A smile lurked at the

corners of his perfect mouth as he said, "I'd tell her what she wants if I were you."

"Very well." Nadine clenched her teeth. "Since you think it's a good idea, dear boy."

"I've heard you weren't pleased with your son's engagement to Joelle." I quickly began my interrogation before she could change her mind.

"It's no secret I wasn't happy." She shrugged. "But I knew Noah would come to his senses and never go through with the wedding."

"Really?" I raised my right eyebrow, a trick that I had mastered in graduate school and put to good use in my previous career. "How about that faux wedding invitation you passed around at your prayer circle meeting? That sure sounded like you were upset."

"That was just a little joke." Nadine's expression remained serene. "No one took it seriously."

"But you didn't like Joelle." I gave her my most maddening grin. "Did you?"

"I didn't have anything personally against her." Nadine crossed her legs and stretched her arm across the back of the settee. "But she wasn't right for my son. He needs someone who can be a hostess for him. Someone with the right background with whom he can start a family. Someone like you were before your father let greed and stupidity ruin your name. Joelle couldn't even recognize a fish knife."

"So you're saying she was out of her depth at a

formal dinner party." I ignored the dig about my father, wondering instead if Joelle's lack of table-setting knowledge was significant. "That's not exactly unusual in this day and age."

"Joelle Ayers would have been out of her depth in a mud puddle."

I was ambivalent about hearing Nadine tear down Noah's deceased fiancée. Part of me, the part that had never let him go, was glad his mother didn't like Joelle any better than she had liked me. The more compassionate side of me winced at hearing the dead woman being maligned.

Nadine must have taken my silence as a sign of weakness, one she was quick to exploit. Her smile was like an ice pick when she said, "As you know, my dear, Noah tends to make poor choices when selecting his girlfriends. So naturally I was concerned."

"You know, Nadine, dear, if I've learned anything in the past thirteen years, it's that you can't change the length of your legs, the width of your hips, or what your parents did in the past."

"How Zen of you. Of course, you have no choice, considering your background."

"Exactly." I saw her countenance darken when I didn't fall apart at her attack on my lineage, and used her displeasure to my advantage. "But enough about me. Back to Joelle and your relationship with her."

"I don't know why you're so interested in her.

She's dead." Nadine's voice was teeming with triumph. "Joelle is no longer anyone's problem."

"Except for the person who killed her." I shouldn't have been surprised by Nadine's attitude, but I was. "Which brings me to my last question. Where were you Saturday night between six and seven?"

"Are you accusing me of murder?" Nadine's self-control snapped. "I wouldn't dirty my hands on that little piece of white trash."

"White trash?" I glanced at Boone, who seemed as confused as I was. "I had heard that Joelle was part of the country club set."

"Be that as it may." Nadine's eyes glittered with loathing. "No matter how expensive her clothes were, where she lived, or what kind of car she drove, she was nothing but a two-bit tramp."

"Really?" Interesting, but then again maybe not. Nadine had probably said the same thing about me. "What makes you think that?"

"Because unlike my son"—Nadine gave an elegant snort—"I am able to tell the genuine article from the ones who are just pretending."

Not having an answer to that statement, I repeated the most important question. "So, where were you Saturday night between six and seven?"

"I was at an anniversary party, as were our esteemed police chief and his charming wife." Her words rang with confidence, but I could sense the relief coming off her as I walked away.

# CHAPTER 8

Couldn't you have just died at Nadine's expression when you walked in the parlor?" Boone chortled as we drove away from the party.

"That was a moment to treasure, all right." I felt a surge of satisfaction at having bested a longtime nemesis. Even if she had an alibi, Nadine had spilled her guts to us.

"She sure hated Joelle." He curled his upper lip in an imitation of his hero, Elvis Presley. "Not that that was a big shock."

"Nope." I stared out the windshield as we zipped past the old homesteads—their neat barns, railed fences, and snow-covered fields reminding me of a simple, less-complicated time.

Boone was taking the long way back so we could rehash our triumph, but I was worried that Jake might arrive at my house before we did. Just before we'd left the mansion, I had slipped into the bathroom to call him, and I told him I was on my way home. Not that it was a big secret that Jake was coming over; I just didn't want Boone to jump to the wrong conclusion. Or even the right one.

"Nevertheless, it was still good to hear Nadine's take on Joelle."

"Yep." I blew out such a gigantic breath of regret that condensation formed on the inside of the Mercedes' passenger-side window. "But I wish she had been alone that night. I really, really wanted her to be the murderer."

"Nadine could have hired someone," Boone offered, reaching over to pat my knee. "She doesn't seem like the type who's willing to get her own hands dirty."

"Maybe." I leaned my head against the back of the seat. "But the way Joelle was killed seems too personal for that. Too full of hatred."

"True."

"Will you call Poppy when you get home and fill her in?" I knew our friend would be chomping at the bit to hear about our evening.

"Sure." Boone looked at me strangely. "I thought you'd want to talk to her."

"Uh." Shoot. I should have had an excuse ready. "My cell is dead. I forgot to charge it. And if I use the landline, I might wake Gran up. Her bedroom is right off the kitchen."

"I keep telling you to get a new cordless system like mine. It has three bases that you can plug in at any electrical outlet." Boone steered the big sedan into the lane leading to my property. "That antique you have on the wall is from the Stone Age. I can't even imagine living with only one phone."

"And I keep telling you, not only can't I afford

unnecessary extras, but Gran has problems coping with changes."

"Oh. Right." Boone stopped the car in front of the steps. "Sorry."

*Phew!* There was no strange vehicle parked in my drive. Now I just had to get rid of Boone before Jake arrived. "Thanks for giving me the fund-raiser ticket and for the ride and for helping me with Nadine." I quickly hopped out of the car. "I'll talk to you tomorrow. And tell Poppy I'll call her in the morning."

I breathed a sigh of relief when Boone's Mercedes vanished into the shadows, but before I made it into the house, a set of headlights pierced the darkness. Had Boone seen my late-night visitor's arrival?

Even if I hadn't been expecting him, I would have known Jake was the owner of the truck that pulled up next to me. The massive Ford F-250 exuded strength and toughness and determination, traits it was clear that Jake possessed in spades.

The pickup was as shiny as if it had just left the dealership, and since I knew that unlike a lot of men who drove huge trucks, Jake actually used his on a working ranch, I wondered if he had washed it just for me. However, I quickly dismissed that thought as wishful thinking. There might be a physical attraction between us, but polishing his truck would imply more than that. Which was silly, since we'd met less than twelve hours ago.

The passenger door popped open, and Jake leaned out. "Hop in."

"Uh." My heart pounded erratically. Yep. The magnetism was still there. "Why? Uh, I mean, why don't you come into the house?"

"We might disturb your grandmother." He grinned. "If she's anything like Tony, she hits the sack right after the ten o'clock news."

"Good point."

Jake was even more stunningly handsome than I remembered. His thick ebony hair curled over the collar of his denim shirt, giving him an untamed, rebellious appearance that his full, tempting lips reinforced. The close quarters in the pickup's interior were not a good idea if I wanted to maintain control. "But—"

"Come on." His voice held a silky persuasion. "We'll go for a ride."

"Um." I searched for an excuse. "I should check on Gran. She's had a rough time with what's happened."

"We won't be long."

"Well, it is a pretty night." Giving in, I gathered the full skirt of my dress, placed my foot on the lighted step, and used the grab handle just inside the doorframe to hoist myself up. Geesh! It was like scaling a rock wall to get into the damn cab. Which was probably no problem for Jake, who was redwood tall and superhero muscular. But for me at five-six, with no upper-

104

body strength, it was a major undertaking. Maybe I should start lifting weights.

"Need some help?" His sapphire eyes glinted with amusement as I settled myself into the brown saddle-leather passenger seat.

"Not now," I huffed. "But next time maybe you can throw down a ladder."

He chuckled good-naturedly. "So how was the shindig at the Lee Mansion?"

"Decadent, but interesting." The cab was toasty warm and I unbuttoned my leather coat. "Nadine Underwood detested her son's fiancée."

"From what you told me this afternoon, I'm sure her dislike of her future daughter-in-law wasn't a revelation to you."

"No." I studied him as he turned down a gravel road that wound charmingly between stands of snow-laden fir trees. His striking blue eyes were fringed with dense black lashes that any woman would envy, and that I could achieve only with an eyelash curler and several coats of expensive mascara.

"Did you get anything else from her?" Jake stopped the pickup in front of a frozen pond, but didn't turn off the engine.

His blatant waste of fossil fuels and flagrant disregard for our environment shocked me for a moment, until I realized that I had been so brainwashed by everyone in the city preaching about "going green," I had forgotten that those of us who lived in the country were green long before most people ever thought about it. We'd been growing our own food, composting, using windmills for power, hanging clothes out to dry, drinking well water rather than bottled, borrowing from neighbors, and using natural cleaning products for hundreds of years. To my mind, every once in a while we were entitled to keep our motors running.

"Nadine claims she was with the chief of police during the time of the murder."

"Alibis don't always prove someone is innocent," Jake assured me.

"That's what Boone said."

"Boone?"

"Boone St. Onge," I explained. "He's the guy who came into my store just before you left. I forgot that I didn't get a chance to introduce you."

"Are you and St. Onge involved?" Jake's voice was even, but a crease had formed between his eyebrows and his hands were fisted.

"He was the one who took me to the fund-raiser and helped me question Nadine." I considered claiming Boone as my boyfriend in order to combat the ripple of excitement I felt at the realization that Jake was interested in whether or not I was free. But knowing how fast he would find out the truth, I discarded the idea. "He's been one of my best friends since he sliced off my braid in kindergarten."

Jake quirked an eyebrow, so I explained, "We were playing cowboys and Indians. I was the cowboy."

"Ah. That makes sense. I guess you were lucky he didn't go for true authenticity and scalp you." Jake unfastened his seat belt so he could turn toward me. "I'm glad that's all he is."

"Oh." I felt a shiver of awareness, but fought to ignore it. I had to keep my mind on the fact that I was the number one suspect in a murder investigation.

"Do you have someone special in your life?" Jake's tone was casual, but there was something about his expression that made my mouth go dry.

"No." It felt as if I were sucking on a cotton ball, and I had to clear my throat in order to continue. "Not right now."

In truth, although I would never admit it to anyone, I'd only ever had three lovers. None of them had particularly turned me on, which was fine with me. They were calm and sensible, and after the drama and chaos of my teenage years, the last thing I wanted was a tumultuous romance. Or so I had told myself at the time.

Apparently my desire for a tranquil existence had changed, since, without realizing I was going to ask, I heard myself say, "How about you?"

"Nope." He stopped, then abruptly added, "It's tough having a relationship in my line of work, and I'm not the easiest guy to get along with."

"Oh." I was captivated by the silent sadness of his face, and wondered what or who had put it there. "I think that can be said for most of us, especially if you're used to being on your own."

"Maybe." Jake flipped up the console between us, creating a bench seat. "But what I don't understand is how all the guys in Shadow Bend let you get away." He slid over next to me. "Or maybe you're too many horses for them."

I stared straight ahead, not allowing myself to be beguiled by the enthralling scent of what I was coming to think of as eau de Jake—a mixture of lime, saddle soap, and sexy man.

He pushed the button to release my seat belt, then cradled my cheek in his palm.

I tried to breathe normally, but his lips were a fraction of an inch from mine and his gaze searched my face. The feel of his body pressed along the length of mine made me hotter than a flatiron. The warmth of his palm as he slid my coat off my shoulders made me gasp. And when he moved his hand to the neckline of my dress, his fingers trailing over my collarbone, a delicious shudder ran down my spine.

His face was so close to mine, his blue eyes so dark with desire, that I was mesmerized. I was waylaid by an attraction more potent than any I'd ever felt before, and erotic images flashed through my mind.

I tried to tell myself that I didn't want him.

That he wasn't my type. That I needed to concentrate on finding out who killed Joelle so I didn't end up in prison. But a rebellious voice in the back of my mind urged me on.

Before I could gather my resolve, his head dipped and he kissed me, hard. This wasn't a tentative first-date kiss. He took my breath away as he licked into my mouth, making me squirm against him as he pressed me against the warm leather seat. And all the while, he moved against me, his shirt and skin and heat creating a friction that made me quiver. Unable to keep from pulling him closer, I surrendered and scraped my fingernails hard down his back. Suddenly my earlier waxing episode didn't seem quite so foolish.

I knew this was too much, too soon, but he drew me like chocolate-dipped sin. My common sense was beginning to lose the battle it was waging against my lust, and his hand was heading toward the triangle of black silk that covered ground zero when his phone rang. It took us both a long moment to understand what we were hearing, but the repeated strains of "Yellow Rose of Texas" finally penetrated our fog enough for him to lift his head.

With one last kiss he reached into the backseat, grabbed his cell from his jacket pocket, and growled, "Yeah?"

From the phone's speaker, I heard a distinctively feminine voice purr, "Hope I'm not interrupting something hot and heavy, sugar britches. You sound out of breath. You better not be messing around behind my back."

Nothing like being slapped in the face with the competition to douse your desire faster than a cold shower. I slid my arms into my leather coat, buttoned it, and refastened my seat belt. Playtime was over.

"Can it, Meg." Jake frowned, watching me. He narrowed his eyes, then turned his attention back to the cell and asked, "What's up?"

"The trail on Joelle Ayers begins about a year ago in KC when she used a birth certificate belonging to a deceased infant to get a driver's license." Meg rattled some papers, then said, "Prior to that, nada. It seems your vic is a Jane Doe."

"Shit!" Jake tapped his fingers on his knee. "Okay, this is what I want you to do. Tell the local LEOs you got a tip she was involved in a federal crime and request her fingerprints. Maybe she's in the system and we can come up with her real identity that way."

"Won't the detective investigating the case do that for us if we tell him that Joelle Ayers is an alias?"

"He's fixated on a particular suspect, so I don't trust him to be thorough in pursuing other leads."

"Gotcha." Meg paused. "Oh, I also checked out that other name you gave me. Dev—"

"Gotta go." Jake pressed the OFF button as he hastily slid back behind the wheel and shot me a guilty glance.

Between Meg and his checking up on me—not that I really blamed him for the latter—I was finally able to drag my thoughts back to the investigation. Pretending we hadn't just been involved in heavy-duty lip-lock, I commented, "So Joelle wasn't really Joelle. That's got to mean something, don't you think?"

"It's a start." Apparently Jake, too, had decided to ignore our makeout session.

After an awkward silence, I asked, "So, what did you think of Anya Hamilton?"

"Let's just say that if zombies were attacking, she'd be safe."

I snickered. Jake's looks and sense of humor would be hard to resist.

He continued: "Anyway, now that I hear this news, what Anya said makes more sense."

"What did she tell you?"

"Essentially she claimed that Joelle was secretive and never allowed anyone inside her condo."

"Which, if you're hiding your true identity, would be the prudent thing to do." I tapped my chin with my index finger. "I wonder if the cops found anything when they searched her place. They would search it, right?"

"Absolutely."

"Any chance this new information about Joelle

will get Detective Woods off my back?" Maybe I'd misheard what Jake had said to Meg.

"I wouldn't get my hopes up."

"You're probably right." In fact, I knew he was. "Still, a false hope is better than no hope at all."

"Maybe." Jake's gaze was sympathetic. "But we need to stick to our previous plan to find another suspect for Woods."

"I was afraid of that."

# CHAPTER 9

When my clock radio clicked on Wednesday morning, I woke with a smile on my face. It took me a few seconds to figure out why I felt so happy; then I remembered my dream. Jake and I were back in the cab of his truck, but this time his phone hadn't interrupted us.

*Hell!* My fixation on a man I hadn't known for even twenty-four hours was ridiculous. I wiped the grin off my lips and stomped into the bathroom. Having sex with Jake would just complicate my already muddled life. It was time to get hold of myself and concentrate on my impending arrest. Just because I hadn't been this attracted to a guy since high school didn't mean it was okay to forget about everything else— especially when the "everything else" was me ending up in jail.

Gran was folding laundry when I entered the kitchen. I looked around for Banshee and saw him perched on top of the fridge. It was one of his preferred launching pads, so I gave the appliance a wide berth in order to avoid having him leap on my head as I walked by.

My favorite breakfast, puffy French toast with a side of crispy bacon, was waiting in the warming oven, and Gran slid it in front of me as soon as I sat down. She couldn't wait for me to tell her all about the CDM fund-raiser. She loved hearing about the clothes, food, and decorations, but her real interest was in my conversation with Noah's mother.

"Nadine's always been a few cookies short of a dozen, but it sounds as if even the ones she has left are crumbling." Gran gathered up our dirty plates and took them to the sink. "Ignorance of what a fish knife looks like does not qualify someone as an uncouth lowlife."

"Exactly." I put away the butter and syrup. "All it means is that unlike most of the girls who grew up in Shadow Bend, Joelle wasn't forced to go to Miss Ophelia's etiquette classes on excruciatingly correct dinner behavior."

"Hard to believe that parents are still making their children endure such torment," Gran deadpanned.

"Isn't it?" I had hated those lessons.

"And I heard Miss Ophelia required that this

year's young ladies take out all items stuck in their various piercings, other than a single pair of earrings in their ears, and cover up any visible . . . uh . . ."

"Tattoos."

Gran nodded, then handed me a stack of clean clothes and changed the subject. "Who are you talking to next?"

"I'm not sure." It was better if she didn't know that Jake and I planned to interview Noah. She had spent her whole life in a small town where people took family feuds seriously. So despite the fact that Noah had betrayed me more than a decade ago, the mere mention of my high school boyfriend's name usually sent Gran into a paroxysm of cursing that would make a rap singer blush.

"When are you seeing Tony's grandnephew again?" Gran's blasé expression didn't fool me one bit.

"We haven't made any firm plans." Last night, the moment Jake pulled up to my back door, I'd hightailed it out of his truck without giving him a chance to even say good-bye, let alone set up a time to question Noah.

Escaping from the kitchen, I went into my bedroom to get ready for work. Since there was a good chance I'd be seeing both Noah and Jake today, I considered wearing something other than my usual clothes. But I decided that dressing differently for them would be admitting I cared what either man thought of me. I did put on my best, most slimming jeans, and the aquamarine Devereaux's Dime Store sweatshirt that brought out the color of my eyes, but I drew the line at makeup, or changing my hairstyle from its usual ponytail.

As I headed into town, I noticed that the wind had really picked up overnight. It was so strong that the birds were riding their feeders as if they were Tilt-A-Whirls, and sleet blew across the blacktop, making it hard to see where the road ended and the ditch began.

It was a relief to cross into the city limits since there the streets were plowed and salted. The snow-covered village square, with the bandstand at the heart of it, reminded me of everything I loved about Shadow Bend. I had fond memories of playing tag with Boone and Poppy among the eight white cast-iron columns and then, once we had exhausted ourselves, lying on our backs and staring at the summer blue sky through the intricately carved decorative arches that linked the pillars.

I cruised the four blocks, passing the Greek Revival building that housed the bank, the unadorned cinder-block newspaper office, Little's Tea Room in its Queen Anne–style house, and the movie theater with its limestone facade and art deco entrance. Because it was too cold and too early for many folks to be out and about, the sidewalks were deserted, and the area looked like a postcard of an idyllic Midwestern small town.

Shadow Bend had an oddly divided population. On the homegrown side were the farmers, ranchers, and people who worked at one of the three small factories that had managed to ride out both the first recession in the eighties and the more recent economic slump of the past few years.

On the nonindigenous side were the individuals who had moved to the area to raise their families in a more wholesome atmosphere than most city neighborhoods could offer. Although they were willing to face a long, often brutal commute to provide a simpler childhood for their kids, many felt the town should adjust to them rather than vice versa. And that attitude often created problems.

Native Shadow Benders were trying hard to maintain the way of life with which they had grown up. A way of life that meant taking civic responsibility and working hard. A way of life in which it never occurred to people that they were entitled to something just for being born. They wanted their world to remain a safe and orderly place, as it had been for the past hundred years. And they distrusted the change the newcomers brought with them.

Since I had worked in Kansas City for many years but always lived in Shadow Bend, I tried hard to make my store a spot where both factions felt comfortable. Unlike Brewfully Yours, which catered to the commuters, or the feed store, whose sign out front said it all—GUNS, COLD BEER, BAIT—my goal was to offer a neutral zone where the two groups could find some common ground.

And I had been succeeding; Blood, Sweat, and Shears, the sewing club that met on Wednesday evenings at the dime store, had nearly equal numbers of townies and outsiders in its membership. In addition, the kids who hung around after school had accepted my decree that if I saw any evidence of cliques, discrimination, or bullying, everyone would be kicked out, not just the guilty parties.

All of which explained why it was so important for me to protect the respectable reputation that I had been slowly regaining after my previous run-in with the law. I needed to find out who had killed Joelle Ayers, and I needed to find out fast—before Detective Woods pointed all eyes in my direction and ruined everything.

Jake's inquiries had helped by shedding new light on the victim, but as he'd said, it was doubtful that anything he'd discovered would shake Woods's conviction that I was the murderer. Jake's prediction was confirmed when I found the detective waiting for me as I turned down the alley and parked in the small lot behind my store.

Huddled in a puffy dark blue Michelin Man coat, Woods stood by his unmarked Crown Victoria, and as I got out of my car, he silently followed me inside. I stopped in the back room and faced him. Even though the store wasn't yet open for the day, and there weren't any customers present, I wanted to make absolutely sure that this conversation took place in private.

"I had an interesting phone call this morning," Woods said, rocking on his heels. When I didn't respond, his expression soured and he continued. "It was a request from the feds for our victim's fingerprints."

Wow! It was only eight thirty and Jake's girlfriend at the U.S. Marshal's office had already contacted the Kansas City PD. That was impressive.

"Really." I tried hard to sound only mildly interested. "Why would they want that?"

"They wouldn't say." Woods crossed his arms. "Do you want to hear my theory?"

"Knock yourself out." I hoped he knew I meant that literally.

"I've been thinking about it ever since I got the call. I asked myself, who else involved in this case has a history with the feds? And guess what? The only name that came to mind was yours."

"The feds completely cleared me of any

suspicion concerning their investigation of Stramp Investments." It took all of my self-control not to groan. "They are not interested in me anymore." *Damn!* In helping me, Jake had put an even bigger target on my back.

"Or so they told you." Woods's voice dripped with satisfaction.

"This isn't about me." I didn't stamp my foot at his stupidity, but I may have tapped my toe a couple of times. "While you're trying to pin the murder on me, the real killer is laughing up his sleeve at you."

"Oh, *you* won't be laughing once I figure out what you and Joelle Ayers and the feds all have in common," Woods warned. "Was she in on the embezzlement scheme with you and your boss?"

"No. As I've said repeatedly, I wasn't in on the scheme. And as far as I know, Joelle has never had anything to do with Stramp Investments. She definitely was never an employee or client while I worked there."

"Don't think you can hide your connection with Joelle forever." He fingered his gun. "My partner and I are turning over every rock, and eventually someone is going to slither out and spill their guts about you and the vic."

Maybe I had made a mistake in my desire for no witnesses to our encounter. "Look. I'd like to help you out." I edged farther away from Woods. "The door's right behind you."

Ignoring my invitation to leave, Woods said, "And once the department legal eagles clear it, everyone in this town will know you're under suspicion."

*Ah.* So that was why there hadn't been any gossip about me so far. Boone had said he had threatened the Kansas City Police Department with a lawsuit if they leaked my name to the press without any evidence against me.

"You're not getting off scot-free this time." Woods advanced on me.

It was time to get serious. "You need to go." I held up my cell and hit the button for Boone. "I just called my lawyer and he'll hear anything you do or say to me. Unless you have a warrant, this conversation is over and I'm requesting that you leave my property."

"I hate cell phones." Woods whirled around and marched out, muttering, "Your boss may have weaseled out of serving prison time, but someone is going to pay for losing my retirement money."

I was still flustered by the detective's visit an hour later when I opened the front door for Hannah. My anxiety must have shown, because she followed me over to the bookrack and watched as I fumbled with the paperbacks. The ability to slip them into the correct slots was eluding me.

"Are you okay, Dev?" Hannah tilted her head,

and the tiny gold hoop adorning her right nostril caught the light streaming in through the big plate-glass window.

"I'm fine."

"Then why are you putting the new Jennifer Crusie where the fantasy/science fiction books go?" Hannah was more astute than a lot of adults gave her credit for being. The way she dressed— today she had on a pink Hello Kitty T-shirt, black lace knee-length tights, and a white tutu—and her unusual way of thinking fooled them into believing she was too weird to be insightful.

"Well, the happily-ever-after romances Crusie writes are about as realistic as the magical world in the Harry Potter books." My feeble attempt to distract Hannah with humor didn't work.

"Fine." Hannah narrowed her eyes. "But the next time I have a problem, you won't be able to make me tell you about it."

Was that a threat or a promise? Missing out on some teenage angst didn't sound that bad to me. But then, I didn't have a maternal bone in my body.

The morning went downhill from there. After dealing with unhappy vendors, dissatisfied customers, and a ninety-year-old shoplifter who stuffed skeins of yarn down her bra and a floral arrangement into her underwear, I was close to screaming when Poppy arrived at a little after eleven. She took one look at my face, opened her gigantic lime green purse, and handed me a sheet of bubble wrap.

When I raised a questioning brow, Poppy said with a straight face, "Therapy is expensive. Bursting bubble wrap is cheap. You choose."

While Poppy explained her presence, I discovered the joys of popping.

Poppy had been on her way to see the mayor, but realized she needed a witness in case he said anything incriminating, so she asked me to go with her. As I opened my mouth to agree, a part of my mind automatically reminded me of all that I had to do around the store—restock shelves, place orders, pay bills, and select the next candy of the month. But if I was in prison none of that would matter. Despite my enormous to-do list, my priority had to be clearing my name.

# CHAPTER 10

Jake had slept poorly. The pain in his leg and thoughts of Devereaux had kept him awake as he alternated between staring at the ceiling and the clock. By five a.m. he was already dressed and outside doing chores.

It looked as if Wednesday's weather would be a repeat of the past couple of days—cold, windy, and miserable. In the winter, the cows didn't have grass to eat, so they had to be given the hay that had been harvested from the fields during the summer. Jake, Tony, and the hired hands had to haul bale after bale out to the pastures, and the blowing snow made feeding the herd even more difficult.

While he worked, Jake brooded about his actions the night before. After hanging up on Meg, he'd forced himself to keep his expression impassive as he turned back to Devereaux. Poker-faced, he'd coolly discussed the implications of Joelle Ayers's apparent false identity and the results of his interview with Anya Hamilton. Had he made the right decision to hide his frustration and raging lust? Or should he have swept Devereaux back into his arms?

It had been tough ignoring the voice inside his head that insisted he explain to her both why he'd been checking up on her and what the situation was with Meg. In the long run, he knew it was better to let Devereaux think he was a two-timing jerk. That way she wouldn't be tempted to do something he'd no doubt make her regret. Relationships never worked for him, and she didn't seem the type who would be satisfied with just hooking up for a few nights of wild sex.

As he'd driven back to the ranch, he'd nearly managed to convince himself that he was glad they'd been interrupted and that in the future he would keep a professional distance from the luscious Miss Devereaux Sinclair. That is, until he'd leaned over the passenger seat to reach into the glove compartment for his gun and caught a whiff of her perfume. Its crisp, yet sweet scent brought his desire rushing back.

When Jake had stomped into the house a few minutes later, the look on his face must have deterred his uncle from asking any questions, because Tony hadn't tried to detain him. Instead, he'd silently shoved a bottle of Corona into his hand and patted his back as Jake trudged past him into his bedroom.

Now, while Jake took care of the infected navel of one calf, the injured ear of a second, and the snotty nose of a third, then headed back to the house for breakfast, he wondered what Tony would have to say about his behavior last night. The old man usually had an opinion and he wasn't shy about sharing it.

Tony's housekeeper, Ulysses, nodded at Jake when he entered the kitchen, then placed half a dozen slices of bacon on a paper towel, broke three eggs into a sizzling-hot cast-iron fry pan, and popped two pieces of bread into the toaster.

Ulysses was a short, rotund man of unidentifiable age and ethnicity. In the twenty-plus years when Jake had visited his granduncle during each and every one of his school vacations, the housekeeper had looked exactly as he did now: like a silent, golden brown Pillsbury Doughboy.

Jake greeted Ulysses, then spotted his uncle sitting at the table and braced himself for the older man's comments.

Tony glanced up from his newspaper, skewered his nephew with a pointed stare, and asked, "You in any better a mood this morning than last night?"

Jake sighed, knowing his uncle would keep at him until he got the information he wanted. Not out of nosiness, but because of concern. Tony had been more of a father to Jake than his own dad had ever been. Jake's parents had shipped him off to military school when he turned eight and had rarely spent more than a day or so with him since then.

Tony was the one who had taught Jake how to bait a hook, shoot a rifle, and be a man. He was also the one with whom Jake had shared his hopes, dreams, and troubles. The ranch was Jake's real home, not any of his parents' opulent houses, condos, or villas.

"I'm fine."

"You looked madder than a wet hen last night." Tony put aside his newspaper. "Did Birdie's granddaughter give you a hard time? I hear she's as feisty as her grandma."

"Nothing happened." Jake got up and walked to the coffeemaker on the counter. "Want a refill?"

"Don't mind if I do." Tony rubbed his hands

together. "Hard to warm up after being outside on a day like today. It's colder than a corpse's big toe."

Jake grabbed a cup for himself, filled it, then emptied the rest of the pot into his uncle's white crockery mug.

"Thanks." Tony leaned back and took a long sip. "So what's your impression of Dev Sinclair?" He wiped his mouth with the back of his hand. "You know, come to think about it, I'm surprised you two don't know each other."

"We met a couple of times as kids when I went to the grocery store with Aunt Sabina, but you were never one to go to town much, and I liked hanging around with you." Jake shrugged. "Plus, after being surrounded by people all day, every day at school, I liked the elbow room here at the ranch."

"That explains it." Tony nodded before pursuing his original question. "Anyway, what do you think about Dev now that you've finally met her?"

"She's got herself a problem." Jake settled into the wooden slat-back chair. "Her grandmother was right. She's in deep shit."

"Yep." Tony's expression was mournful. "I figured as much if Birdie was willing to ask me for a favor." He quirked his mouth. "I been waiting for that woman to need me for more than fifty years."

"Why didn't you two get together once you

were both free?" Jake asked. "Aunt Sabina's been gone nearly four years and Birdie's husband passed over a decade ago."

"She needed to make the first move." Tony's tone was stubborn. "And we're not talking about me, we're talking about Dev's trouble. Did she agree to your helping her?"

"Yes." Jake thought back to her acceptance. "Though I think she might not have if she wasn't so worried about her grandma."

Ulysses slid a plate in front of Jake and removed the dish Tony had finished with.

"Before I forget, I remembered something I saw a week or so ago." Tony tucked a small red notebook in the back pocket of his overalls. "I was at the bank and the woman in front of me was trying to cash a check, but she didn't have enough money in her account."

"Oh?" Jake wasn't sure where Tony was going, but he knew his uncle didn't make idle chitchat. "Who was the woman?"

"I didn't know her, but the teller called her Ms. Ayers when he suggested phoning her fiancé and having him transfer funds from his account into hers." Tony folded his reading glasses into their case. "She yelled at the teller to mind his own business; that her financial affairs were confidential and she'd get him fired if he told anyone about them."

"Interesting." Jake buttered his toast. "So the

victim was having problems with cash flow." Anya's comment about Joelle wanting to marry a rich guy struck a different chord when that piece of information was added. "I'll have to find out the name of the vic's attorney and check out her estate."

"So what'd you do yesterday afternoon?" Tony leaned back in his chair and crossed his arms. "I figured when you didn't come home, you got right on the case."

Between bites, Jake filled his uncle in on his investigation, ending with, "After I talked to that Hamilton woman, I took a ride into Kansas City to take a look at the hotel where the vic's body was found. I knew I couldn't see the crime scene, but I wanted to get the lay of the land."

"Did Dev go with you?"

"No." Jake dipped his toast into the yolk of a perfect sunny-side-up egg. Ulysses was a genius with a spatula and a frying pan. "She went with Boone St. Onge to a CDM fund-raiser to talk to the vic's future mother-in-law. Devereaux, St. Onge, and that woman who owns that bar just outside of town already had a plan to look into the murder."

"Poppy's smart as they come." Tony nodded approvingly. "And Boone's a good guy."

"Well, I don't like Devereaux and St. Onge going off by themselves like that to confront a possible murderer."

Tony chuckled. "Nadine Underwood is pushing seventy. I'm pretty darn sure, between Dev and Boone, they could take her if she turned mean."

"Not if she had a weapon. She could have shot them both." Jake clenched his jaw. "What's the story with Devereaux and St. Onge?"

"They've been friends since they were little kids. You should have seen . . ." Understanding dawned in Tony's eyes. "You got the hots for Dev, don't you?"

Jake choked on the gulp of coffee he had just taken. *Shit!* The last thing he needed was his uncle deciding to play matchmaker. "What are you talking about? Of course not. I'm just concerned for her safety."

"Really?" Tony raised a brow. "Is that why you went to see her after she got home from the party? To check that she was okay?"

"How—"

"Last night one of the boys saw you turning into her driveway a little past ten."

"We had a lot to discuss."

"It must have been a real intimate kind of conversation." Tony cackled. "You were wearing her lipstick and sporting a woody the size of a baseball bat when you marched through here spitting nails last night." His thick white eyebrows met over his nose. "Looks like the hots to me."

Jake froze as a picture of Devereaux in his truck, her moist pink lips under his, popped into his mind. What would have happened if Meg hadn't picked that moment to phone him? It was almost as if his ex-wife had ESP and had deliberately interrupted them.

"You didn't fool me back when you were a kid, and you don't fool me now." Tony snorted. "Hell, just admit you like her."

"Maybe I do." Jake's tone was stiff. "But I won't be here long and it wouldn't be fair to start something with her when I'm going back to work as a marshal as soon as I'm fit." He mentally shook his head; his uncle was a good one to talk. Tony should have cleared things up with Devereaux's grandmother a long time ago.

# CHAPTER 11

As Poppy and I left the store, I headed toward Poppy's Hummer, which was parked at the curb, but she grabbed my shoulder and said, "The mayor's office is only across the square. It'll be quicker to walk."

I was about to object when the thought of even the remote possibility of getting naked with Jake sometime in the near future made me change my mind. "You're right." I linked my arm with hers. "I should start getting more exercise. I know I'll never be Cosmo Girl thin, but I could firm up my curves a little."

"Really?" Poppy looked at me questioningly, having often heard my negative opinion of any activity that involved sweating on purpose.

"Maybe I'll take up swimming. I hear the high school pool is available in the morning."

"I don't buy it." Poppy shook her head. "If swimming is supposed to be so good for your figure, how do you explain manatees?"

"Excellent point."

As we hiked, Poppy said, "Boone told me all about your adventures with Nadine at the Lee Mansion fund-raiser." Poppy cut her eyes at me. "I was surprised you didn't call to tell me yourself."

"Sorry." I stuffed my mittened hands into my pockets. It was freezing out and the wind was howling. "I was waiting to hear from Jake about what he'd found out from Anya Hamilton." No need to mention that he was delivering the information in person. And I certainly wasn't sharing what had happened in his pickup truck.

"So, what did he have to say?"

I summarized his report on Anya and the news that Joelle wasn't Joelle.

"Wow!" Poppy blew out her lips. "I sure didn't see that coming."

"Yeah." I lengthened my stride, trying to keep warm. "Joelle stealing someone's identity is an excellent lead, but I was really hoping Anya would have more information on her bestie." I paused. "Jake mentioned a woman named Gwen. Should we talk to her?"

"Hm." Poppy pulled her stocking cap lower on her head. "Maybe. She was tight with Joelle, though she didn't seem as jealous as Anya, so I'm thinking some of the other Country Club Cougars, the ones who are lower in the pecking order, might have more to say."

"Any suggestions?"

"Cyndi Barrow."

"Why her?"

"A couple of reasons." Poppy stopped and held up a gloved finger. "One, she's barely a part of the group. More of a hanger-on, really."

"And?"

"And two, she's engaged, so she was one of the few women not chasing Noah."

"Sounds good." I tugged Poppy into moving on before we both became ice sculptures. "Who to, and when, is Cyndi getting married?"

"Frazer Wren, and they've been engaged for five years, with no date in sight."

"That's an awfully long time." I frowned. "What's the holdup?"

"Frazer's got Cyndi on the layaway plan, and I doubt he's good for the balance." Poppy saw my confused look and explained, "All the benefits of marriage with none of the drawbacks of the institution."

"Ah." We crossed the square to the city hall,

and as I pushed open the frosted-glass door for Poppy, I wondered out loud, "How in the heck does Geoffrey Eggers keep getting reelected?"

"Cream isn't the only thing that rises to the top. So does grease."

"Yeah." The heat of the building hit me in the face as we entered, and I unwound the red and black plaid wool scarf from around my throat. "I guess it could be worse. At least he's not an animal." The neighboring town of Sparkville had elected a German shepherd to office after their last mayor was caught trying to sell a city council seat to the highest bidder.

"Have you seen the DNA test that proves Geoffrey is human?" Poppy snickered, then added thoughtfully, "You know, Sparkville could end up having the last laugh on us if our mayor turns out to be a murderer."

The municipal building was divided into four spaces. A postage stamp–size reception area, the clerk's tiny cubicle, and a fairly large conference room accounted for half of the small structure. The mayor's office took up the other half. As we passed through the lobby, a Wagner opera was booming from behind the intricately carved oak door that separated His Honor from the commoners.

A sign on the reception desk indicated that the city clerk would be back at noon, which was why Poppy had timed our visit for eleven thirty. With no one guarding the portal, we could pop in on the mayor unannounced. His Honor wasn't good at thinking on his feet, and he often said things he shouldn't when he was caught unawares.

Poppy knocked once; then, without waiting for a response, she turned the knob, pushed the door open, and strolled over the threshold. I followed her, but hung back when she sauntered up to the nineteenth-century writing table the mayor used as a desk.

Eggers had lurched to his feet at Poppy's entrance, and he stammered as she trailed a fingertip along the tulipwood cross-banding on the tabletop. "Poppy, uh, what a surprise. Was I expecting you?"

"Geoffrey Eggers." Poppy pushed out her bottom lip in an adorable pout. "You sound as if you're not happy to see me."

"Don't be silly." His Honor smoothed the sides of his black pompadour and tugged at the collar of his shirt. "You know I encourage all Shadow Benders to stop by, especially the pretty ones."

Either the mayor was ignoring me or he hadn't noticed my presence. I was used to being eclipsed by Poppy's ethereal beauty; it had been happening since our first-grade play when she got to be the Sugar Plum Fairy and I played a Christmas tree. So instead of being upset, I used the opportunity to study my surroundings. I'd never had a reason to visit Eggers's office before, and I was shocked at how extravagantly it was decorated. Were the taxpayers footing the bill for this palace?

Off to one side, a gold satin tuxedo-style sofa was positioned to face two Hepplewhite chairs upholstered in crimson damask. Between them, a Queen Anne table held curly willows arranged in a crystal vase. Behind the divan hung a gilt framed Louis XV mirror that reflected the rich wood paneling on the opposite wall.

Poppy was softening the mayor up with her coquettish act, so I wandered over to the fireplace and gazed up at an oil painting of His Honor above the mantel. He looked a little like an extremely dapper scarecrow. At well over six-six, with an estimated weight of less than 170 pounds, he appeared uncomfortable with his physical self. Even in his formal portrait, he was slouching and ducking his head.

Eggers must have finally spotted me, or maybe he decided he'd been as rude to a voter as he could afford to be, because he suddenly appeared beside me and said, "Ms. Sinclair, Devereaux, I'm honored you've taken time from your store to come visit me. Please sit down and tell me what I can do for you ladies."

Poppy and I allowed him to seat us on his prized antique chairs; then she said, "Geoffrey, we wanted to get your opinion of Joelle Ayers's murder. Did my father fill you in on the situation?"

"Of course he did." Eggers sat awkwardly on

the edge of the couch; he was too tall for such a low piece of furniture. "The chief knows I like to be kept apprised."

It was all I could do to keep a straight face as he talked. With his knees sticking up almost to his ears and his hands pressed together from fingertips to palms, His Honor looked like a praying mantis.

"And?" Poppy prodded him.

"That poor girl." Eggers's expression was solemn. "Her death is a tragedy, of course."

"Any idea who may have wanted her dead?" Poppy crossed her legs.

The mayor licked his lips, watching Poppy swing her foot back and forth. She was wearing tight leather boots over black leggings, and he appeared hypnotized by the sight of her shapely calf.

Finally he focused and answered her question. "I couldn't say. I didn't know Ms. Ayers all that well, so I have no idea if she had enemies."

"Now, Geoffrey." Poppy wagged a finger at him. "How can you say that when you caused that huge scene at the New Year's Eve ball?"

"I don't know what you're talking about." His voice rang with ersatz honesty.

"I was there." Poppy's tone was no-nonsense. "As were at least a hundred other Shadow Benders and their guests. We all saw you."

His Honor opened his mouth, closed it, and

repeated the process. In his eyes, I saw his thoughts as clearly as if I were reading them from a teleprompter. He was searching for a plausible denial.

When the mayor didn't speak, Poppy prodded him again. "Come on, Geoffrey. You got drunk and challenged Noah Underwood to a duel."

Knitting his scraggly eyebrows together over his beaklike nose, he pursed his thick, rubbery lips and thought hard—at any rate, as hard as he was capable of thinking. At last His Honor said, "I admit it. I admired Joelle, and I thought she returned my feelings."

"Even though she was engaged?" I asked, finally joining the conversation.

"Yes." The mayor smiled at me condescendingly. "Although you might think highly of Dr. Underwood's charms, Joelle indicated that she was reconsidering her choice. She wasn't certain the good doctor was right for her, but he refused to listen to her when she told him she thought they should call off their engagement until she was sure."

"Did you hear anything about that, Poppy?" I asked. "Any talk about Joelle wanting to end things with her fiancé or him giving her a hard time about it?"

"Nothing."

"Be that as it may." His Honor shrugged. "The humiliation of my indiscretion on New Year's

Eve made me reconsider my affection for Joelle, and I never approached her or Dr. Underwood again." Eggers straightened his silk tie. "Why would I? I've always been popular with the ladies and definitely don't have to pursue a woman who doesn't return my interest." Before he could continue, the phone rang and he excused himself to answer it.

While he was gone, I whispered to Poppy, "Why would Joelle flirt with someone as unattractive and old as His Honor when she already had Noah?"

"Hedging her bets?"

"That would mean Joelle was using Eggers." Frowning, I added, "Which makes me feel a little sorry for him."

"Don't." Poppy smiled maliciously. "The mayor may have learned a valuable lesson. If you're going to go flitting from flower to flower, you should expect to be treated like a son of a bee."

"He does seem extremely confident of his romantic prowess." I peeked over my shoulder and watched him paw through the stacks of papers covering his desktop. "What in the world do women see in him?"

"His position and his family's money." Poppy succinctly summed it up. "He thinks he's God's gift to women." She blew out a deep breath. "Too bad you can't return him for a nice cashmere sweater or a designer purse."

When the mayor rejoined us, he said, "As I was about to advise you before the phone interrupted, I've recently begun dating a lovely young lady, and we were together right here in Shadow Bend during Valentine's Day weekend. So, as I stated before, I no longer had any interest in Joelle."

"Really, I'm surprised I haven't heard about it." Cynicism turned Poppy's angelic amethyst eyes to gunmetal gray, and scorn curled her perfect rosebud mouth. "What's your new girlfriend's name? Is she from around here?"

"I see no reason to share my personal information with you." He produced a white handkerchief and a snuffbox. Taking snuff was one of his many unpleasant eccentricities. "And I certainly don't want my friend's privacy invaded."

"Say we believe you." Poppy shot me a glance that said he was right—there was no way to force him to tell us anything. "Then who else might have had a motive to kill Joelle? Were there other men interested in her? Maybe someone from before she moved here?"

"She never talked about her past, and the one time I was in her condo, there were no personal items of any kind visible." Eggers took a pinch of snuff, inserted it in one nostril, sneezed, and blew his nose. "I got the impression this was a fresh start for her, and she didn't want any reminders of before she arrived in Shadow Bend."

# CHAPTER 12

When I got back to the dime store after talking to Geoffrey Eggers, Mrs. Ziegler, the high school principal, was standing in front of the locked door, pulling on the handle. Her face was twisted into an impatient frown; evidently she assumed the CLOSED sign in the window was intended for mere mortals and not for her.

She had been the principal of Shadow Bend High even before I graduated from its esteemed halls of learning. Although she'd always been addressed as Mrs. Ziegler, no one seemed to remember a Mr. Ziegler. And believe me, nobody had the nerve to question her about him.

"Mrs. Ziegler." I approached her cautiously. She wasn't someone you wanted to offend or provoke. "Let me open that for you."

"Thank you." She nodded regally and stepped out of my way. "The placard states that this establishment's hours are from nine a.m. to nine p.m. on Wednesdays." She crossed her arms. "Is it incorrect?"

"No, ma'am." I searched my mind for an excuse. "I only have a few minutes and I need to discuss something with you."

"I'm terribly sorry." Deciding to go with the

truth, or at least part of it, I explained, "I was called to a meeting with the mayor."

She sniffed, the tilt of her nose indicating that her opinion of His Honor matched mine.

I finally managed to insert my key into the lock and turn it. "There you go." I held the door open for her while she swept past toward the back of the store with me trailing her like a baby duck. I wondered what was up, but kept my mouth shut.

While I admired Mrs. Ziegler, she scared the crap out of me. I had never seen her less than immaculately dressed in a well-tailored skirt, a perfectly pressed blouse, and impeccably shined shoes. I halfway believed she wasn't entirely human.

Pointing to my worktable, where I, thank God, was assembling the basket for the Cline baby shower and not the one for the Stewart bachelorette party, she announced, "The high school needs you to show the Athletic Booster Club members how to make Easter baskets for their equipment and uniform fund-raiser."

I had automatically opened my mouth to refuse, since teaching others how to become my competition didn't seem like a very smart business move, when I realized that pissing off one of the town's most respected citizens was not good business, either.

Thinking fast, I said, "I could do that. Or I could put together three samples, take photos, and design a leaflet from which the Boosters could sell the baskets for twenty or thirty percent over their cost." I didn't mention that their cost included my profit.

"Hmm." Mrs. Ziegler tapped the toe of her low-heeled black pump.

"Think about it this way." I could tell she wasn't sold on the idea, so I upped the ante. "If we do what I suggest, there's no capital outlay, there's no storage problem, and there's no mess."

"Well." Mrs. Ziegler slapped her leather gloves against the palm of her hand. "That group does tend to be untidy."

Seeing that she was close to agreeing, I went in for the kill. "And I'll donate a deluxe basket that they can raffle off at their next event." I'd hide the cost of that prize in the price of the other baskets.

"It's a deal." Mrs. Ziegler adjusted her purse strap to sit more securely on her shoulder. "I'll expect the brochures on my desk first thing Monday morning." She paused, tapping the index finger of her ringless left hand on her chin. "Two hundred and fifty copies should be sufficient." She turned to go. "No, better make it five hundred."

Great! Another thing to add to my to-do list. I slumped against the counter.

"Devereaux."

*Oops!* Mrs. Ziegler hadn't left. I twisted my head to look at her.

"Stand up straight." She winked at me. "Slouching makes your breasts sag."

I swallowed wrong and choked. When I stopped coughing, she was gone and I questioned my hearing. Had Mrs. Ziegler really said the word *breasts?* Shaking my head, I shrugged out of my coat and hung it in the back room. I didn't have time to worry about what the principal did or didn't say. I had to get to work.

Good thing that those of us in retail always worked well ahead of the coming season. I already had boxes of Easter supplies stacked in my stockroom. My original plan had been to use this week to sell off the remaining Valentine's Day merchandise at a hefty discount. Once it was gone, I'd begin displaying the pastel plastic eggs, bright green artificial grass, and chocolate rabbits. But with all that had happened since Monday, and now Principal Ziegler's bombshell, I wasn't sure when I'd have a chance to get the cute little chicks and bunnies on the shelves.

Checking the clock, I saw that it was already going on one o'clock, and I hadn't accomplished anything yet today. Better get moving. If I ate my lunch while I finished the baby shower basket, I might still have time to prep the sewing area for tonight's Blood, Sweat, and Shears meeting before the after-school crowd descended on the soda fountain and candy counter.

A half hour later, I popped the last bite of my boiled ham sandwich into my mouth, wiped my hands on a paper towel, and stepped back to admire my creation. For this basket, I had found an original copy of *Bootsy*, published by Wonder Books in 1959. The adorable black and white kitten on the bright blue cover seemed to be smiling his approval as I gathered up the cellophane and tied it closed with an enormous yellow and green bow.

While I was restocking the magazine shelves, the sleigh bells over the front door jingled and I looked up just in time to see Jake striding over the threshold. His expression was guarded, and he looked as exhausted as I felt. His chin was stubbled with twenty-four hours' worth of beard, and his eyes were deeply shadowed with fatigue. Maybe he hadn't slept well, either.

"Hi." He took off his Stetson, fingered the brim for a moment, then put his hat next to the register and unbuttoned his jacket. "About last night . . ." He trailed off, seeming to be at a loss for words.

I flashed back to our steamy encounter in his pickup and felt my cheeks redden and other parts of me tingle. Quickly, almost afraid he could read my thoughts, and because I definitely did not want to hear the end of his sentence, I interjected, "Let's just chalk what happened up to chemistry or proximity or too many cosmos at the fund-raiser, and forget all about it."

"Why? Because you like guys who wear designer suits, drink champagne, and take you to the ballet?" His blue eyes were as hard as the Hope diamond. "I'm not your type, am I?"

Was he serious? He had to be aware of how attractive he was. I'd bet there was at least one woman, maybe more, who lost her head over him on every case he worked. I just had to make sure I wasn't the one this time. A love-'em-and-leave-'em kind of man didn't work for me.

When I saw his jaw tighten, I realized that he was still waiting for an answer, and I quickly assured him, "That's not it at all." His expression of disbelief made me add, "I just think we need to concentrate on the matter at hand. Emotions only mess people up."

Jake didn't appear entirely convinced, so before he could probe further, I elaborated. "See, the thing is that I'm in a good place right now. I've accepted that there are things I may never have in my life, but at least I'm not getting my heart broken."

"You can't make time stand still." Jake seemed to be talking to himself as much as to me. "If you don't keep moving forward toward a goal, you'll fall back to where you were to start with."

"I'm not trying to make time stand still," I protested, fighting the intensity of his gaze. "It's just that I'm tired of men disappointing me, and I don't want to get hurt anymore."

I was considering what he'd said when it dawned on me. Why was I the one on the hot seat? It was Jake's girlfriend who had interrupted us. A girlfriend he had denied having only moments before kissing me. If anyone should be explaining himself, it was him.

Before I could say all that, he stepped toward me. My back was to the magazine rack and he put his hands on either side of my shoulders, resting them on the wooden shelves. A shiver shot through me at the realization that I was trapped and had no desire to break free.

With his face close to mine, he teased, "So it sounds as if you're planning to live the rest of your life as a nun."

"No." My voice held an uncertain tone that I didn't recognize. I was rarely unsure of my decisions. What was this guy doing to me?

Jake's lips brushed mine, and I knew I was less than a nanosecond away from lust overtaking my good intentions, so with my last rational thought I confronted him. "Detective Woods paid me a visit this morning. Your girlfriend called him about Joelle's fingerprints, and now he's more convinced than ever that I'm the murderer."

"Shit!" Jake jerked away from me as if I had stuck a cattle prod in his groin.

I took the opportunity to move away from him

and walked to the register. Flipping open the counter, I stepped behind it and quickly closed the opening. Putting some distance, not to mention a physical barrier, between Jake and me seemed like a prudent move.

"What in the hell did she say to him?" Jake ground out the question between clenched teeth.

As I began cleaning up the basket-making paraphernalia, I repeated Woods's accusations, ending with, "Then when he was leaving, he said, 'Your boss may have weaseled out of serving prison time, but someone is going to pay for losing my retirement money.'"

"What a jerk."

"Yep."

Once my work space was spick-and-span, I hauled out the first of four long folding tables that needed to be set up for the sewing circle. Jake mutely brought out the other three while I put them up.

He finally broke the silence between us by saying, "Meg's my ex, not my girlfriend."

"You called your ex-wife for information?" I nearly dropped the sewing machine I was carrying. "Did you ever consider she might not want to help you? Even if you had one heck of an amicable divorce, there are usually some hurt feelings or resentment. Didn't you think it was possible that she'd want to sabotage you and set off Woods on purpose?"

"She's the best researcher in the service." His expression was a mixture of stubborn and sheepish. "Besides, she left me, not the other way around. She has no reason to want to get back at me."

"Okay." I drew out the word, indicating my incredulity at his utter lack of understanding of the female mind, but I didn't bother to argue. If Jake really believed his ex-wife didn't have any ill will about their failed marriage, then there was no point wasting my breath trying to persuade him otherwise. "If you say so."

"I'm sure whatever happened when Meg spoke with Woods wasn't intentional on her part." Jake rubbed the back of his neck. "She wouldn't be that unprofessional."

"Uh-huh." I made sure he didn't see me roll my eyes. "Anyway, considering how well our investigation has gone so far, I think it's probably best that we stop now before we make things worse for me. Maybe if I don't draw any more attention to myself, Woods will lose interest."

"You know that's not what will happen." Jake shook his head. "Woods is like a rock. And it doesn't matter if the rock hits the glass or the glass hits the rock—it'll be bad for the glass."

"Yeah." He was right, even though I hated to admit it and really wanted the whole situation to go away without any further effort on my part.

Still, it was always better to be proactive than reactive. At least that's what I told myself as I admitted, "You're probably right."

"I spoke to Joelle's attorney, Riyad Oberkircher, just before I came over here." Jake explained about the scene his uncle had witnessed at the bank.

"How did you know he was her lawyer?"

"There are only three attorneys listed in the Shadow Bend phone book. Since I assume St. Onge would have mentioned to you if he represented the vic, I went to see the other two." Jake shrugged. "I had to flash my badge to get the information, but Oberkircher finally told me that Joelle had no next of kin listed in her will, but there's not much money or property involved, and everything goes into a trust for her dog."

"So, just as you and Tony suspected, she was nearly broke." I digested that tidbit, then said, "Do you think she was only marrying Noah for his money and he discovered that and killed her?"

"The only way to find out is to talk to Dr. Underwood."

I knew that, but I didn't want to accept what had to be done. Facing my high school boyfriend after so many years of avoiding him would be awkward at best and very possibly downright excruciating.

Noah and I had been friends since the first time we'd been paired up for dance lessons when we were six years old. Our ancestors had been among the five founding families of Shadow Bend, and we were constantly together at town social functions. Once we became teenagers, it had seemed natural for us to become sweethearts, and once we started dating we were inseparable. Each of us became the most important person in the other's world. Until Jake walked into my life yesterday, I had never felt that same passion toward any other man.

Jake put his hands in his jeans pockets. "What time will you be finished here?"

"The meeting ends at nine, but it'll take me fifteen or twenty minutes to clean up and get the store ready for tomorrow."

"I'll pick you up at quarter after."

"That's not a good idea." I rubbed the bridge of my nose. Explaining Shadow Benders to folks who hadn't grown up here was always tough. "People around these parts keep to a pretty rigid schedule. 'Early to bed and early to rise' isn't just an old proverb to them."

"Fair enough." Jake buttoned his coat. "Since the store's only open half a day tomorrow, how about I come by to get you at noon?" He picked up his hat. "I checked, and the Underwood Medical Clinic closes at eleven thirty on Thursdays." As he left, he said, "You need to figure out where the doc will be after he finishes there."

"How am I supposed to do that?" I called after Jake, but he was already gone. I muttered to myself, "I'm not even sure he's back at work. After all, his fiancée died just a few days ago."

# CHAPTER 13

At quarter to six the sewing circle members started to arrive. The first to pull up, squealing into the prime front-of-store parking spot, was a dented old muscle car with a duct-taped front grille and a spiderweb crack on the windshield. Between the primer and the rust, it was hard to determine the vehicle's original color.

A girl in her early twenties unfolded from the driver's seat. With her carrot red hair and bright clothing, she was a dead ringer for a grown-up Pippi Longstocking. People often under-estimated Zizi Todd, just as they did Hannah. Zizi's appearance suggested an airhead, but in fact she was in graduate school studying to become a clinical social worker.

I greeted Zizi, but she rushed past me, calling over her shoulder as she thrust open the bathroom door in the back of the store, "Traffic was heinous and I've had to pee for the past hour."

A few minutes later she joined me in the craft corner just in time for the arrival of Winnie Todd, Zizi's mother. Winnie was the original flower child. Her long gray hair was a froth of frizzy curls down her back, and her tie-dyed T-shirt sported a peace symbol.

She'd left Shadow Bend to live in San Francisco during the mid-sixties, but had returned, sans husband, in the late eighties to have her only child. Several of the townspeople had expressed concern that she was not only a single mother but also pregnant at forty-three.

Winnie made it clear that she had plenty of money, having inherited a sizable estate from her grandparents, and that the doctors had assured her the fetus was healthy, but her words fell on deaf ears. Which was no surprise to me. Being of sound and logical mind in Shadow Bend doesn't necessarily mean you'll be understood or appreciated.

I put down the tape measure I'd been holding and relieved Winnie of what looked like a mutated sewing machine, asking, "What do you have here?"

"It's a serger so we can finish the edges of the blankets," she explained. "Did you get the satin binding I e-mailed you about?"

"Yep." I pointed behind me. "It's on the cart with the bolts of fleece and the thread."

Both Winnie and Zizi cared deeply for their

fellow human beings, and together they had cofounded this sewing circle dedicated to supporting the county's homeless shelter. Currently the group consisted of twenty women ranging in age from sixteen to eighty-three. Each member paid for her own materials and donated the finished products either directly to the shelter or to the shelter's resale shop.

While Zizi and Winnie hugged and exchanged news of their day, I slipped into the storage room and phoned my grandmother. I hated leaving her alone for twelve hours, but at least Wednesday was the only day the store was open past six. Birdie assured me she was fine, and she seemed disappointed to hear I would be coming home right after work rather than meeting up with Jake.

By the time I returned to the craft area, most of the other seamstresses had arrived. Coats were off, fleece was being cut into two-and-a-half-yard lengths, and sewing machines were whirring.

As I moved closer to the tables, I noticed that there was an unusually high volume of whispering and clucking going on. My heart skipped a beat. Had word of Woods's investigation of me gotten out?

Ducking behind a rack of scrapbook pages, I listened to the discussion.

Cyndi Barrow, the Country Club Cougar whom

Poppy had suggested we interview, was one of several women whom I hadn't expected to join the sewing circle, yet she had shown up for the first meeting and faithfully attended all the subsequent ones. She finished touching up her lipstick and said, "I really wasn't at all surprised to hear that someone had killed her."

Zizi paused in midcut, her shears half open. "Why is that?"

Cyndi tucked the golden tube into her purse and said, "I hate to speak ill of the dead."

"But . . . ?" Winnie's unconventional features rearranged themselves into an encouraging smile.

"Well." Cyndi's voice sank to a whisper and I had to abandon my cover and move closer to hear her next remark. "She was just so mean."

"That's a little harsh, isn't it?" Zizi frowned. "I thought you two were friends."

"We were, but . . ." After a predictable show of reluctance Cyndi continued. "About a month ago a bunch of us were shopping in Kansas City, and when we came out of the restaurant where we'd had lunch a guy walked up to Joelle and said, 'I haven't eaten anything in four days.' The rest of us were searching our purses for change, but she stared him straight in the eye and said, 'God, I wish I had your willpower.' Then she and Anya and Gwen just strolled away, laughing their heads off."

"Okay. You're right." Zizi nodded. "She was a pathetic excuse for a human being."

Apparently word of Joelle's murder had spread, but my involvement had not. Since no one had taken any notice of me, I allowed myself a relieved sigh.

After that exchange, talk turned to the weather, how bad it had been; television, how bad it had been; and children, how bad they had been. The women took a fifteen-minute break at seven thirty, and for five dollars each, I provided coffee, tea, and a selection of cookies and pastries.

Payment was on the honor system—the women put their money in an old cigar box—so after making sure there were plenty of cups, plates, utensils, and napkins, I went back to working on the store's books. I sat on a stool with my laptop on the smooth marble counter and lost myself in the world of Quicken.

Only a few minutes had gone by when I jerked my head up, suddenly interested in a conversation between Zizi and her mother.

"Are you coming to the lunch meeting tomorrow for the shelter committee?" Winnie took a sip from her mug, then a bite of chocolate chip cookie.

"I thought it was canceled." Zizi licked the icing off a red velvet cupcake.

"Me, too." Winnie frowned, spreading

155

wrinkles across her face like ripples in a pond. "But Dr. Underwood insisted we have it. Do you know that since his fiancée's death, he didn't even take a day off from the clinic? He said Joelle wouldn't want his patients to suffer on her account."

"He's such a good man." Zizi had a dreamy expression on her face.

I ground my teeth. Noah had everyone fooled. His choirboy good looks were such a deceptive image. It might have been thirteen years since he dumped me, and he might be a good doctor, but I still didn't trust him. Maybe if he'd apologized once we were adults, I would've been able to forgive and forget, but he hadn't, so my hurt feelings had never healed.

Winnie smiled fondly. "Yes, he is." Her smile turned rueful. "If his mother wasn't such an ogre, I'd suggest you ask him out once he's over losing his fiancée."

At least Nadine's true colors were evident to others, and I now knew where Noah would be tomorrow afternoon. Correction: I would know as soon as I found out the luncheon location.

At eight fifty, I announced that the sewing circle had ten minutes to finish up, and then I returned to the register to handle any final purchases the women might have. I loved ringing items up on the old brass cash register. Its distinctive ding always made me smile.

Winnie was the last to leave, and when she came over to say good-bye, I said as casually as I was able, "I heard you and Zizi talking about the shelter lunch meeting. Where's it being held?"

"The Manor." She smiled. "Are you thinking of joining our committee?"

"Uh." *Crap!* I should have thought of an excuse before I asked. "Well . . ."

"Wait a minute." Winnie scrunched up her face, obviously replaying the conversation she'd had with Zizi, then gave me a sharp look. "Are you hoping to run into Dr. Underwood? Everyone in town thinks you two should be together. Do you still have feelings for him?"

"No!" I shook my head so vehemently I felt my eyes cross. "But a friend of mine wants to talk to him, so when I overheard you mention his name . . ."

"I see." Winnie's expression softened. "I always thought it was a shame that things didn't work out between you two."

"We were too young." I repeated the same words I'd been saying for the last thirteen years.

I loved living in a small town, but Shadow Bend had better data storage than the Internet. The memory in the collective brain of its residents was both an amazing and a cruel phenomenon. There were wonderful memories of victorious high school sports teams, lovely summer festivals, and other good times. But there were also pitiless memories of poor choices, appalling judgment, and pure bad luck. Unfortunately, once such events were etched in the town's memory there was no erasing them. The DELETE key didn't exist, and fresh starts were hard to come by. Shadow Benders never forgot.

Winnie must have seen through my bland expression because she said, "You know, everyone in town is thrilled you bought the dime store since we all love it. And nothing that your parents did, and nothing that that awful Mr. Stramp did, was your fault." She reached out and patted my hand. "Sometimes we have to accept that we can do all the right things and there's still a terrible outcome."

"I understand that." I smiled at her, then shook my head. "I just wish fate wasn't such a bitch."

The Manor was located on a man-made lake midway between Shadow Bend and Sparkville. It attracted diners from as far away as Kansas City, catering to the affluent for both a fine-dining experience and elaborate parties. I had attended a wedding reception there many years ago, but I'd never eaten in the restaurant. My vague memory of the place warned that it was both elegant and intimidating, so I had dressed accordingly in camel wool slacks and a sea green sweater set.

As Jake turned his pickup into the long driveway, a fox ran out of the trees and paused at the edge of the pavement. He eyed the truck warily, sniffed the air, turned, and with a twitch of his tail scampered away. His fur gleamed russet red in the afternoon sun, and I twisted my neck so I could watch him out of the pickup's rear window. I straightened in my seat only after he disappeared into the woods.

Jake handed his keys over to a valet; then we climbed one of the twin marble staircases and went through the imposing brick entrance. Stepping into the stunning lobby, I admired the Thomas Moser chairs and a sideboard displaying a collection of Murano glass. From the dining room came the sound of a harpsichord playing a Bach prelude, and it took me a moment to realize the music was live.

As Jake approached the hostess podium, I studied a pair of large gilt-framed paintings on the side wall. They may not have been original works of art, but they could have fooled me. Which said a lot, considering that as part of my previous occupation I had been required to possess a working knowledge of the value and authenticity of artwork, antiques, and the other trappings of wealth. It was an odd job qualification to insist on, but Mr. Stramp had wanted his employees to be able to judge a client's bank account by his or her possessions.

The hostess told us that the shelter committee was meeting in the King Charles salon, located on the other side of the dining room. While we made our way past the generously spaced tables filled with well-dressed diners having serious discussions, I put on my game face and braced myself for what was sure to be a painful encounter.

The group was already seated and the server was placing plates in front of them when we walked into the private room. I had wondered why people whose task it was to raise money for a homeless shelter were meeting at such a posh restaurant, but I understood when I saw all the Tahari dresses, Di Modolo jewelry, and Manolo Blahnik shoes worn by the majority of the members. Those folks were willing to work for charity as long as they didn't have to experience any discomfort while doing so.

Zizi and Winnie's off-the-rack, casual attire made them stand out in this bunch like partridges among peacocks. However, neither appeared uncomfortable in the crowd, and both waved to me. Winnie shot me an interested grin and lifted one eyebrow.

Heads ping-ponged as Jake and I approached Noah. I had tried to persuade Jake that since we had no authority—he wasn't there as an official law enforcement agent—we should be more discreet and perhaps wait to grab Noah until the meeting was over. But Jake had insisted that suspects were more likely to cooperate and tell the truth if they were interrupted during the course of something public like a meeting. And since he was the professional, I had reluctantly acquiesced.

Now, noticing several of Nadine's cronies whip out their phones and start to text, I was sorry I had agreed. While it was nice to see that the older generation was keeping up with technology, I would have preferred not to be the one on whom they were practicing their skills.

Far worse than being electronically gossiped about was facing my former boyfriend. Noah took me in from the tips of my brown high-heeled boots to the top of my less than perfect ponytail. He offered a tentative smile, but when my expression remained blank, his gaze slid away from me and he tightened his jaw. Poking viciously at his endive and arugula salad, he appeared oblivious to the blonde on his left, who leaned over and murmured in his ear.

The young lady looked at me, then at Noah, then back at me. Her face a picture of confusion, she turned to the woman on her other side and whispered a question.

*Wow!* There was actually one person in the tri-county area who hadn't heard the story of my father's arrest and Noah's consequent dumping of me in high school.

Needless to say, this was not the Shadow Bend set I hung around with. Although I recognized most of them, and had seen several of the women a couple of days ago at the CDM fundraiser, my only real interactions were customer/vendor-related. At one time or another, I'd created erotic baskets for nearly all of them. Often they were for the same man—although, at least until Joelle's order, never for Noah. I wondered how many of these ladies had set their caps for him, now that he was free again and ripe for the picking.

An impeccably groomed brunette in her late thirties sprang from her chair and said, "May I help you? This is a private meeting."

She laid her hand on Noah's shoulder, but he subtly twitched it off and moved out of her reach. I caught Jake's eye and gestured unobtrusively with my chin.

He nodded imperceptibly, acknowledging that he also had observed their behavior, and whispered to me without moving his lips, "That's Gwen."

"Oh." I had seen her around, but never knew her name.

"We're sorry to interrupt, but it's important that we have a word with Dr. Underwood." Jake's tone was neutral.

"That's not possible," Gwen said. "Dr. Underwood is a very busy man, and we're extremely lucky he was able to give us this afternoon. As the chairwoman of this committee, I have to insist that you speak to him another time." She glanced down at Noah, giving him a possessive smile.

"Thank you for your concern, Gwen." Noah rose to his feet. "But I'm sure you can spare me for a few minutes." Turning his back on the woman, he stuck out his hand to Jake. "I'm Noah Underwood."

"Jake Del Vecchio." The men shook and Jake jerked his chin to the left. "I noticed an empty room next door. Let's talk in there, Doctor."

The sole other male committee member, Vaughn Yager, checked his diamond-studded Rolex and joked, "If you're not back in a half hour, Doc, these beautiful women and I will mount a search party." He winked. "But we might get lost." Turning his attention to me, Vaughn invited, "Dev, honey, why don't you stay here with us and let me buy you a drink? Everyone knows that Underwood already had his chance at you. Give me a whirl."

"No, thanks." I tempered my refusal by adding, "Besides, you already have your quota of women, all of whom are far more beautiful than me."

"But not half as smart or interesting."

"Flatterer." I smiled; then for the women who were openly listening I added, "This is strictly business."

Vaughn had been in my high school class, but back then he'd been the son of the custodian, and as shunned and picked on as I had become after my father's debacle. In recent years, Vaughn had made a fortune playing professional poker. He'd returned to town, purchased one of the few factories in the county that had survived the bad economy, and was now a big shot.

I had liked him better before. Back then, I'd appreciated his drive and wit, but now that he had had his nose straightened, added a chin implant, and sported a manicure, he was no longer the boy I had admired.

As I followed Jake and Noah into the other room, I thought about Noah's instant, protest-free compliance with our request. Did he know that Jake was a U.S. Marshal? Surely he had no desire to speak to me.

Once we'd taken a seat at one of the small round tables scattered around the Queen Mary salon, Noah said to Jake, "You're Tony's nephew, right?"

"I'm his grandnephew, yes." Jake didn't seem surprised that Noah knew who he was.

"Is Tony all right?" Noah asked. "I told him he needs to start taking it easier, which was why I was happy to hear you were helping out on the ranch."

"He's fine," Jake said, then sat mutely staring at Noah, clearly hoping the other man would be intimidated enough to want to fill the silence.

I looked between the two guys. Jake was large and muscular and powerful, while Noah was sleek and elegant and aristocratic. Both gorgeous, but in utterly different ways. Dark versus fair. Stunningly masculine versus boyishly handsome. Wolf versus greyhound.

Lost in my own thoughts, I nearly missed Noah's question. "Not that I'm ungrateful for your help in escaping Gwen and the other ladies' attentions for a few minutes, but what's so urgent?"

"Your fiancée's murder." Jake's expression was indecipherable.

"What about it? Do you have some information about her death? Have they found the person who killed her?"

When Noah finally ran out of questions, Jake said, "I'm unaware of any arrests." He continued, his eyes hooded. "Actually, we were hoping *you* might be able to shed some light on what happened."

"Me?" Noah's broad shoulders stiffened under his perfectly tailored black suit jacket. "I've already told the police everything I know."

"Maybe you'll remember something more if you tell us." Jake's expression was unbending. "Now that you've had a few days to think about it."

"Why are you interested?" His voice caught for

a moment, and his glance flickered between Jake and me. "Did you know Joelle?"

It hadn't occurred to me before, but it was odd that no one else we'd talked with had asked that question. I made a mental note to mention that fact to Jake once we were alone. Maybe he'd have some insight.

"No. I never met her," Jake said. "You may have heard that I'm a deputy U.S. Marshal, and although I'm currently on leave, I'm unofficially looking into Joelle's murder on behalf of Devereaux." Jake tilted his head at me. "Her connection to you has made her a target, and she's being harassed."

Jake and I had discussed my not wanting Woods's suspicion of me to get around, but Jake had argued that since Noah was the type of guy who seemed to like to rescue women, his desire to save me would make him more cooperative. I had grudgingly agreed that we would tell Noah, but no one else, that I was prime suspect number one.

"Dev?" I heard the guilt in Noah's voice. "Who's harassing her and for what?"

Before Jake could answer, I decided I'd rather spin the story my way, so I quickly said, "The detective on Joelle's case has decided that because you dumped me in high school, I'm still carrying a torch for you. His theory is that I murdered your fiancée in a jealous rage in order to free you to marry me." I took a breath and added, "And I'd appreciate it if you kept this confidential."

"Of course." Noah's smoky gray eyes clouded. "But the detective's notion is ridiculous. Everyone knows you've hated me since then, and that you have no desire to rekindle our romance. Right?"

I turned away, unable to cope with the pain etched on his face. "Right."

# CHAPTER 14

Apparently, Jake realized how much I didn't want to discuss the past, because he immediately stepped in and said to Noah, "So I assume you're willing to help us out." He leaned back in the delicate gilt chair, his face set in hard lines. "Tell us what happened last Saturday."

"Joelle wanted our first Valentine's Day weekend together to be special. Occasions like that were extremely important to her."

*Hmm.* That sure didn't sound like a woman who wanted out of an engagement. Had the mayor lied to us or had Joelle lied to him about her relationship with Noah?

Noah stared at the tabletop. "She arranged everything."

"What do you mean by 'arranged'?" Jake prompted him.

"She made the reservations at the Parkside Hotel, planned a special room service menu with the chef, and cleared my late-afternoon schedule with the clinic receptionist. The night before, she packed my overnight bag." Noah studied his clasped hands. "That morning she drove to Kansas City, checked in, and drove back to give me one of the key cards so I could avoid any delay at the registration counter."

"Check-in at most hotels is three or four o'clock," Jake observed.

"She said she cherished our time together too much to waste even a second of it, so she slipped the clerk a tip to get the room earlier," Noah explained.

I barely stopped myself from making a face, gagging at the idea that Joelle had allowed Noah to believe that his time was more valuable than anyone else's. She had found the ultimate doctor ego trip and reeled him in like a striped bass on a fishing line.

"What time did she give you the key card?" Jake's question broke into my thoughts.

"I'm not sure. She left it at the clinic's reception desk." Noah's tone was self-lacerating. "I was too busy to come out and get it from her."

"Then what did she do?" Jake's voice was nonjudgmental, but I could see his lips tighten.

"I guess she went back to the city." Noah shrugged. "She wanted to do some shopping and get her hair done." He looked at Jake. "You know that detective asked these same questions, right?"

"Yeah." Jake scowled. "But the police aren't exactly eager to share information with us since Devereaux is their main suspect."

"Of course. How stupid of me." Noah's knuckles whitened as he gripped the edge of the table. "I'm still not thinking straight."

"Joelle picked up the gift basket from me a little after one o'clock, so she probably came straight to the store after stopping at the clinic," I offered, fighting the sympathy I was beginning to feel for Noah. "When I was putting the basket in her car, she mentioned she was heading into the city as soon as she stopped for gas."

"Maybe we can locate the station she stopped at," Jake said. "Her credit card usage would give us the time." He turned to Noah. "Did she have a favorite place to gas up?"

"No." Noah shook his head. "Whichever one was most convenient."

"Okay. I'll drive her most likely route and see which filling stations are located along the way." Jake fished out a notepad and pen from the pocket of his flannel shirt. "We also need to find out when she first checked in to the Parkside and when she got back." He turned to Noah. "What time did you arrive at the hotel?"

"I was supposed to be there at six. My last appointment was at four, and I figured thirty to forty-five minutes with the patient, then a quick shower. My plan was to be on the road no later than five o'clock. But we got a call about a medical emergency coming in, so I stayed."

"What time did you finish with that patient?" Jake glanced up from his note taking.

"I didn't. She never showed up." Noah frowned and blew out a regretful sigh. "When we tried the number the woman had left, no one answered. And there was no voice mail or answering machine."

"How long did all of this take?" I asked. I was beginning to think Noah had been deliberately delayed, which would imply that Joelle's murder was premeditated. "Did you go directly to the Parkside afterward?"

"Yes. But I didn't leave town until after six." Noah looked at me as if he were begging me to understand his decision. "I had to wait. I had no choice. What if it had been a real emergency and her arrival was delayed by car trouble or some other circumstance? The nearest hospital is forty miles away, and ours is the only clinic that's open past noon on Saturday. I couldn't risk letting a patient die because I was anxious to start my weekend."

"So the room service guy had already found Joelle's body when you got there?"

I winced at Jake's bald statement. Noah's face was pale, and beads of sweat had popped out along his upper lip. He seemed to be truly suffering. I reached out to comfort him, but caught myself before my hand made contact with his, reminding myself that Noah had deserted me during the worst experience of my life. His defection, coming on top of losing both of my parents—one to jail and one to California—had devastated me. He didn't deserve my compassion. Or did he? Was it time to forget the past?

"Yes." Noah's ragged voice interrupted my trip down memory lane. "There was heavy traffic going into the city, so I didn't get to the hotel until nearly seven thirty. I think the police said the waiter found her about a half hour before I arrived." Noah inhaled sharply. "If I had left when I was supposed to, not waited around for a phantom patient, maybe I could have saved her." His Adam's apple moved convulsively as he tried to swallow his remorse. "It's all my fault."

"Because you were late?" Jake clarified.

Noah nodded.

Once Jake was assured that Noah was speaking metaphorically and not literally, he said, "Just one more thing, Dr. Underwood. Think back. Was there ever anything odd about Joelle that you ignored at the time but thought later was a little hinky?"

"Hmm." Noah closed his eyes and pursed his lips. After a minute or two he said, "There was one strange incident. Once when we were out in

171

a crowd someone shouted out the name Jolene and she reacted as if they were calling her. She explained it away, saying the two names were so similar she'd just misheard with all the noise."

"But you didn't quite believe her?" Jake probed. "Did you ever ask her about it again or do any checking on her background?"

"No." Noah gazed at me thoughtfully. "For once I was determined to trust someone. I'd made the mistake of letting my doubts ruin another relationship, and I wasn't about to do that this time."

When he didn't go on, I wasn't sure if I was relieved or disappointed. We all sat silently for a moment. It was clear that Jake wasn't going to reveal that we had discovered Joelle's false identity, so I changed the subject and asked Noah, "Have you heard anything about the mayor having a new girlfriend?"

"No one has mentioned it to me." Noah shook his head. "And after what happened at the New Year's Eve ball, I'm sure someone would have told me."

I could tell that Jake had run out of questions for Noah, so I asked him to give me a few minutes alone with him. Throughout our interview, I had begun to see that it was long past time to clear the air with my high school ex. We had both been so young, and lacking in the maturity to handle the situation. Now that we were adults, I needed to let go of my bitterness and start fresh. Or at least I had to give it a try.

Once Jake was gone, I told Noah, "I just want to say I don't hate you. I never really did." I faced him across the table and steeled myself against his heartrendingly tender gaze. "All I ever wanted was for you to say you were sorry for what you did to me." The words leaked out of me like air from a balloon, leaving me feeling deflated. "For you to admit you were wrong."

"But I did." Noah wrinkled his smooth brow. "Don't you remember?"

"No." I blew out a puff of exasperation. Here I was, giving him a second chance, and he was trying to wiggle off the hook. "When did this supposed apology take place?"

"The day you came back to school. When we were working on the yearbook that afternoon." A stubborn expression settled on his face. "After everyone else left, I said that I was sorry. I explained that I didn't have any choice. If I didn't stop seeing you, my mother—who was a member of the bank's board of directors—had threatened to bring even more charges against your father, and to involve your grandmother in the investigation, too."

"That's not what you said at all." I couldn't believe he was looking me in the eye and lying to me. "You said you were sorry, but it was too much of a risk to be seen with me anymore."

173

There were other corrections I could have made to his account of what had happened, but I chose to hit the highlights. "Admit it; the danger was to your reputation, not to my family."

"That is not true." Noah's face had turned brick red. He took a deep breath, started to speak, stopped, then said, "If you had loved me even a fraction of how much I loved you, you would remember that conversation like I do. I memorized every word."

"But . . ." Noah's words burned into my skin, leaving a bleeding wound behind, and I rose from my chair, turning away from him. Had he really apologized and I'd been too angry to hear him? Had the pain of the past thirteen years been avoidable? No. It couldn't be. The ache in my chest swelled into my throat, and I had to bite my lip to keep the tears away. "I don't think . . ."

"That was the problem." Noah came up behind me. "You weren't thinking back then. You were miserable and didn't want anyone to comfort you. You erected a shield that no one could breach."

"How can you say that after you abandoned me?" I rounded on him. "You took your mother's side over mine and left me to face the town's ridicule without you. Boone and Poppy were the only ones who stood by me. You were too worried about your reputation to continue dating the daughter of the town's biggest criminal."

"That's not what happened at all." Noah ran his fingers through his dark blond hair. "You turned away from me. That's why I never approached you in all these years. You made it clear you wanted me to leave you alone."

"I don't believe that. If you'd wanted to see me or try to reestablish our relationship, you would have."

"When I tried to call you a few days after that last fight of ours, you called me a stalker, so I thought it was best to wait for *you* to contact me."

"What are you talking about?" I shook my head. "There was no phone call."

"Yes, there was." Noah's voice rang with sincerity. "And since I would never do anything to hurt you, not then and not now, I respected your wishes to be left alone. But you have to believe me. You have to stop being so stubborn and open up yourself."

I could see the wounded teenage boy in his eyes, and the love I'd once felt for him tried to escape the place in my heart where I'd sealed it up tight. I parted my lips to say I believed him, but then I stopped.

Memories of the past flickered like a slideshow in my mind. Finally I murmured, "You know, now that I think about it, I was always the one who had to change and trust and be different. And at fifteen and sixteen, I was willing to do that. But I've grown up since then. I've learned that trying to earn someone's love is a lot like trying to lose weight—eventually you always end up right back where you started from, or worse."

Noah shook his head. "All I ever wanted was for you to be the best you could be."

Taking a deep breath, I nodded. "I know, but perhaps what you think is the best me, and what I think is the best me, are two different things."

"Maybe you're right." The words fell from Noah's lips like broken glass. His head drooped and he said almost to himself, "I had hoped, if you ever gave me a chance to really talk to you, it would mean that you were ready to forgive and forget."

"I do forgive you," I said as I walked toward the door. "I just don't think I can forget." The words left my mouth tasting of regret. "And right now I can't waste time reliving the past. I need every minute to worry about my future."

Without waiting for Noah's reaction, I hurried out of the restaurant, panting with the effort not to cry. By the time I made it to the parking lot, I had gotten myself under control. Which was a good thing, since Jake was sitting in his truck and I didn't want him to see me acting like a lovesick teenager.

On the pickup's CD player B. B. King was singing "The Thrill Is Gone" and Jake was resting his head against the seat with his Stetson tipped over his eyes. I wondered if he was asleep, but the moment I opened the door to climb into the cab, he straightened and gave me a searching look.

Before he could ask any questions I didn't want to answer, I said, "Thanks for letting me speak to Noah alone. I hope I didn't keep you too long."

"You're welcome. After you've been on as many stakeouts as I have, waiting for someone any less than twelve hours is a breeze." He switched off the CD and put the truck in gear. "Everything go okay?"

"Fine." My reply was terse, but I couldn't afford to think about what had just happened. "What's your impression of Noah's story?"

"Hard to say." Jake pulled out of the lot and onto the drive leading to the road. "But what he told us sure didn't paint him in a flattering light, and most people who lie make themselves look like the hero and everyone else like the villain."

"That's true." I narrowed my eyes. "But did he really make himself look bad? Think about it. The heroic doctor selflessly sacrificing his own pleasure to take care of a patient."

"That would be a smooth move on his part." Jake turned right on the blacktop and headed back to town. "Making us ask ourselves how can he be the killer if saving lives is so important to him?"

"Until we verify his account of Saturday, I'm keeping him in the suspect column." I twisted my neck and glanced at Jake to gauge his reaction to my declaration. Would he think I was acting like a woman scorned? "Noah's nurses and receptionist doubtlessly are not my biggest fans, and they know Boone and Poppy are my friends, so you'd be the best one to have a word with his staff."

"Too bad the clinic is closed this afternoon." Jake slowed as he approached a corkscrew turn in the road. "It would be good to speak to them before Noah has a chance to talk to them and influence their memories."

"You're in luck." The seat belt was cutting into my neck and I adjusted it before going on. "Noah's staff moonlights at the county hospital during the times his office is closed. They work the Baby Wellness Center there."

"Great." Jake smiled at me. "Want to go with me, and we can get dinner afterward?"

Tempting as a meal out with Jake was, I shook my head. "I'd better not. I haven't spent much time with Birdie lately, so I should go home and see how she's doing."

"Yeah." Jake's expression was unreadable. "That's probably a good idea."

We were both silent for a few seconds; then it occurred to me that I hadn't told Jake what the mayor had said, so I filled him in on that conversation. As I spoke, I wondered what else I had forgotten to tell whom.

I thought back. Did Boone know that Joelle wasn't really Joelle? Had I told Poppy? Did she tell Boone about our conversation with the mayor? And, of course, neither of them knew what Noah had just told Jake and me.

We needed to have a group meeting and make sure we were all on the same page. But did I really want Jake to get to know my friends? What if they didn't like him or he didn't like them? Worse, what if he liked Poppy too much? He wouldn't have been the first man who looked at Poppy and me side by side and chose her. Not that she'd ever purposely steal someone I was interested in, but she was so incredibly lovely she didn't have to do anything to have guys fall for her.

I knew I was being ridiculous. First, the most important issue was finding out who killed Joelle so I didn't end up behind bars. Second, why did it matter to me what happened when Jake met my pals? He was just someone helping me out because his uncle and my grandmother used to date. Heck, except for the physical attraction, I wasn't even sure I wanted him. I glanced guiltily at him.

He turned his head at that exact moment, meeting my eyes and cocking a brow as if to ask, "What?" When I didn't speak, he shrugged, looked back at the asphalt, and concentrated on driving.

At last the rational part of my brain won, and I said, "We should get together tonight with Poppy and Boone so we can all catch up with what we've been doing." Jake didn't answer right away, and I added, "Unless, of course, you have other plans."

"No, I'm free." He drove on for a minute or so, then pulled the pickup into the driveway of a ramshackle farmhouse. He shifted into park and turned to me. "Why don't you want me to meet your friends?"

"What are you talking about?" Had he read my mind? "I'm the one who just suggested it."

"I've been watching your face. From the moment you remembered you hadn't told me about your visit to the mayor, you've been wrestling with whether to get your friends and me together."

"That's ridiculous." I turned my upper body and looked out the side window.

"Like hell it is." Jake put his hands on my shoulders and gently eased me toward him. "Why don't you want to introduce me to them?"

"I do." I cleared my throat. "I was just considering whether it was a waste of your time or not." There, that sounded plausible.

"Bullshit." Jake pulled me closer. "Tell me the

truth. Why do you want to keep me out of your personal life?"

"I don't," I protested. "Except, well . . . we're not . . . I mean . . ." Squeaking, I finally got the word out. "Dating." I swallowed. "Are we?" He had asked me to dinner.

"Not yet." Jake seemed surprised by his answer, and he added slowly, "But we might be if you weren't so intent on keeping me at arm's length."

Was I? Was Noah right? Did I close myself off from people? The realization that it might be my fault that I'd been unable to form any lasting relationships with men tore down the final vestige of my self-control. It had been thirteen years since the last time I had allowed myself to cry, and once the tears started, I couldn't stop them. Suddenly I was sobbing so hard I couldn't catch my breath.

I tried to twist away, but Jake drew me against him, wrapping his arms around me as if to shield me from anyone who might hurt me. He stroked my hair and murmured soothing words until I had exhausted myself. Then he grabbed a napkin from the glove box and handed it to me.

Once I'd blown my nose and wiped my eyes, he asked, "What's wrong?"

"Noah." I gulped. "He . . ."

Before I could continue, Jake said, "What did that bastard do to you?" Without waiting for my answer he growled, "Don't worry, sweetheart.

He won't get away with hurting you this time."

"He didn't do anything." I pulled myself together and shook my head. "And I've learned that when you try to get even with someone, you're only allowing that person to continue to harm you."

# CHAPTER 15

Jake sat in his truck watching as the dime store's door closed behind Devereaux and wished she was still beside him. Better yet, still in his arms. Why was he allowing her to affect him this way? He whacked his head against the back of the seat and stared at the ceiling.

Things were going way too fast, and his life seemed to be careening out of control. How had he gone from deciding not to tell Devereaux about his ex-wife to asking her out on a date? What happened to letting her think he was a two-timing jerk so she'd keep him at a distance? Had he completely lost his mind?

When he'd stopped by the store to talk to Devereaux yesterday afternoon, she'd given him an out for their interrupted lovemaking Tuesday night. But had he accepted her rationalization and let the matter drop? No. Instead he'd accused her of being a snob. She had voiced his feelings exactly—emotions only mess people up. So why didn't he agree with her and pretend nothing had happened between them?

That would have been the smart thing to do. Instead he'd kissed her, and would have continued kissing her if she hadn't chosen that moment to tell him about Woods harassing her. Jake whacked his head against the back of the seat again. Was he going crazy?

Maybe so. A sane man wouldn't have a burning desire to go back to the restaurant, find Underwood, and beat him to within an inch of his life for making Devereaux cry. A sane man wouldn't allow a woman he barely knew to crowd his every thought. A sane man would be able to control himself, and stop thinking about laying her down and tasting her sweetness.

Jake pounded the steering wheel. He was leaving town as soon as he was healed. He repeated what he'd told himself the previoius day: Relationships didn't work for him and it wouldn't be fair to Devereaux to hook up with her for just a few nights of wild sex.

Despite having just told himself all of the good reasons to cool things between them, Jake closed his eyes and savored the memory of her soft warmth in his arms. A long shudder traveled over him and he felt something deep in his chest. It wasn't an itch that could easily be scratched and forgotten, but more an all-consuming craving. A wanting beyond anything he'd ever felt before.

This was not good. Frowning at his own weakness, he scrubbed his face with his fists. He couldn't allow this feeling to override his common sense. The safest course would be to avoid Devereaux—at least until he had himself under better control.

Instead of meeting up with her and her friends that night as he'd promised, he would call and cancel. He'd claim an emergency on the ranch, and report his findings from this afternoon's interviews via the telephone.

Jake took a deep breath and pulled himself upright. It was time to go to work. He checked the crude map that Devereaux had drawn for him on a paper napkin, threw his truck into reverse, and backed onto the street.

Snow clung like white moss to the trees that lined the country road connecting Shadow Bend with the county seat. Jake drove the speed limit, giving himself a chance to collect his thoughts and figure out a strategy for approaching Underwood's staff.

Even going a sedate fifty-five, his F-250 ate up the miles, and he arrived at the hospital at three fifteen. The Baby Wellness Center, a government-subsidized program, was housed in the oldest part of County General. As Jake crossed from the hallway of the recently remodeled part of the building into the corridor of the untouched wing, he noted that there was nothing cheerful or even new inside the clinic. Instead of fresh paint and modern equipment, there was only a bleak sense of constantly having to scrape by. Whoever had been in charge of disbursing the grant money had been tightfisted, seeing no need for frills.

Entering the waiting room, Jake realized he was in luck. The center closed at four, and there were only one mother and baby waiting to be seen. As he walked past the exhausted-looking woman, she glanced up from trying to soothe the screaming infant she held in her arms. He gave her an encouraging nod and she smiled wearily.

From her perch behind the check-in desk, the receptionist peered up at him for a long moment, then asked doubtfully, "Can I help you, sir?"

"I hope so, Madison." Jake leaned in, reading the ID card hanging from a lanyard around her neck. "I sure could use some help."

Madison was in her early twenties and wore a pastel smock printed with baby animals. Blond curls framed her heart-shaped face, and there was a vase with a single pink rose next to her computer.

"My name is Jake Del Vecchio." He held out his hand and she tentatively shook it. "I'd like to ask you a few questions. Do you have a minute?"

"Sure." She pointed to the monitor. "I was just doing some paperwork. Nothing that can't wait. What would you like to know?"

"A friend of mine had an accident last Saturday and called Dr. Underwood for help." Jake rested a hip against the counter. "Do you remember that?"

"I do." Madison gazed at Jake, her solemn baby blue eyes never leaving his. "We were almost out the door when the call came in."

"But you came back, right?" Jake's posture remained relaxed and his tone casual.

"Yes."

"That's a shame." Jake's expression became remorseful. "As it turned out, my friend wasn't as badly hurt as she thought and she ended up not going to his office after all. Now she feels bad and wants to know if the doc waited around a long time for her."

"Gee." Madison screwed up her face. "I don't know how long Dr. Underwood waited. He told me I could go ahead and leave, so I did."

"Well, shoot." Jake glanced around. "Did anyone stay with him?"

"Yes." Madison bobbed her head. "Yale—the physician assistant—left with me, but Mom stayed."

"Do you think I could have a word with your mom?" Jake asked.

"Sure." Madison stood. "You wait right here and I'll go get her."

"I'd appreciate it." Jake smiled. "By the way, what's her name?"

As she disappeared into the back, Madison called over her shoulder. "Eunice Vogel."

Jake decided that Madison must take after her dad's side of the family because he couldn't see any of her soft prettiness in Eunice. They were both petite and blond, but that was where the resemblance ended. Eunice's white uniform hung on her thin frame as if she'd recently been ill, and her face looked as if it had been carved from the side of a mountain.

Her eyes were full of censure when she marched up to Jake and admonished, "It was extremely rude of Ms. Brown to ask the doctor to wait and then not show up for the appointment." Hitting the palm of her hand with the business end of a stethoscope, the nurse stared at him as if daring him to deny her statement.

Eunice's disapproval was sharp enough to slice a decade-old fruitcake and Jake wondered if he was bleeding from her cutting stare.

"Yes." He hurried to assure her. "I know. And she is very sorry."

"Well, she should be." Eunice jabbed a finger at Jake's face. "The doctor had an important personal engagement that evening and she made him late for it with horribly disastrous consequences."

"That's terrible." Jake pretended that he had no idea to what the nurse was referring. "How long did the doctor wait around?"

"Long enough." Eunice's stance oozed contempt. "Wasting even a minute of that saintly man's precious time is a sin."

"Ms. Brown *did* try to call and say she wasn't coming after all, but no one picked up." Jake took a chance at lying since Madison had said she wasn't at the office to answer the phone. "Why didn't you or the doctor get the telephone? Surely if you were waiting a long time . . ." He trailed off, hoping she'd reveal something.

"Well." The nurse's voice held a lot less conviction than it had a moment ago, and red stained her cheeks. "Actually, since it was Valentine's Day weekend and all, the doctor told me to go. I had tickets for a play, and my husband was waiting in the parking lot."

"What time was that?" Jake asked immediately, not giving her a chance to think.

"A few minutes after five." Eunice's voice faltered.

"Let me see. The call came in at what, four thirty?" Jake thought out loud. "And Madison and Yale left a few minutes later, and you followed at five." Jake stared at the nurse. "Dr. Underwood may have stayed another hour. Or he could have left as soon as you were out of sight, which would explain why no one answered the phone." Jake stepped closer to the older woman and gazed down at her. "You have no idea if his time was wasted or not, do you?"

188

The nurse didn't admit her lack of knowledge, but neither did she duck his accusation. Instead, she pursed her lips, gave him a withering look, and said, "We're through here. You need to leave right now."

# CHAPTER 16

My cell rang as Gran and I were eating dinner. The phone was on the table between us, and Birdie's eyes lit up when she saw Jake's name appear on the tiny screen. I must admit my heart accelerated a little, too.

At first it sounded as if he was opting out of the evening's plan to get together, but after a few minutes of confusing chitchat, he finally confirmed Boone's address and said he'd see me later.

Boone's was the only place where we could be assured of complete privacy. I, of course, lived with Gran, and although Poppy had an apartment above Gossip Central, I didn't think this kind of discussion should take place when the bar was open for business. There would be too many curious eyes speculating on Jake's presence, and how he fit into our group.

Before Jake hung up, he mentioned that he might be a little late. Considering that we weren't meeting until nine because Poppy had to work until her relief bartender came in at eight thirty, I wondered what could delay him at that time of night.

Gran and I played poker for a couple of hours— she wiped me out of toothpicks. Then at eight I left her watching a rerun of *CSI* and went to change out of my sweatpants and T-shirt. I didn't allow myself to think about why I was changing outfits, but I suspected it was because Poppy would be dressed to seduce—her usual style when she tended bar—and I didn't want to look like her ugly stepsister. I also managed to convince myself that I was only putting on makeup so Boone wouldn't give me a hard time. It's amazing how much bullshit I can persuade myself to believe.

Sadly, my hair required more effort than I had the patience to give it. Although I tried setting it in hot curlers, evidently I had forgotten how to do that, because an untamable cloud of ringlets sprang forth when I unwound the little white rods. Giving up my attempt to appear glamorous, and choosing not to look as if I were auditioning for the role of Little Orphan Annie, I wound the whole mess into a loose bun on top of my head.

After stopping in the living room to check on Gran, who was snoring mightily in her La-Z-Boy with Banshee curled on her lap, I hopped into my car and headed toward town. I wasn't sure if supper hadn't agreed with me or if I was getting the flu or if the stress of the last few days had settled in my stomach, but it felt as if pterodactyls were playing paintball in my intestinal tract. Maybe I should have brought along a barf bag.

Boone lived in the best part of town—where all the old money resided. He'd inherited the Prairie-style house from his grandmother, and the only changes he'd made were to enlarge and remodel the master bathroom, convert one of the four upstairs bedrooms into a walk-in closet, and add a detached garage out back.

It was a relief to see that I was the first one to arrive, and I parked in the empty driveway. As I did almost every time I visited Boone, I stopped for a moment to admire the grouping of multipaned windows that was the focal point of the second floor. They were the crowning touch on what otherwise would have been a rather humdrum facade.

Boone was waiting for me in the foyer. He greeted me without commenting on my spiffier-than-usual appearance, which I deemed a good omen.

While he hung my jacket, I peeked in the mirror opposite the coat closet and cringed. Smoothing the black lace of my shirt over my hips, and tugging up the deep V of the neckline, I wished I'd worn something else. I was sporting way more cleavage than I was comfortable exposing, and the top's stretchy material clung to my generous curves.

Since my body type was more apt to be seen in a Rubens painting than in a *Vogue* photo spread, I liked my clothes loose. It was my opinion that the only entity that should cling to another entity was plastic wrap. Which made me wonder why I had ever bought the damn shirt in the first place, let alone worn it tonight.

"You look fine." Boone pulled me away from the mirror and into the library.

Draperies the color of expensive brandy pooled on the hardwood floor, and a nutmeg-colored leather sofa and matching chairs were arranged in front of a fireplace. An oak table held a crystal vase full of chrysanthemums and asters, and brass lamps gave off a warm glow.

"Have a seat," Boone invited. "So at last we get to meet the mysterious cowboy who rode in on his white horse to rescue you."

"What do you mean 'at last'?" I chose the chair nearest the warmth. "You met him Tuesday afternoon, not ten minutes after I did."

"Right." Boone sank gracefully into the other chair.

I frowned. That left the couch for Poppy and Jake to share. *Geesh!* When had I become such a jealous shrew? I had never cared before who sat next to the men in my life. Which, by the way, Jake was not.

"He couldn't get out of there fast enough that day." Boone adjusted the creases in his khakis.

"And you've been strangely reluctant to talk about him."

"That's not true," I protested. "There've just been more important things to discuss. Like how to keep me from going to jail."

Before Boone could respond, we heard Poppy yell a greeting as she let herself in. She burst into the room, gave me a hug, and plopped down on the sofa.

Poppy had come directly from the bar and was wearing skintight jeans that laced up the side, exposing tantalizing glimpses of porcelain skin, and a black bell-sleeved knit shirt held together by a single satin ribbon tied between her breasts. Suddenly my choice of clothing didn't seem quite so risqué.

After we all had helped ourselves to a drink—I stuck to soda, but my friends had martinis—Boone and Poppy tried to grill me about Jake. When I didn't cooperate, they changed tactics and interrogated me about the case. I put them off, saying we'd go over everything once Jake arrived.

Usually the three of us found enough to say to occupy us for hours, but tonight the conversation seemed forced and stilted. It was as if we were all waiting for the main event. I hated that Jake had already changed the dynamic among us.

Squirming, I checked both my cell phone and my watch. No messages, and Jake was already nearly twenty minutes late. Maybe he'd changed his mind and wasn't coming after all.

Sad to say, I realized that might be best after all. Jake and I needed to keep our relationship impersonal. Meeting my friends and becoming a part of the group was not the way to do that. So why was I upset by his absence?

The next ten minutes dragged by as I tried to pay attention to Poppy's story about her father's latest outrage against humanity. Finally the doorbell rang, and relief surged through me. When Boone sprang from his seat, it was all I could do not to follow him out to the hallway.

Gripping the arms of my chair so I'd remain seated, I heard the front door open and a muffled exchange between the men. A few seconds later Jake stepped into the den. His eyes immediately found mine, and he shot me a devastating grin.

I beamed back at him, not sure why we were both so darn happy.

After Boone introduced Jake to Poppy, he asked him, "What can I get you to drink?"

"A beer would be great." Jake seemed distracted as he studied the brimming bookcases built into three of the four walls.

"Sam Adams okay for you?" Boone asked, and when Jake nodded, Boone ordered Poppy, "Help me bring in the munchies."

"Let me." I put down the ginger ale I had been sipping to soothe my traumatized gastric system.

I started to rise, but Poppy was already up. With a wave and a wink, she followed Boone into the kitchen.

Once my friends were out of earshot I said to Jake, "If you were busy tonight, we could have postponed this meeting." As soon as the words left my mouth, I realized they sounded petulant. "I mean, I know you have other things to do than just help me." Shoot! That hadn't been much better. "Anyway, what I'm trying to say is that I don't know if I ever thanked you, but I really am grateful for everything you've done for me."

"You're very welcome." Jake's deep voice filled the room and I felt goose bumps form on my arms. "Sorry I was late, but I had to wait for a call."

"No problem." Was the call from his ex-wife? I clamped my lips shut and concentrated on not asking that question. "Have a seat."

Jake examined the options, then folded his long frame onto the chair opposite mine. For a moment, he rested his head on the back and closed his eyes, a position that displayed his handsome profile.

My mouth went as dry as a week-old doughnut, and I drank in the appealing picture he presented sitting there. Studying him like that, I saw the lines of pain around his eyes and mouth. He never spoke about his injured leg, but I'd bet the dime store's next mortgage payment that reminders of it were seldom far from his thoughts.

I glanced up and caught Jake looking at me, his expression unreadable. At that moment Poppy came in with a serving platter full of hors d'oeuvres, saving me from having to come up with something to say.

She held out the silver tray to Jake with her right hand and offered him a napkin with her left. "See anything you like?" Her voice was sultry and she fluttered her eyelashes. When he froze, she giggled and said to me, "Boone was right. He's quite a hunk."

Jake tipped an imaginary hat at Poppy and said, "Why, thank you, ma'am."

Poppy giggled again, then put the platter down on the table and curled up on the couch. A second or so later, Boone returned. He handed a bottle of beer to Jake and refilled Poppy's martini glass from a silver shaker before settling next to her on the sofa.

Poppy looked around brightly. "So, who wants to go first?"

Three pairs of eyes turned to me and I said, "I guess I will." It took me a minute to organize my thoughts. "Let me see, we all know everything up until when Boone and I came back from the fundraiser, right?" All of them nodded their heads. "Well, since I can't remember who knows what, let's go over the whole lot from that point on."

"Wait!" Boone's cry made me choke on the sip of soda I had just taken.

Poppy sprang to her feet and pounded me on the back, while Boone darted to the desk in the corner of the room and dragged back a poster-size white rectangle. He snapped open the easel and set the board in front of us. Dashing back to the desk, he rummaged in the drawer. "I think it's a good idea for us to write everything down," he explained as he rejoined the group, handing us each a different color erasable marker.

"Good idea." I loved a good list, and charts always made me happy. As I explained about Joelle's false identity, recounted Woods's second visit to the dime store to harass me, and outlined the mayor's claims of a new girlfriend providing an alibi, I jotted the information on the whiteboard using bullet points. I finished with, "Any questions or anything you all want to add?"

"Nope." Poppy licked the Brie oozing off the edge of her cracker.

"That about covers it." Jake took a swig of his beer.

"Hardly," Boone snapped. "What about the good doctor? Don't tell me no one talked to him. I'm sick and tired of everyone giving him a free pass."

"They don't," Poppy objected. "It's just that he's had such a hard time with that mother of his, and he does so much good for the community."

Boone ignored Poppy's protest and demanded of me, "Did you or did you not go to see Dr. Do-Right? I bet you chickened out, didn't you?"

"No. I did not chicken out." I hesitated. Talking about Noah was still hard and my already upset stomach clenched at the prospect of describing our encounter. I looked hopefully at Jake, but his expression said it was my story to tell.

"I heard Noah would be at the Manor for a shelter committee meeting today." Sticking out my chin, I straightened my spine and prayed my voice wouldn't betray my feelings. "So Jake and I drove out to the restaurant and talked to him this afternoon."

"Oh, my God!" Boone cried happily. "You faced off with him in public?"

"It was perfectly civilized," I corrected.

Boone fanned himself with both hands. "I wish I had been a fly on the wall for that reunion. The women on that committee must have been all atwitter in overdrive when you walked in the door."

"Yes," I replied tersely, hoping to move on. "They were surprised."

"That has to be the biggest understatement of the year." Boone didn't even try to suppress his grin. "I bet the fussin' and whisperin' could be heard all the way into the next county. I'm surprised I didn't receive a Tweet about your appearance."

"Maybe you missed it." I scowled at my friend and muttered, "They were certainly texting. I'm sure if you check Facebook, you'll get the full report."

"So?" Poppy stuffed the cracker into her mouth and spoke around it. "What happened?"

"Did Noah agree to talk to you?" Boone jumped in. "Was he jealous you were with someone as hot as Jake?"

I shifted uncomfortably and answered before they could embarrass me further. "Noah was very cooperative. He told us that he'd been delayed at his clinic and didn't arrive at the hotel until after the room service waiter had already found Joelle's body."

"Really?" Boone drew out the single word and rolled his eyes, indicating his skepticism. "And you two believed him why?"

"Not necessarily," I replied, in our defense. "I'm just telling you what he said."

"Good." Boone nodded to himself, satisfied. "Dr. Devious fools a lot of people into thinking he's a selfless martyr, but not me."

Poppy playfully whacked Boone's upper arm with the back of her hand and said to me, "I take it if you didn't trust Noah's account of what happened that day, you checked it out? Talked to his staff?"

Jake, who had seemed lost in his own thoughts up until now, said, "I did. Is there something wrong with Underwood's nurse?" he asked. "She seemed sort of sickish, like a strong wind might blow her away."

"Not that I've heard." Poppy shook her head. "But about a year or so ago, Eunice decided to improve herself and lost a lot of weight." Poppy drew her legs up and wrapped her arms around her knees. "Unfortunately, she's one of those women who looks better chubby. Now she resembles a flattened piñata—one with all the candy gone."

Boone and I nodded our agreement.

"Did Eunice or Yale verify Dr. Deceitful's version of what happened?" Boone eyed Jake thoughtfully. "Or wouldn't she even talk to you?"

Jake explained how he'd gotten Noah's staff to tell him about that day, ending with, "So, although Eunice couldn't say how long Underwood stayed around waiting for the phantom patient, Madison was able to vouch for the fact that a Ms. Brown had indeed called."

Poppy furrowed her brow and said, "But his behavior does sound sort of suspicious, doesn't it? I mean letting his staff go like that. You'd think he'd at least want his nurse to hang around, since it was a female patient." She took a sip of her martini before adding, "I guess that means Noah's still on our suspect list."

"Hey, don't look so sad," I chided her. "There's

no such thing as too many other people with good motives." I smiled, but a part of me mourned the news. Just when I thought I might have misjudged Noah, Jake's interview with Eunice indicated that there was a good chance he couldn't be trusted.

"Definitely," Boone agreed, visibly happy that Noah's innocence couldn't be proved.

"So, what do we do next?" I asked, eager for a change of subject.

"I need to take a closer look at the hotel and the crime scene." Jake's expression was sober. "I just wish I knew how I could do that without revealing my interest to the Kansas City cops. I don't want Woods to get another burr up his butt."

"You'll think of something." Poppy tilted her head. "From what Dev tells me, you're a wonderful investigator and extremely clever."

"Right," Boone chimed in, with a conspiratorial grin. "Dev says she's really impressed with how you handle yourself in situations."

"I did not say that." I looked back and forth between them, incredulous at their outrageous lies. What were they up to? Next thing I knew they'd be telling Jake about their plan to throw Woods off my scent by showing him I already had a boyfriend, and thus had no interest in Noah.

Boone turned back to Jake. "Dev doesn't want

you to know how much she admires and likes you."

"That's nice to hear." Jake cocked a brow at me, plainly amused by my friends' blatant attempts to play matchmaker. "I never would have guessed."

"Well, we figured you should know." Poppy's expression was virtuous.

Narrowing my eyes, I lasered them both a warning look. One that said I'd kill them if they didn't stop this immediately.

My visual threat didn't faze them. Poppy and Boone went on while I searched my mind for something to distract them. Finally I said, "Poppy, weren't you going to talk to Cyndi Barrow about Joelle?" It was lame, but the only way I could think of to change the subject.

"Shoot!" Poppy sobered. "I forgot all about it. I'll try to track her down tomorrow."

"What should I do?" Boone asked.

I looked at Jake, who shrugged and said, "I can't think of anything right now. We've talked to everyone you three thought might be a suspect. Unless you've come up with someone else?"

Boone and Poppy shook their heads.

I heard the quaver in my voice when I asked, "Does this mean there's nothing more we can do?" A flicker of fear darted up my spine. Would Woods have his way and see me in prison?

"No," Jake assured me. "The crime scene will

probably give me some new leads to follow."

After that, the conversation became more general and Jake joined in. His wit and ability to laugh at himself made it seem like he'd been a part of our group forever.

Boone shared lawyer stories, Poppy told about some of her more outrageous bar patrons, and Jake gave us an idea of how dumb criminals could be.

I was talking about my adventures in the world of high finance and investing when I yawned; Boone and Poppy quickly followed suit.

Jake stretched and said, "Looks like it's time to call it a night."

We all agreed. Before we separated, Boone, Poppy, and Jake exchanged cell phone numbers, and Jake cautioned us not to tell anyone about Joelle's false identity.

After we promised, Boone picked up the empty appetizer tray from the coffee table and said, "Poppy, could you grab the glasses for me, please?"

I stood to help with the cleanup, but Poppy gently pushed me back down. "I've got it," she whispered. "You keep Jake company."

Choosing not to argue—embarrassment was inevitable if I did—I agreed, then sat tongue-tied, unable to think of anything to say to Jake.

Finally, he cleared his throat. "I had a good time tonight."

"Me, too." I blushed. "I could tell my friends really liked you."

"I liked them, too." He stood. "I should get going. Ranch work starts early."

"Sure." I got up, too. "I'll show you out."

We walked into the foyer, and after I handed him his coat and hat it looked as if he was about to kiss me.

Sticking to my resolve, I stepped out of his reach, so instead he touched the brim of his Stetson and said, "I'll call you tomorrow."

"Great." I forced myself to look away from the warmth of his eyes.

"That was stupid." The front door had barely closed when Poppy berated me. "Why didn't you let him kiss you? It was clear he wanted to."

I faced her. "The last thing I need in my life right now is a boyfriend. Think about my track record with the opposite sex."

"Phooey!" Poppy blew a raspberry. "Your problem is that you think the perfect guy will turn up on your doorstep like an already-assembled piece of furniture. But a good man doesn't just happen."

"No?"

"No. They have to be put together by us women. First you have to eliminate all the bad habits his mom taught him. Then you have to get rid of that macho crap they pick up from beer and truck commercials. And finally, you have to delete all the data his friends entered. Only at that point are they worth spending any amount of time with."

We both giggled a little; then I said regretfully, "A relationship with Jake would be too much of a risk."

"Life is a risk." Poppy poked my shoulder for emphasis. "Your only choice comes down to whether you're the taker or the taken."

# CHAPTER 17

B ingo?" I heard my horrified tone and started over, trying not to sound quite as appalled as I felt. "You want me to go to bingo with you tonight?"

I had been heading to work when Gran ambushed me in the front hallway.

"If you're not too busy." Her voice quavered suspiciously; then she went for the kill. "I just thought it would be fun since we haven't been spending much time together."

Gran's Friday evening bingo games were a sacrosanct part of her life, but she'd never before invited me to accompany her.

"Really?" Either she was dying and not telling me, or this was some sort of scheme. Gran liked her space, and enjoyed the chance to let her hair down with her friends. What was she up to?

"You said you and Jake weren't working on the murder tonight." Gran compressed her mouth into a thin white line, then, like a ventriloquist, muttered without moving her lips, "Although I can't imagine why not."

"Because we haven't decided on our next move yet," I explained, folding my arms across my chest and waiting for her next volley.

"Right." She narrowed her pale blue eyes, then smiled sweetly. "I believe you mentioned that Boone has a business dinner." Banshee was draped around Gran's neck like an ermine stole, and she stroked his tail before adding, "I imagine Poppy's working at her bar."

She had me there. "True." My friends were busy and I had no intention of being alone with Jake. Not that he had asked, although he had said he'd call. "You're not sick or anything, right?"

"No," Gran snapped and Banshee hissed, all traces of sweet little old lady and cute kitty vanishing. "Is it too much to ask that you spend a couple of hours with me, doing something I enjoy?"

"Of course not." She was right, and I felt guilty for doubting her. "Sorry." Sucking it up, I said cheerfully, "I'd love to play bingo with you tonight. The store closes at six. How about I pick you up a little after that, and we can go right there."

Gran shook her head decisively. "I better meet

you. If you're not at the hall by five o'clock all the good seats are taken."

"Good seats?" I knew Gran liked to go early, but I had always assumed it was to visit with her pals, not to stake out her territory.

"The ones up front," Gran explained. "Father mumbles and you can't hear him from the back." She groused, "They need to buy one of those . . . uh . . ."

"Microphones?"

She shook her head, but I was stumped.

"You know, one of those thingies that show what numbers have been called." Gran sneered, "But the Altar and Rosary Society is too cheap to spend the money."

"Oh." I was already in the doghouse with Gran, so I didn't mention the hearing aid the audiologist had suggested. Why borrow trouble?

"Come in the side entrance," she ordered. "Only newbies use the front."

"Gotcha." I eased the door open. "Is there food available?" I knew I'd be starving if I had to wait until after nine to have supper.

"Certainly." Gran inserted herself between the threshold and me. "The ladies of the church sign up to bring stuff to sell."

"Terrific." I brightened at the thought of homemade goodies.

"Don't get too excited." She sniffed. "Half those women use box mixes."

"Okay." I wasn't discouraged. Even a not-from-scratch brownie would taste mighty fine if you were hungry enough. "I better get going."

"Not so fast." Gran didn't budge when I tried to step around her. "Maybe you should take a nice outfit to change into after work."

"Why would I do that?" My guard immediately went up. Clothing suggestions from a woman who wore a flowered muumuu one day and an authentic 1920s flapper dress the next were a little suspect. No doubt about it, she was up to something. "I wasn't aware bingo was a formal event."

"Sweet Jesus! I'm not suggesting a ball gown and dyed-to-match slippers," she retorted. "Just a top that doesn't have writing across your chest."

"Fine." I spun on my heel, stomped into my room, grabbed a white blouse from the closet, and returned to the foyer. "Can I go now?"

"Be my guest." Gran stepped away from the door. As I walked out, she yelled after me, "Don't forget to put on some lipstick and take your hair out of that stupid ponytail."

Damn! I had been mean to my grandmother, and I was still stuck playing bingo tonight.

The day went downhill from there. Hannah arrived for work looking pale and as if she was about to pass out. She finally admitted she was too sick to stay. Soon after her departure, a customer came to pick up a wedding shower basket that she had ordered for her daughter.

The mother of the bride hated my creation, especially the book I had selected—*The Joy of Sex*. She insisted that I do it over immediately and include a book that would help her daughter learn to bake, rather than help her learn how to put a bun in the oven. She also demanded that I deliver it to her home as soon as the dime store closed.

Then the phone rang. And rang. And rang. After too many annoying calls to count, I almost didn't answer the next one, especially when I saw it was Jake. Finally I reminded myself that he was helping to keep my butt out of jail, and I picked up.

"Devereaux?" His voice sounded like well-aged scotch, smoothly intoxicating, and sent a ripple of awareness through me.

"Yes." My hand tightened on the receiver and I had to clear my throat. "It's me."

"It took some doing, but I've arranged to get access to the crime scene."

"That's incredible." I was impressed. "How did you pull that off? Did you have to reveal you were a U.S. Marshal?" I crossed my fingers, hoping he hadn't. I didn't want Woods to get wind of our investigation.

"No. I located a colleague who has a CI on the hotel staff."

"CI?"

"Confidential informant," he explained. "Someone law enforcement officers pay for their information and cooperation."

"That's terrific." I wedged the phone between my ear and shoulder so I could continue to work on the Easter baskets for the Athletic Booster Club's fund-raiser. I was nearly done, but still had to photograph them and make up the brochures. "When are you leaving?"

"I can't tonight. It turns out Uncle Tony needs me for something or other." He sounded puzzled. "Anyway, how about we go tomorrow afternoon?"

"We?" I zeroed in on the important part of his announcement as I propped a tiny bag of Jelly Belly candy against a fluffy pink rabbit.

"Yes. The hotel contact is the night main-tenance man, and he says he can only do this if we check in, so he can claim he had no idea who we were if down the road there's any problem with his boss or the local cops."

"Why can't you check in alone?" I measured out a length of yellow satin ribbon.

"Because it's the honeymoon suite." Jake's voice was amused. "The CI insists it has to be a couple or it will look suspicious."

"Yeah, I can see how a single guy staying in the honeymoon suite might seem peculiar," I admitted. "Okay. I'll go." If Jake made a pass while we were at the hotel I'd just say no. I'd close my eyes and pretend that I wasn't attracted to his handsome face or turned on by his sexy body, and I'd just say no. Yeah, right. "Let me look at my calendar."

"By all means." His tone became distant. "I wouldn't want to interfere with your social life."

I was about to explain that I was checking to see if I needed to stay after the store closed to make any baskets when I stopped. Maybe it was better to let him think I was seeing someone else.

"So." Jake interrupted my racing thoughts. "Can you fit me in?"

"Yes. I'm free after four." There was nothing urgent on my basket-making schedule. "Do you want to pick me up here, or would you like me to drive?"

"I'll drive."

Before I could say good-bye, he hung up and I stood there listening to a dial tone.

Having, as ordered, changed into my white blouse, combed my hair down around my shoulders, and applied peach lipstick, I was ready to report for bingo duty. That is, as soon as I dropped off the remade wedding shower basket to Mrs. Fussbudget.

Thank goodness, the mother of the bride was satisfied with my second attempt. Unfortunately, now that she was happy with it, she wanted me to stay and chat. She insisted on showing me the bridal gown and all the wedding gifts that had already been delivered for her daughter, and then she led me through her house, which had been turned into a shrine to the happy couple's upcoming nuptials.

Since a delivery that should have taken a couple of minutes had turned into a nearly half-hour encounter, I was now seriously behind schedule. As I sped toward my bingo date, I resigned myself to a boring evening with the support-stockings-and-dentures crowd.

*Ouch!* Where had that snarky thought come from? I mentally apologized to the senior citizens I had maligned and vowed to play nice.

Gran's game was at St. Sagar's Catholic Church. As a child, I had asked the priest about the name. Although he'd explained who Saint Sagar was, further probing revealed he had no idea why Shadow Bend's Catholic church had been christened for a martyred bishop from Turkey. Not surprisingly, the parishioners called it St. Saggy's.

St. Saggy's had had a recent spate of bad luck, which started when the six-foot-tall fiberglass figure of Jesus that stood in front of the building was struck by lightning. The statue went up in flames, like a giant roman candle, leaving nothing but a blackened steel skeleton.

Understandably, people did not find this an uplifting display, and, according to Gran, attendance at Sunday Mass was way down. Father Flagg, a different priest than the one I had annoyed with my questions during catechism classes, was frantically trying to raise the funds to replace Jesus, but the cost was prohibitive and few people were contributing to his pet project.

There was something disturbing about the burnt effigy, and I parked my car as far from the twisted hunk of metal as I could get. Turning my head to avoid looking at the unsettling image, I hurried past it toward the fellowship hall on the far side of the lot.

The hall was a faded green pole building divided into a trio of gathering rooms, with a long kitchen accessible to all three. It was a bare-bones structure serving the congregation's needs for catechism classes, weddings, showers, and funeral luncheons. As I pushed through the glass door, I saw a notice tacked to the bulletin board on my right. It read: THE FASTING AND PRAYER CONFERENCE INCLUDES MEALS.

I was still chuckling at the sign when Gran met me a few steps down the hall. She was dressed in a 1950s black linen sheath that had white arrows on either side of her still tiny waist. Matching black pumps and her hair in a French twist completed her outfit. I paused for a moment, thinking that this is how she must have looked the year she graduated from high school.

"You're late." Her disapproval was evident in

the steel grip she took on my arm. "Hurry up."

It always amazed me how fast Birdie could move, considering her size and age. Trailing her down the corridor, I had trouble keeping up. She led me to the largest of the three rooms and steered me over to one of the five long tables at the front.

"We're sitting here." She gestured at a spot with four sheets of paper bingo cards taped to the table's surface, and an array of brightly colored markers known as daubers lined up ready to help make us rich. "Put your coat on these two chairs so no one takes them."

Birdie's jacket was already draped over two other seats, so although I followed instructions, I wondered why. Mentally shrugging, I checked the old-fashioned round wall clock. There were still seventeen minutes until the game commenced, so I looked around.

People were six-deep at the rear of the room, chatting. They'd created a human wall that blocked the sight of whatever was behind them, but the delicious odors of roasted meat, pickled peppers, and baked goods beckoned me. I was hoping for Italian beef sandwiches on homemade rolls and chocolate cupcakes with vanilla icing.

Following my nose, I sauntered over to the mob. I could smell the food. Now if I could just get close enough to taste it.

Gran accompanied me, and as I reached the

group, she announced in a loud rah-rah voice, "Here's Devereaux."

The crowd turned as one and stared at me as if they were waiting for me to perform a song-and-dance act. I felt like a guest on a late-night talk show. Either that or the crazed killer in a Stephen King novel. I wasn't sure which prospect horrified me more.

As I was pondering that choice, the throng swarmed around me. They were all talking at once, and it was difficult to hear any one individual, let alone answer all their questions about my health, business, and social life.

I was trying to focus when a woman who barely came up to my chest tugged on my sleeve and in a stage whisper announced, "I heard you and Dr. Underwood made up at the homeless shelter meeting."

I shot a worried glance at Gran. I hadn't told her about my encounter with Noah. "No." I tried to hush the pint-size troublemaker. "We didn't make up—I mean," I stammered, "we were never fighting—so there was nothing to make up about."

The woman patted my arm and tutted. "Of course not, dear. But it's good you cleared the air with him, especially since he's free again. Someone told me that after you left yesterday, Dr. Underwood said you were as pretty now as you were at sixteen."

Really? "How sweet of him." I struggled to

keep the smile off my face, ridiculously pleased that Noah thought I was still pretty.

"Will you be dating him now that his fiancée is dead?"

I recoiled. "No!" All I needed was for Detective Woods to hear a rumor like that.

"Definitely not." Gran put her arm around me. "My granddaughter has moved on to bigger and better men than Noah Underwood ever was or will be." She gave me a look that said once we were alone, we'd be discussing my failure to keep her apprised of my activities. "In fact, you'll get to meet her new beau tonight."

Before I could process Gran's statement, a voice boomed across the bingo hall, "Birdie Sinclair, where in the Sam Hill are you?"

# CHAPTER 18

At seventy-seven Tony Del Vecchio was an imposing figure. Like his grandnephew, he was tall and handsome, with the same intoxicatingly blue eyes. Hard work had kept Tony lean and muscular, but his hair was silver rather than black.

I had, of course, met Tony on many occasions, but now that I knew he and Birdie had nearly gotten married, I looked at him differently. Previously, he and Birdie had been cordial, but there had been no hint that they'd ever been anything but neighbors. Now he was beaming at her.

He marched over and swooped her into a bear hug, whispering something in her ear.

"Tony." Birdie's face softened into a smile and she squeezed him back, murmuring, "I'd forgotten all about that day."

Apparently, he had taken Birdie's calling him to ask that his nephew help me as a signal that she was ready to change their relationship. And from her expression, it appeared he'd been right.

So that was why Gran had wanted me to come to bingo. She needed my moral support in order to take this new step with Tony. I could certainly understand that. But since it seemed to be going well, maybe I could sneak away and wouldn't have to stay for the whole evening.

Lost in thoughts of my getaway plan and having the house to myself for a couple of hours, I failed to notice the next arrival. That is until a familiar voice near the entrance said sharply, "What are you doing here?"

Birdie's friends closed ranks around me as smoothly as a precision drill team. I appreciated their show of support, even though it was probably more for Birdie's sake than for mine.

In the interim, Jake waded through the crowd and now stood in front of me.

The miniature firebrand who moments ago had

been quizzing me about Noah marched up to him and poked him in the stomach. "She's with us. Who are you? And what are *you* doing here?"

"You all remember my grandnephew, Jake." Tony joined us and slapped his nephew on the back. "The one who's a U.S. Marshal and was injured in the line of duty." Tony puffed out his chest. "He's helping me out on the ranch."

"Oh." My defender melted and grabbed Jake's hand. "What a sweet boy."

Sweet? Seriously? Jake? I shook my head. Sexy. Handsome. Hot. Yes. But not sweet. And certainly not a boy. Unfortunately for my state of mind, he was all man.

While the bingo ladies turned their attention to Jake, I pulled Gran aside and hissed, "Is this why you wanted me here so badly?"

"I don't know what you mean." Gran's face was wreathed in an innocent smile.

"You set this up with Tony, didn't you?" I was beginning to put together the conversation I'd had with Birdie in the morning with the one I'd had with Jake in the afternoon.

"Sweet Jesus!" There were bright circles of pink on her baby doll cheeks. "What are you talking about, child?"

"Oh, please." I gave a choked scream of frustration. "This. Matchmaking." I only just managed to stop myself from stalking away. "Jake and me."

"Sweetie. I swear." Gran put her hand on her heart. "I'd never interfere in your . . . uh . . ."

"Love life," I supplied with a raised brow.

"Exactly." Gran nodded.

I started to point out that she wasn't anywhere near as good a liar as she thought she was, but Tony materialized at Gran's side and glared at me as he asked, "Everything okay, ladies?"

"She thinks we planned this whole evening just to get her and Jake together." Gran pointed at me accusingly. "Tell her we'd never do something like that."

"I'd like to hear this, too." Jake had freed himself from his admirers and joined us. "Is she right, Tony?" He gazed at his uncle accusingly.

"Yep." Tony twitched his shoulders. "Dev is tee-totally correct. Birdie and I think you two would be perfect for each other, so we decided to help things along." He grinned. "You should thank us. We discussed it, and it's clear you both have the hots for each other. And you're both single. So what's the problem?"

I stared at Gran and Tony with equal amounts of incredulity. Finally I threw up my hands in speechless frustration.

Jake and I stood in glum silence, digesting the fact that our loved ones had conspired against us behind our backs. It wasn't until I heard a titter that I looked around and saw that we had an audience.

• • •

LADIES: PLEASE REMAIN SEATED FOR THE ENTIRE PERFORMANCE. I gazed at the oval sign adorning the back of the bathroom stall door. The words were framed by a drawing of parted stage curtains, and although the sentiment was amusing, I wasn't smiling. However, I was perfectly willing to follow the instructions and stay exactly where I was.

A few minutes ago, when I realized that several of the oldest raisins on the Shadow Bend grapevine had heard Tony's comment, I had run away to the ladies' room. Now I was afraid to come out.

After reminding myself that I had survived much scarier circumstances, I stood, swung open the door . . . and immediately regretted my decision when I saw Vivian Yager in front of the sink.

She was not only Vaughn's aunt; she was also the owner of the Curl Up and Dye beauty salon. The women in town went to Vivian's for all the news that didn't make the weekly paper.

It was too late to go back into the stall. If I did that, it would be all over town that I had irritable bowel syndrome, or some other gastric embarrassment. Instead, I said, "Hi, Viv," and braced myself for her questions.

"Dev." She jumped. "You scared the pants off me. I thought I was alone."

"Sorry." I washed my hands, even though I hadn't used the facilities.

"I was running late tonight," Vivian said. "I just got here."

"Oh." That explained why she wasn't interrogating me. Now I just needed an innocuous topic until I could gracefully make my exit. "Hope your friend liked the Valentine's Day basket I made for you."

"He loved it." Vivian winked. Then as she watched me smooth an errant curl behind my ear, she said, "I know you probably think I'm just a small-town blue rinse and Final Net jockey, but if you give me half a chance, I could make your hair look amazing."

"I'm sure you could." I started to demur, then paused. Vivian's own short, sleek style was terrific, and I hadn't had a cut since I'd quit my investment job. Maybe I should take her up on her offer—at the very least get my split ends trimmed.

"I have an opening Monday morning at nine, and since your store doesn't open until noon . . ." Vivian let her voice trail off.

"Well . . ." I was about to take the appointment when a thought occurred to me. "Was Joelle Ayers a client of yours? Her hair was just beautiful."

"No. None of the country club crowd come to me." Vivian addressed my image in the mirror, concentrating on applying her lipstick. "They all go to a place in the city called Imagination."

"Cool name," I responded automatically. Now that Vivian mentioned it, I remembered that Noah had said Joelle was getting her hair done in the city after she left the hotel key card for him last Saturday afternoon.

"Yeah." Vivian tucked the gold tube in her purse. "Those women think I'm not good enough because I charge a quarter of what they pay at that salon." She chuckled. "Funny thing is, the stylist who does their hair there went to beauty school with me, and I graduated number one while Melanie, aka Sarin, was at the bottom of the class."

I assured Vivian that although I couldn't take the Monday slot she offered, I would let her do my hair when I had a little more time. What I didn't share was that before then, I would be getting a cut from Sarin.

When I emerged from the bathroom, Father Flagg was hurrying down the hall. He stopped and asked, "Devereaux, how have you been?"

"Fine, Father." As a lapsed Catholic, I was uncomfortable with the priest's scrutiny.

But before he could ask why I wasn't coming to church or about any of my other sins, the bingo ladies descended on him. The women were a force of nature, kind of like a tsunami; chiding him for his tardiness, they swept him away to call the game.

Relieved at my narrow escape, I didn't see Jake looming in front of me until he said, "I'm sorry Uncle Tony shanghaied you like that." He shook his head. "I don't know what got into him."

"No problem." I felt my cheeks heat up. "It was probably Gran's idea."

"Maybe." Jake stared at the floor, not meeting my eyes. "But Tony could have said no. In fact, up until a few days ago, I would have sworn he wouldn't have any part of something like this."

"I don't know what's with Gran, either." I rubbed my temples. "She's never shown the slightest interest in matchmaking before."

"Weird." Jake stuck his hands into the back pockets of his jeans.

"Too bad everyone heard." I toyed nervously with the tiny pearl buttons on my blouse. "The whole town will know by noon tomorrow."

"Maybe that's not a bad thing." Jake kept his voice low against eavesdroppers. "Your friends told me about their idea to get Woods off your back by making him think you were already involved with another guy, and thus would have no reason to want Underwood's fiancée out of the picture." His lip curled. "Considering Woods's mentality, it might be a pretty good idea."

"Maybe." I tried to read Jake's expression, but as usual, it was impossible to decipher. He had one of the best poker faces I had ever run across, which was annoying when I was trying to gauge his feelings. All I could hope was that he had just as much trouble reading me. "Although I'm not sure anything will deter Woods's quest to see me behind bars."

"It's not like we can undo the fact that fifty people just heard Tony and Birdie declare we were hot for each other." Jake's tone was resigned.

"True." Was he unhappy to have his name linked with mine? "I guess it wouldn't hurt to let people think we were dating." I let my eyes drift up to meet his. "But that would mean we'd have to act like we were really into each other when we're out in public."

"I doubt that'll be difficult." Jake's gaze burned into mine.

I licked my lips and sighed. That was the problem.

Although I had agreed it was a good idea to allow everyone to think Jake and I were involved, I still tried to pretend an indifference to him for the rest of the evening. But sitting beside me, with his thigh occasionally brushing mine, he was too intense and too compelling to be ignored.

During halftime, or whatever they called it for bingo, I finally made it to the food table. Jake followed me and I carefully avoided looking at him as I passed him the dishes he requested. I needed to get my libido under control and remember the only reason we were spending time together was to keep me out of jail. Otherwise, when we checked in to the hotel tomorrow afternoon, I would end up tackling him the minute we stepped through the door of the suite.

Just before we went back to the game, I excused myself. This time I wasn't running away; I truly did need to use the restroom. A few seconds after I sat down, I heard the outer door squeak open. As I peered through the gap between the stall door and the frame, I saw two women walk up to the sinks.

They were in their late fifties or early sixties, and clearly old friends, since they seemed in perfect sync with each other. Almost as one, they withdrew combs from their handbags.

The women's conversation wasn't so much a discussion as a stand-up comedy routine, with one of the ladies doing all the talking.

The nontalker's laugh was like the shrill squeal of a telephone receiver left off the hook for too long. Someone needed to hang her up before the mirror cracked.

I was about to stuff toilet paper into my ears when I heard the comedian say, "Did I tell you that the cops were out at Miss Ayers's condo again?"

"No," Ms. Hyena said, raising both of her painted-on brows to indicate her surprise. "How do you know that?"

My question exactly.

I drew my legs up so they wouldn't realize I was there and willed the stand-up comic to explain herself.

"Remember after the first time, her attorney, Mr. Oberkircher, told me to go ahead and clean up the mess they left, because the landlord wanted to rent it out again as soon as Ms. Ayers's lease was up?"

The funny lady must be Joelle's housekeeper. I needed to have a chat with her somewhere private. Birdie would probably know her name.

"Uh-huh," Ms. Hyena replied. "You said she had left all her money to that dog of hers. Too bad she didn't name you as his guardian, instead of her fiancé. You would have been sitting pretty getting all that money to take care of the little mutt."

"Yeah. That would have been a sweet setup." The comedian paused to dig through her purse. "Anyway, Mr. Oberkircher called again yesterday and said to go back. Seems the cops found out something new—Mr. Oberkircher said he didn't know what—and took the condo apart again."

*Hmm.* I wrinkled my forehead. Jake's ex must have informed the KC police that Joelle wasn't who she had claimed to be. Jake had said his ex would have to notify them. But if the cops hadn't told her attorney, that meant that they were keeping her false identity a secret.

"Did it take you long to put the place to rights?" Ms. Hyena asked.

"A lot longer than last time." The stand-up comic grimaced. "This time they got fingerprint dust everywhere, and that stuff is tough to wipe off."

"So we need to talk to Joelle's housekeeper and hairdresser," I explained to Jake as he walked me to my car after bingo.

"Okay." He waited until I was seated. "See if you can make an appointment at that beauty shop for five o'clock."

"I'll try, but salons like that one book really far ahead, so there might not be any openings."

"Do your best. We'll tackle the cleaning lady once we find out her name. By the way, the CI at the Parkside said that Joelle originally checked in at eleven a.m. and came back at five p.m. There was no gas purchase on her credit cards, so she must have paid in cash." Jake started to close the Z4's door, then stopped and leaned forward.

Suddenly the air around us seemed electrified and I knew he was about to kiss me. My pulse skittered alarmingly. Another second and it would be too late to stop him.

"Devereaux?"

"Yes?" I loved the way my name sounded rolling off his tongue. My full name, not the shortened version nearly everyone else used.

Suddenly a horn honked and the sound of voices calling good night drifted over us. We both seemed to realize where we were, and Jake withdrew, slamming the car's door without another word.

# CHAPTER 19

You know, you could do a lot worse than Jake Del Vecchio," Gran commented as we sat watching Julia Roberts play a hooker with a heart of gold on TV later that night.

"I'm sure I could." *Pretty Woman* was one of Gran's favorite movies, but I thought the message it gave about women sucked. "But he's a Mr. Right Now and I want more than that."

"Sweet Jesus!" Birdie exclaimed. "Do you think you can find a man who's handsome, charming, witty, well dressed, financially successful, and a romantic lover anytime you decide?"

"No. But it would be nice." I was amused by Gran's list. I would settle for someone not leaving town as soon as he got his job back.

"You know, you'll be thirty soon, and what you look for in a guy will have to change."

"Really?" I decided two could play matchmaker. "How about when you reach the ripe old age of seventy-five? What do you want then?"

"He needs to be breathing and not miss the toilet when he pees."

After I stopped laughing, I asked, "Well, Tony Del Vecchio certainly exceeds your wish list. Heck, he has most of what's on my list."

"Some things aren't meant to be." Birdie's voice was sad, and a few minutes later she decided to go to bed.

I had thought about asking Gran about her relationship with Tony back when they were teenagers. Why she had married so soon after he was declared MIA. And why she and Tony hadn't gotten together after both their spouses had passed away. But I wasn't ready for any more emotion in my life right then. I would discuss it all with her later—once I was no longer in danger of joining my father behind bars.

The first thing I did when I arrived at work the next morning was call Imagination for an appointment. I stated that Joelle had referred me and I wanted her stylist. For once, luck was shining on me. Sarin had just had a late-afternoon cancellation and she agreed to slip me into that vacant slot.

Saturday was a busy day at Devereaux's Dime

Store, and my weekend clerk, Xylia Locke, and I were kept hopping. Xylia was the complete opposite of my high school helper. While Hannah dressed like a Hello Kitty girl, Xylia wore khakis and sweater sets. Hannah planned to study graphic arts, while Xylia was majoring in business administration. However, both young women were hard workers, intelligent, and loyal to me and the store.

With Xylia's assistance, I was able to help shoppers locate the items they were searching for, work the soda fountain, and still photograph the baskets for the Athletic Booster Club's fund-raiser, create the flyers, and e-mail the brochure file to the OfficeMax nearest the Parkside Hotel.

It was three thirty, and I was making what I thought might be the fiftieth hot fudge sundae of the afternoon when I realized that Gran would be by herself overnight. Why I hadn't thought of this sooner, I'm not sure. Maybe because I hadn't been away from home since I'd bought the dime store.

*Shoot!* Gran would have a hissy fit if she got the notion I had arranged for someone to babysit her, so I couldn't ask Poppy or Boone to spend the evening. What I needed was a way to make sure she was okay without making it seem I was unwilling to leave her alone.

*Hmm.* An idea was forming, but would it work? Handing a bowl of ice cream to the eager ten-year-old customer standing across from me, I put the CLOSED sign on the soda fountain counter and hurried into the back room. It took me a few seconds to find the number, but when I punched it in, Gran's friend Frieda answered on the first ring.

After identifying myself, and suffering through a few minutes of chitchat, I cut to the chase. "I've got a proposition for you."

"Oh?" Frieda's tone was cautious. She'd worked the midnight shift at the local liquor store for too many years to be overly trusting or optimistic.

"How would you like to go to the Argosy casino in Riverside this afternoon and stay overnight in its hotel? I'll pay for gas, your room, and stake you a hundred dollars gambling money."

"What's the catch?" Frieda had had a hard life; losing a husband before she turned twenty-one and dealing with a no-account son had probably taught her that there was no such thing as a free lunch.

"You take my grandmother with you, but don't let her know our arrangement. Tell her you won the trip."

"Why?"

I explained that I had to be out of town, without saying why or with whom, then added, "And I don't think she should be alone for so long."

"Birdie is fine. You really don't have to worry

231

about her, but if it will make you feel better, okay." Frieda paused. "How should we do this?"

"Call Gran as soon as we hang up and don't take no for an answer. Tell her you won't go if she doesn't come with you because it won't be any fun alone." I swiftly calculated the logistics. "I'll make your hotel reservation right now and drop the money and your confirmation number off in a half hour or so."

"You've got a deal."

I thanked Frieda and said good-bye, then got online and booked a double room for her and Gran. Although it was still ten minutes until the store was officially scheduled to close, there were no customers present, so I walked Xylia to the front door and switched off the neon OPEN sign. Once I was alone, I took six twenties from the register for Frieda and two hundred dollars for me before locking the rest of the contents in the safe. Not that there was much left after my pilfering.

I paperclipped Frieda's money to the reservation printout and stuffed it all into an envelope, then stuck it in my purse. I carefully tucked the remaining cash into my wallet, reserving a fifty, which I stashed in my bra.

With only a few minutes left, I grabbed my tote bag and dashed into the restroom to change clothes. It wasn't that I cared about being attractive for Jake. Really. But I knew from my days of patronizing upscale hair salons that I needed to look the part of their usual affluent clientele when I arrived for my appointment.

The antique black distressed jeans and scarlet V-neck sweater were the perfect attire for a Saturday afternoon visit to the salon, especially when I added my cropped leather motorcycle jacket. The asymmetrical ruffle-covered zipper gave the jacket a chic flair. Thank goodness I hadn't gotten rid of *all* my "city" clothes—only the ones that reminded me of the office.

Jake was precisely on time. I met him at the door and hustled him into his truck while explaining, "Sorry to rush you, but we need to run a couple of errands before you take me to the hair salon, and I don't want to be late for my appointment."

"No problem." He backed out of the parking space and asked, "Where to first?"

"White Eagle Trailer Park." I was pleasantly surprised that he didn't question me about what we were doing, but wondered why he was so silent.

After I delivered the money and confirmation printout to Frieda and she assured me that Gran had agreed to accompany her to the casino, I settled back into the F-250's comfy leather seat and gave Jake the address of the OfficeMax. I waited for him to say something about the errands or our mission, or even about my outfit, but he just nodded, put the truck in gear, and headed toward the highway.

His silence as the miles rolled by was beginning to get on my nerves, but when I tried to start a conversation, he responded with only a word or two. The man plainly didn't want to talk, and that confused me. The previous night at my car, I was sure he was about to kiss me. Now, in the light of day, I wondered if he was regretting his offer to help me.

Between the quiet and the motion of the pickup, I must have dozed off, because I startled awake when he pulled up in front of the OfficeMax. When my eyes opened, I saw that Jake was studying me, his expression impossible to read.

After a few seconds I gave up trying to figure out what he was thinking and said, "I'll only be a minute."

"Fine."

As promised, the flyers were waiting for me. I paid for them and was back in the Ford before my seat got cold. As I settled in, I asked, "Do you know the way to the salon?"

"Yep."

Why wasn't he talking? Had I done something wrong? Maybe he was sorry he had agreed to act as if we were a couple. *Grr!* Even if his brooding was about something else, the least he could do was be sociable.

When we pulled up to Imagination, I asked, "Are you coming inside with me?"

He shook his head. "I'll go take another look at the hotel before we check in, and be back for you in an hour."

"Don't bother." His impersonal attitude was beyond exasperating and I snapped, "I'll grab a cab and save you a trip."

He didn't respond, just waited for me to get out, then merged smoothly into traffic. I thought I saw him glance in his rearview mirror, but that may have been purely wishful thinking on my part.

Before I entered the salon, I took a deep breath, determined to put Jake's disturbing behavior out of my mind. I needed to have my wits about me in order to find out all the dirt on Joelle. No one knows more about a woman's secrets than her hairdresser.

Imagination was exactly what I expected—sleek, modern, and featuring shampoo that sold for thirty-six dollars a bottle. Although I didn't really want to, I was getting highlights. I figured that procedure would give me twice as much time to grill Sarin.

Once I made it through the gauntlet of receptionist, beverage girl, and stylist assistant, who directed me to change out of my sweater and jacket and into a short, silky kimono, I was finally seated in front of a mirror. Before I finished getting comfortable, a glamazon appeared in front of me.

She was six feet tall and reed thin, a platinum blonde with a bone-white complexion, dressed from head to toe in black leather. In a thick Romanian accent, she said, "I am Sarin. You will leave everything to me and I will make you beautiful enough to marry a prince."

*Uh-oh!* "Actually, I just want a few highlights. Nothing too extreme."

"Of course." Sarin clapped for her assistant. "Let us begin."

As Sarin ran her fingers through my hair, holding up what appeared to be random strands, I scanned my surroundings. The salon had an air of luxury. Thick rolled towels were artistically arranged in brass trays, flutes of champagne sparkled in the clients' hands, and scented air was puffed from hidden nozzles.

I was shocked to realize that I had forgotten what this kind of life was like, and happy to recognize that I hadn't missed it. When I quit my job and bought the dime store in order to spend more time with Gran, I knew I'd never regret that decision. But I had been afraid I'd mourn the loss of my huge salary and all the things I was used to buying with that money.

"You have good hair." Sarin refocused my attention on the task at hand. "You should let me style it for you after I finish the highlights."

"Not this time." My sales resistance was extremely high, having used all the tricks myself when I was trying to get people to invest with me. "Although I do like my friend Joelle Ayers's cut." I crossed my fingers that Sarin hadn't heard about Joelle's death.

"Yes. It is striking." There was something calculating in Sarin's tone. "But her hair takes a lot of maintenance. She comes in every other week to keep it up. Are you willing to do that?"

"Not really." There was certainly no way I could afford that. "Why does Joelle's style take so much work? It looks fairly simple to me."

"I can't really say." Sarin's jet-black eyes kept sneaking quick peeks sideways, as if what she was saying was for the record rather than her true inclination. "Client confidentiality."

Nodding sympathetically, I said, "Of course. I completely understand."

She dismissed her assistant, then walked around me so that her back was to the mirror, and said in a low voice, "You wouldn't believe the stories I could tell you."

"Oh?" Was she asking for a bribe? "Joelle was in last Saturday, right? Did she have anything interesting to say?"

Since Sarin's Ferragamo sandals probably cost upwards of four hundred bucks, I wasn't sure fifty dollars would impress her, but I reached into my bra and handed her the folded bill

237

anyway. Crossing my fingers, I lied. "I promise not to divulge anything you tell me."

"No. Nothing that stands out." Sarin tucked the money into her pocket.

"So what stories do you have?" I hoped I hadn't just wasted my money.

"Joelle demands that no one ever be able to tell that her hair is colored or permed." The stylist picked up the stack of foil squares her assistant had left for her, and started working on me. "She freaks out if she sees any of her natural shade at the root or, God forbid, a gray hair showing."

"Wow!" I noticed that Sarin's accent had disappeared and her cheeks were rosy. "That's certainly over the top." The stylist no longer looked or sounded like the queen of the vampires, which was a huge relief.

"And don't get me started about her extensions and her need to have them be perfect." Sarin shook her head. "If one comes loose, it's as if the apocalypse has begun and one of the horsemen is breathing down her neck."

"I wonder why?" I mused, thinking that even for a woman hiding her identity, Joelle's obsession had been a bit much. "Who cares if people know you dye your hair or add to it? In this day and age it's no big deal."

"It is to her boyfriend."

"Really?"

"Yes." Sarin's smile was mean. "He's some

kind of hotshot doctor, and he made a big deal about being honest in a relationship. He told her that plastic surgery and fake hair were a lie."

"I didn't realize Joelle was so insecure." Interesting. Everyone had said Noah was wrapped around her little finger, but Sarin's information suggested otherwise. "She seems so confident."

"Maybe in other matters." Sarin shrugged. "But she told me that she doesn't feel like this guy's true love. More like a fill-in."

"Who is she a fill-in for?"

"Some old teenage crush." Sarin finished painting the highlighting solution on my hair and set the timer. "Before he asked Joelle to marry him, he told her that he had to be honest with her. He knew he could never get this high school chick back, but he'd love her forever, and Joelle would always be second in his heart."

# CHAPTER 20

I walked out of Imagination in a state of shock. Both Sarin's bombshell about my ex-boyfriend and the cost of her service had stunned me. I wasn't certain which was more disturbing, but a hundred and fifty bucks for highlights that I wasn't sure I even liked was edging out the news about Noah's declaration.

The beep of a horn jerked me back to the

present, and I saw Jake's truck double-parked in front of the salon. He waved, then leaned across the seat and opened the passenger door. My first inclination was to ignore him and grab a taxi. His cold-shouldered attitude on the ride in had upset me more than I cared to admit, and I wasn't ready to face him.

Too bad I had already blown through the money I took from the register. That meant twelve dollars and change was all I had left. Taking a taxi to the hotel would leave me close to broke. Since I had shredded my debit card, an ATM was out of the question, and because I'd kept only one credit card—which currently resided in the dime store safe—for emergencies, Jake was my only way home.

Pride warred with common sense, and for once common sense won. I grudgingly stomped over to the Ford, climbed into the cab, and buckled up.

Jake flicked a quizzical look at me, then pulled into traffic.

When he kept glancing my way, but remained silent, I said, "What?"

"You seem different."

"Duh." After finishing the highlights, Sarin had somehow managed to form my curly hair into a waterfall of ringlets. "I just spent an hour and beaucoup bucks in a salon. I'd better look different."

"Oh." Jake shrugged. "I thought you'd just get a trim or something."

I didn't bother explaining my motive to him. Instead I said, "Don't be concerned. The color will grow out in a couple of months, and the style will be gone as soon as I shower in the morning."

"I wasn't worried." Jake's appreciative smile and sexy dimples almost made me forget I was ticked off at him. "It looks good." Under his breath, I thought I heard him mutter, "Too good."

"Thanks." Since I couldn't think of anything more to say on that subject, I demanded, "Guess what I found out?"

"The beauty shop gal killed Joelle because she used the wrong shampoo."

"I wish." I bit back a giggle. Jake's good cop, bad cop routine wasn't about to work on me. I was determined to hang on to my mad until he explained himself. "Joelle's hair was as phony as her identity."

"So?"

So, indeed. Did her fake hair have anything to do with the murder? The only one who would have been upset by her deceit was her fiancé, and since I wasn't sure I wanted to share the information Sarin had revealed about Joelle being a fill-in for me in Noah's eyes, I kept silent.

While I pondered, Jake turned the pickup into the entrance of the hotel's parking garage. He rolled down the window, plucked the ticket from the machine, and when the gate lifted, drove into the darkness. It took a while, but he finally found an empty space on the top floor. Grabbing my tote bag and his duffel from the backseat, he met me by the elevator and punched the DOWN button.

The doors opened immediately and we stepped inside. When we arrived at the ground level, Jake took my hand and tucked it into the crook of his arm.

I tried to draw away, but he murmured into my ear, "Try to act like we're in love. Remember, we're supposed to be sweethearts."

"How could I forget?" I sneered. "You've been so pleasant all afternoon."

It wasn't a big surprise when he only grunted.

The Parkside was a boutique hotel, which meant it was small in comparison to a Hilton or Hyatt, and its decor made a statement. No cookie-cutter furnishings or predictable artwork was allowed. Instead, uncomfortable-looking chrome chairs were grouped in pairs, trios, and foursomes throughout the ultramodern lobby.

The exposed redbrick walls and burnished-steel light fixtures reminded me more of a warehouse than a luxury hotel. And the wrought-iron reception desk seemed like something that might be found in a torture chamber rather than in downtown Kansas City. I sure hoped the rooms weren't furnished the same way.

As we waited for the clerk to finish speaking on the phone, I whispered to Jake, "When do we meet your contact?"

"His shift starts at eight." Jake lowered his voice. "He'll come to our room when he's ready to talk."

Once Jake had handed over his parking ticket and credit card, he signed on the dotted line and we were given a paper folder containing a single plastic key card. I guess since we were in the honeymoon suite, the clerk figured we'd never leave the room without each other and didn't need two cards.

Jake put his arm around my waist and said, "Ready, darlin'?"

"Of course, love muffin." I bared my teeth in a fake smile. "Lead the way."

The suite turned out to be one cavernous open space, and I had to hide my dismay. I had counted on a separate bedroom and living room, figuring I could sleep on the couch. Clearly, Cupid was conspiring against me.

I tried to think optimistically. One—Jake hadn't insisted on carrying me over the threshold, which would have revealed how much I weighed. Two—maybe the maintenance man would give us the info we needed and we could check out early. And three—in his present mood Jake didn't seem interested in getting me naked and having his way with me.

Jake shed his hat and shearling jacket and began prowling around the suite with a "do not disturb" expression on his face. Happy to leave him alone, I took off my coat and studied the massive room. Black leather and chrome Barcelona chairs and an unframed oil painting of a matte red sun against a shiny ebony background carried out the lobby's minimalist motif.

The stainless-steel wet bar, sleek black-lacquer entertainment center, and übermodern TV also went along with the industrial theme, as did what I guessed had to be the sofa—although that particular piece of furniture resembled the examination table in a doctor's office more than a comfy couch.

A pair of doors led to a small terrace. It was too chilly to stand outside, but I did slide open the glass and take a deep breath of the cold air. In the early-evening darkness, only the illuminated downtown buildings were visible. They obscured the twinkle of the stars, and having thoroughly transformed back to a country girl, I found that I preferred the view from my porch in Shadow Bend.

Lost in my own thoughts, I didn't notice Jake's approach until he startled me by saying, "Did you discover anything else at the beauty shop?"

"Well . . ." I explained what Sarin had told me about Noah's dislike of artificially achieved beauty, then paused. I still wasn't sure whether to tell Jake about Noah's supposedly undying love for his high school girlfriend. Jake knew enough about Noah and me and our history to realize that I was probably that old flame.

"What are you leaving out?" Jake demanded, reading my no-doubt guilty expression.

Sighing, I told him, then asked, "What do you think of that?"

"I think," Jake answered without hesitation, "that we now have another solid motive for the good doctor." Rubbing the back of his neck, he continued. "And if Underwood wasn't already at the top of our suspect list, he sure is now."

"You mean if he found out that not only was Joelle's appearance fake, but everything else about her was bogus, too?"

"Exactly." Jake stroked his chin. "Joelle's murder was a crime of passion. Sticking a champagne bottle down someone's throat and driving a stiletto into her chest are not the acts of a burglar. They're the behavior of a murderer with a very personal motive, which points to the doc. He discovers her secret, goes berserk, and attacks her with whatever is handy."

"Which is unfortunate for me, since one of those weapons was part of the basket I made."

"Yeah. That is a piece of bad luck, unless . . ."

"Unless?"

Jake spoke slowly, as if testing out a theory.

245

"Unless Underwood intentionally incriminated you."

"But why would he do that?" I shook my head. "I can't see Noah deliberately setting me up to take the rap, and the more I think about it, the more I can't see him in a homicidal rage. If he was going to kill someone, the murder would be planned down to the last second. Besides, it's not as if they were already married. It's pretty easy to break off an engagement. There was no need for him to kill her."

"Okay. Purposely implicating you is probably a stretch, but why all of a sudden do you think the good doctor is innocent? You were certainly willing to consider him a suspect up until today."

"True." I reluctantly admitted the flaw in my logic. "But now that I'm actually trying to picture Noah losing control like that, I see how ridiculous it is. He's always been the most controlled person I know. He makes *Star Trek*'s Mr. Spock look impetuous."

"Maybe." Jake shoved his hands in his pockets. "Or maybe it's because now that you think Underwood still loves you, he can't be guilty of anything."

"Of course not." That wasn't true. Was it? "My feelings have nothing to do with my opinion that Noah isn't capable of impulsively killing someone."

"Given the right circumstances, you'd be surprised what folks are capable of doing."

"Hardly," I scoffed. "In my previous occupation I saw exactly what people were willing to do if they thought it was in their best interest."

"Including you?" He lifted a brow. "Are you still willing to do anything if it benefits you?"

"What are you talking about?" I had a bad feeling that I knew the answer, but I wanted to hear him say it.

"It took me a while to figure out your little act—first you're hot for me; then you keep me at arm's length; then you start the tease all over again." He glowered at me. "That's your way to ensure I keep helping you, isn't it?"

Jake's words cut into me like flying glass. Unwilling to let him see me bleed, I ran into the bathroom. That was why he'd been so cold to me all day. But how could he think that of me? After all the duplicity I'd endured at the hands of my father, mother, high school sweetheart, and boss, the last thing I would ever do was treat anyone like that. I wondered what, or who, had put that toxic idea in his head.

Staring into the mirror, I was appalled to see tears in my eyes. Devereaux Sinclair did not cry, yet I was on the verge of doing so for the second time in a week. What was happening to me? Why was I suddenly allowing my emotions to rule my head? I was a dispassionate businesswoman, not some hormonal teenager. It was time to get a grip.

Trying to regroup, I gazed at the creamy ivory walls and ocher ceramic tiles of the bathroom. The dispassionate part of my brain noted that this décor was a soothing contrast to the rest of the suite's provocative design.

The cold water I splashed on my face helped clear my mind. And then it occurred to me: Could there be a reason, other than the one Jake had already stated, why he had gone from ardent to aloof to accusing in less than twenty-four hours?

Now that I had time to think it over, I wondered if my supposed use of feminine wiles on him was just an excuse to keep me at arm's length. Or maybe there was still another reason for his behavior.

After considering what his motive might be, I decided that I didn't care what was behind his mood swings; I was sick of them. And although I was probably guilty of the same thing, I resented the mixed signals he'd been sending me since we had first met.

Resolved, I marched out of the bathroom and up to Jake, who was gazing darkly out the terrace doors. "What crawled up your butt since last night? And don't try to tell me it was the realization that I was leading you on, because that's a load of crap." Okay. That was a crude way of putting it, but he deserved even worse.

"You seem upset," Jake's tone was smug. "Did I hit a little too close to home?"

Even as my fury erupted and I kicked him in the shin, I was thinking that I couldn't fault Jake's observational skills. Not the part about me flirting with him because I wanted him to get me off the hook with Woods—that issue was way more complicated—but all the rest. I *had* sent mixed messages to Jake, and maybe knowing that Noah still loved me *had* changed my opinion of him

"Of course I'm upset." I glared at him as he nursed his leg. "You've been jerking me around since the day you strolled into my store and announced you were there to save me."

"Yeah?"

"Yeah." I stared down my nose at him. "First you kiss me, then you freeze me out, then you insult me. Did you really think I'd take that kind of treatment without reacting? And then to accuse me of using you . . ." I trailed off, unable to complete the sentence without either punching him in the nose or breaking down and crying. "How about you cowboy up and tell me what's really wrong? Believe me, it's better to admit you're wrong right away, because it's a lot easier to eat crow while it's still warm."

Blue eyes blazed into mine as Jake strode

toward me. I could see that each step he took shot a bolt of pain up his leg. *Damn!* I should have remembered his injury and never kicked him. Now I was the bad guy, and I could feel my righteous anger trickling away with every flicker of discomfort that he fought to hide.

In less than a nanosecond he was so close to me we were almost nose to nose, and despite the fact that I was still upset with him, I found myself fascinated with every detail of his face.

The muscles in the strong column of his throat worked as he struggled to speak. "I had an appointment with my doctors here in Kansas City this morning before I picked you up, and I'm not healing as well as they hoped." Jake gripped my shoulders. "They told me they'd give me another month, but if there's no improvement, I'll have to either take a disability retirement or a job at headquarters."

"So you could still work for the U.S. Marshals?" I wanted to make sure I understood.

"Yes, but being a desk jockey isn't the same as fieldwork." His grin was brief and rueful. "It just feels so damn good when you get to tackle the perp, handcuff him, and bring him in. If I can't do that, I'd rather take Tony up on his offer to run the ranch."

"I'm so, so sorry. And I do understand that news like that must be devastating." My adrenaline spent, I leaned my cheek against his.

"Yeah." Jake's breath was warm against my ear. "It threw me for a loop, all right."

We were silent for a moment, then I raised my head and said, "What I don't understand is how did you go from that awful report about your injury to me not really being attracted to you?"

"Someone may have mentioned the possibility." Jake stared at his boots.

"And that person would be . . ."

"Meg."

"Right." I stepped away from him. "You called her to tell her what the doctors said?"

"I had to." Jake moved his gaze from his feet to his belt buckle. "She's my supervisor."

"Oh. That has to be awkward." Had I known his ex-wife was his boss? Definitely not. I would have remembered that nugget of information. "And you didn't think she might have an ulterior motive?"

"Now that you mention it, I should have." He smiled sheepishly, then frowned. "She caught me at a bad moment. She was always good at finding any weaknesses and exploiting them to her benefit."

"Look—I'm sorry I've been blowing hot and cold, but you have, too."

"Sorry about that." He dimpled. "I guess we both have our battle scars."

"You think?" It wasn't the apology I'd hoped for, but his appeal was undeniable. "When I was a teenager and upset about Noah dumping me, Gran told me that hurt can soften you like a flannel shirt that's been washed over and over again, or it can turn you into a dried-up rose, ready to crumble the first time anyone doesn't handle you with care."

"Which are you?"

"I think I've been the flower, but I don't want to be like that anymore." I sighed. "Can we start over? Maybe try to trust each other a little?"

"That might be good." He put his arms around me. "That might be real good."

The warmth of his voice and his embrace melted my resolve to go slow this time, and I said into his shoulder, "I'm game."

"Care to prove it?" His invitation was a passionate challenge I found hard to resist.

Jake pulled me closer and I arched against the solid length of him. The pressure of his chest against my breasts sent tingles to other sensitive areas of my anatomy. I closed my eyes because it was too easy to get lost in the way he was looking at me.

Jake's heartbeat thudded against my own. I knew we should stop and really think about whether we wanted to take this step. We had both learned a piece of life-altering information today—his career might be over and my ex-boyfriend might still love me. Right now we should be stepping back, considering our options, and regrouping. Certainly we shouldn't be taking any kind of emotional risk.

But Jake's husky voice telling me everything he wanted to do with me was interfering with my resolve. He hadn't even touched his sexy lips to mine, yet I was weakening.

One of his hands brushed a curl away from my face, and his caress was so tender, a sigh escaped before I could control myself. His other hand massaged my hip. Why did his touch feel so good? Readying myself to break away from his embrace, I took a deep breath. *Shoot!* He smelled like fresh hay and clean air and leather—a thoroughly masculine version of heaven.

Tendrils of alarm slid through my brain, entwining with a longing that was swiftly erasing all my good intentions. My voice cracked as I asked feebly, "Wouldn't it be prudent for us to take things more slowly?"

"Probably." Jake trailed kisses along my jawline. "But I've never been a prudent guy. If I were, I'd have become a CPA or an engineer, not a deputy U.S. Marshal." His mouth moved to my ear, nipping at the lobe. "And I doubt someone who was a hotshot in the investment world is always cautious, either."

"It's all about measuring risk versus return." I let my head fall back, a silent invitation for him to continue his exploration. I knew there was a good reason why I shouldn't do this, but darned if I could remember what it was.

"So, should I stop?" He nibbled down the cord in my neck as he peeled off my sweater. "We could watch TV until the CI gets here."

"Maybe in a little while," I suggested, threading my fingers through his hair. "There's nothing good on television Saturday nights."

"How about Pay-Per-View?" Jake taunted, stopping and putting a little space between us, but not taking his arms from around me.

I saw his gaze wander to my mouth, and I knew he was going to kiss me. "I'm not in the mood for a movie or a ball game." If I was ever going to call a halt to our lovemaking, now was the time, but a sudden flare of heat made me moan.

"Well . . ." His tongue slid against the seam of my lips. "We could do this."

He teased me with gentle but insistent kisses, inflaming a primitive need in me that was so powerful it shredded both my caution and my common sense. My mouth opened, and he deepened the kiss, tasting me as if I were a fine Merlot. I moved nearer, until I was cradled between his thighs. The intimacy of the situation was making me lose all restraint.

It was my turn. I tussled Jake's shirt over his head, then intensified our kiss. Arching my spine, I tried to burrow closer to him. While his hands were busy with the clasp on my bra, I pulled his belt through the loops, allowing it to slither to the floor.

Somehow, during my quest to get Jake naked, I had lost my jeans. And a small part of my mind, the tiny portion that could still think, was thankful that I had worn black satin underwear.

Then, just before we approached the point of no return, there was a knock on the door and a voice called through the metal, "It's me, Leon Jones. Let me in."

# CHAPTER 21

Son of a bitch!" Jake watched Devereaux disappear into the bathroom. She was clutching her discarded clothes as if they were a lifeline, so it was a good bet she wasn't coming out anytime soon.

Kicking his belt under the couch, he buttoned his shirt, then took one last look around before letting the CI in. The guy's timing sucked.

The maintenance man was exactly what Jake had expected—weaselly, hyper, and sporting several prison tattoos.

"Hey, man, what took you so long?" Leon scuttled over the threshold, peering down the hallway behind him before slamming the door shut. "You need to call and demand that your toilet be fixed immediately. Act real mad and threaten to check out. The clerk will beep me, and then my time is accounted for and it will be okay if someone saw me coming in here."

Jake complied as ordered while he tried to forget the sensation of having Devereaux in his arms. He had expected to be turned on, but he wasn't prepared for the tenderness he felt for her. She had wrapped herself around his heart like a silky web, one that grew tighter the more he fought it. How could a few kisses have such an impact?

Once his alibi had been established, Leon asked, "Hey, where's the chick? I told you that a couple needed to check in to this suite or it would look suspicious." He strutted forward, his finger pointing toward Jake. "You better not have screwed me."

"My *friend,* whom you will address in a respectful manner, should you be honored enough to meet her, is in the bathroom." Jake's voice dropped to a dangerous growl. "And don't ever stick a finger in my face again."

"Sure. Okay, man. No need to get all Dirty Harry on my ass." Leon backed away until he was beyond Jake's reach. "Are we cool?"

"We're cool."

"So, what you want from me?"

"Did you see the crime scene before it was cleaned up?"

"Not the body, but the mess that was left

behind." Leon puffed his chest out and led the way to the bed. "It all happened right here."

"Show me," Jake ordered, glad Devereaux didn't have to hear the gory details. She put up a strong front, but she hadn't had to face the horrors of violent death as he had during the past ten years.

"See these scratches?" Leon pointed out four burnished-chrome rods, one at either end of the headboard and one at either end of the footboard. "This is where the handcuffs were attached. The cops cut them off her."

"Was there anything else?" Jake looked around the stark space, wondering how the perp had gotten in. Had he been hiding? The only places he could have concealed himself were the bathroom and the closet.

"No blood or nothing anywhere but the mattress," Leon said, shaking his head, "but the cops got that fingerprint powder shit all over the place."

"I heard the door was ajar and that's how the room service waiter was able to get in." Jake waited for Jones's nod before continuing, "Any idea how someone could gain access if the door was locked?"

"There's no way, man." Leon hooked his fingers in the loops of the gray work pants that barely clung to his skinny hips. "Unless the dude was Spider-Man and climbed seventeen floors up the outside of the building, he needed a key."

Jake knew that according to the hotel's electronic records, the last key card to open the suite's door was one of the pair given to Joelle when she checked in. Since she had one and Underwood had the other, unless someone had figured out a way to make a duplicate key card's electronic signature look like it belonged to the victim, Noah Underwood was involved in the murder of his fiancée.

"Did any of the staff report a missing key card?" Jake asked. If someone had borrowed a card, changed the electronic signature, and returned it, the altered signature would have been noticed.

"Nope." Leon's bony shoulders moved uncomfortably beneath his gray work shirt. "And believe you me, the cops made every damn one of us produce ours to be checked. We were all fingerprinted, too. They claimed it was to eliminate us as suspects, but I think they just wanted to hassle us."

Jake rubbed the bridge of his nose. "How about the garage? When I registered, the guy took the parking ticket. He said that all my parking info would be transferred to my key card and I could use it to get in and out of the garage. I assume there will be a record of the time I parked and how long I stay there."

"Sure. The hotel insists that you put your parking on your tab," Leon confirmed. "Only guests are allowed to use the garage."

"Can you get me a list of all the cars parked in the garage last Saturday?" Jake figured the police had seen it, but maybe they had missed something, especially considering Woods's determination to convict Devereaux. "And any other hotel security records for that night."

"Probably, but I'll have to wait until the night manager takes his supper break." Leon edged toward the door. "And I don't know when that will be. Anything else? 'Cause I got to get going."

"No." Jake smiled to himself. Maybe he and Devereaux could pick up where they had left off. "Slip those copies under the door when you get them."

"Sure." Leon bounced on the balls of his feet. "But it may be a while."

"No problem. Just don't forget." Jake held out his hand, a fifty folded in the palm. "Thanks for your help. I'll leave another thank-you at the desk for you when you get me the lists."

"Always a pleasure doing business with the Marshals. Unlike the Feebs, you guys pay up front." Leon grinned, showing a gold front tooth. "Too bad the cameras on this hall were jacked up that night."

Jake was immediately alert. "What happened?" Malfunctioning cameras were too big a coincidence to be just a fluke. "Was it just this floor?"

"Yeah. A breaker tripped, and since the

cameras are the only things on that particular circuit, and the hotel management is too cheap to have redundant circuits or a backup battery, no one noticed until the cops asked to see the tapes."

"Okay. I'll need to see the layout of those circuit breakers."

"And how am I going to explain that if someone sees us?" Leon demanded.

"Tell them I'm your parole officer," Jake suggested. "I'm checking up on your work situation. Making sure you're doing a good job."

"Hell, no!" Leon crossed his skinny arms. "I ain't on parole and I'm not pretending to be. I done my time. I'm a free man."

"Fine." Jake snuck a peek at the closed bathroom door. If he could hurry this guy along, he still might have a chance to continue what he had started with Devereaux. "If anyone asks, I'm the fire marshal."

"Yeah." Leon's mouth moved from side to side. "That might work."

Before they left, Jake knocked on the bathroom door and explained where he was going. Devereaux's muffled response was not reassuring.

As Leon led him into the bowels of the building, Jake thought about Devereaux. What was it about her that rocked his world? Was it because she made him feel alive and energized? With her he felt the way he had when he first became a U.S. Marshal: as if the world was a good place where anything was possible.

When they were together, he found it hard to keep from touching her, even in public. He wanted to hold her hand, stroke her cheek, and press her warm curves against his side. He made a face. When was the last time he had felt that way about a woman? Had he ever?

The feelings Devereaux brought out in him were dangerous. Jake loved being a deputy U.S. Marshal, and he had every intention of resuming his job. It was important that she understand that before they went any further. He couldn't let anyone change his mind. Not even someone as beautiful and sexy as Devereaux.

Absentmindedly, Jake put his hand into his pocket and froze. When had he stuck Devereaux's bra in there? His fingers caressed the silky material. Was it his imagination or was it still warm from her body? He groaned and shook his head. It was time to get his mind back on the business of finding the murderer.

When the service elevator doors opened at the subbasement level, Leon stuck his head out, looked both ways, then gestured for Jake to follow him. The gray linoleum floors of the well-lit corridor were worn but clean, and the cinder-block walls had helpful arrows directing them to various operations. It would be fairly easy for someone to find their way around, and if that person wore gray work clothes, they'd fit right in and no one would notice them.

A few feet down the hallway, Leon flung open a door and pointed to a vast display of circuit breakers, all neatly labeled. Jake frowned. It sure wouldn't have taken a rocket scientist to figure out how to disable a particular floor's security cameras.

"Did the cops dust the breaker for prints?" Jake asked. He couldn't remember from the report Meg had sent him.

"Yeah. They didn't find anything but smudges." Leon peered uneasily over his shoulder. "Man, we got to get out of here before someone catches us. The more I think about it, the less you look like a fire marshal."

"Sure. I guess there's nothing else here to see." Jake allowed himself to be herded toward the elevator, but stopped Leon from punching the seventeenth-floor button. "How about checking on our way back to see if the night manager's on his supper break?"

"Yeah. Why not get it over with?" Leon poked the LOBBY button. "Pretend to be yelling at me about your toilet and demanding to talk to the manager when we walk past the front desk."

Jake did as Leon asked, and they waltzed past the reception area with no one the wiser. Their luck held—the manager's office was both unlocked and empty. The garage and security records were easy to find on the computer and Jake printed out a copy while Leon kept watch.

They were in and out in less than ten minutes, and when they parted company, Leon was clutching another fifty-dollar bill. As Jake rode the elevator to the seventeenth floor, he was whistling. Not only did he have all of the hotel's security information for the night of the murder, but he also had a plan for the rest of this evening.

He was going to make sure Devereaux understood that it was only fun and games between them, and that he'd be leaving Shadow Bend as soon as he got the go-ahead to return to work. Then, once she was clear on that matter, they would get to know one another on a whole new level.

Anticipation warming his blood, Jake inserted his key card and flung open the door.

# CHAPTER 22

I was curled up on one of the chairs trying to read *Pride and Prejudice and Zombies*, a novel that Hannah had insisted on loaning me, when Jake walked into the suite. The cooling-off time I had spent in the bathroom had made me realize that no matter how much I desired him, it really wasn't a good idea to sleep with Jake Del Vecchio.

Maybe if he ended up staying in Shadow Bend to run the Del Vecchio ranch, and I was able to clear myself of the murder charge dangling over my head, we could explore the possibilities. But despite the ongoing drought in my love life, I was looking for something more than just a casual fling with a hot guy.

As Jake took a seat on the couch, I was determined to get our relationship back to the business of clearing my name, so I asked, "Did you find anything helpful?"

"Nothing to do with the surveillance camera's circuit breakers—a six-year-old could figure out how to disable them—but I did get the hotel security information we need."

"Great." I kept my gaze on the pages of my book. "Then, since there's nothing more we can do here, I think our best course of action is to return to Shadow Bend. It would be a mistake for us to . . . uh . . ."

"Have sex?"

"Yes." I licked my lips. "I'm a suspect in a murder investigation and you're just passing a little time until your injury heals. If those circumstances change . . ." I trailed off again.

"Right." He nodded. "I understand."

Apparently, he'd had time to think our situation over, too, which was strangely disappointing.

I leapt to my feet, grabbed my tote bag, and looked at him. "Ready?"

"Yeah." Jake got up. "But why don't we have supper before we hit the road? We can look over the garage parking lists and make sure there's nothing more I need to ask Leon."

I agreed, telling myself that since we were both hungry and dinner was business, not pleasure, there was no harm.

We ate in the hotel restaurant, and despite all the ups and downs Jake and I had been through that day, the meal was enjoyable. At least until we got down to the case.

Joelle's time of death had been established using the minute after her call to room service at six p.m. as the earliest point she could have been killed and the minute before the arrival of the waiter with her order at seven p.m. as the last moment the murderer could have struck. With this criterion in mind, we skimmed the list looking for cars parked in the hotel garage during that crucial hour.

"Look." I pointed to two familiar names.

"Interesting." Jake's brows rose. "So Mayor Eggers and Dr. Underwood both lied to us."

"So it would seem." I exhaled. "His Honor claimed he never left Shadow Bend last Saturday, and Noah said he didn't reach the hotel until seven thirty, but this list shows him entering the garage at five forty-five."

It was becoming harder and harder to believe that my ex-boyfriend was innocent. Clearly, he hadn't told us the truth about the time of his arrival, which meant that now, along with a motive, albeit one that still seemed implausible to me, he had had opportunity. My only hope was that Eggers had lied, too, but his motive—insane jealousy because he'd wanted Joelle for himself—seemed even less convincing than Noah's did.

I woke slowly, somewhat surprised to find myself alone and in my own bed back home. Had I made the right decision to keep my relationship with Jake platonic? Gazing up at my bedroom ceiling, I waited for a sign from the heavens. When none appeared, I turned my attention to the ramifications of what we had found on the hotel's parking list. I prayed that His Honor was the murderer and not Noah.

The doorbell interrupted my entreaties, and I dragged myself out of bed. As I shrugged into a chin-to-toe-length chenille bathrobe, I checked the time. It was a little past ten o'clock. Who would come for a visit that early on a Sunday morning?

With Gran gone, I hadn't rushed to get up or dressed, but peering out the peephole, I wished I had. Detective Woods stood on my frontstep, a nasty look on his ugly face. When I didn't respond to his repeated ringing, he began hammering on the oak panels with his fists.

Determined to ignore him until he gave up, I hugged myself and hoped Gran didn't return from her outing until I had gotten rid of the detective.

"I know you're in there. Your car is in plain sight and there are footprints in the snow leading to the door, but not away from it." Woods's self-satisfied voice turned venomous. "Either you let me in or I come back with a warrant for your arrest."

*Great!* He was upping the ante. What was my best course of action? I needed a witness. And not just any witness—preferably an armed one who could get here quickly. That narrowed it down to Jake.

Boone might be my attorney, but since Jake was a U.S. Marshal, he would have a nice big gun. Plus he lived only a few miles down the road. Considering that Woods sounded crazed enough to start shooting, it was no contest between the two men.

Woods let loose another round of threats as I stepped back from the door and located my cell phone. Jake answered immediately, and once I explained the situation, he said he'd be right over.

Trying to stall the detective, I yelled, "Give me five minutes to get dressed."

"Five minutes." Woods stopped pounding. "After that I'll have my partner call the SWAT team."

I took a quick peek out the window. Sure

enough, another man was sitting behind the wheel of a Crown Victoria. He must be Woods's elusive partner. I'd been half convinced the guy was a figment of the detective's imagination.

Woods was probably exaggerating when he threatened to call in reinforcements, but I still kept an eye on the clock as I hustled into a pair of jeans and a sweatshirt, scraped my hair into a ponytail, and swished Listerine around my mouth. Then I returned to the front door, hoping Jake made it before my time ran out.

The detective was counting down the seconds when Jake's F-250 squealed into the driveway. At the last possible moment, I turned the lock and the men went shoulder to shoulder, each trying to be the first to enter.

Jake won the competition and strode over to my side, his blue eyes exuding triumph and concern. When at first I didn't see his pistol holstered on his belt, I glanced down and spotted a reassuring bulge near his ankle.

"So much for that feminist crap you broads are always spouting," Woods snapped. "The princess had to wait for her white knight to come save her before letting down the drawbridge."

Jake ignored Woods and focused his attention on me. "You okay?"

"I'm fine." I fought the urge to collapse against him. Woods's knight-in-shining-armor jab had hit a little too close to home. "Just worried that the detective might do something we'd both regret—probably me more than him."

"Are you saying I haven't acted professionally?" Woods's breath was coming out in angry spurts and his fists were clenched.

I took a step backward, but he darted after me and thrust his face into mine. "What were you doing at the Parkside Hotel last night?"

Before I could speak, Jake moved me behind him and growled, "That's not how this is going to go down. You don't invade her personal space, and she doesn't file a complaint against you."

Jake had a good eight inches on the detective, and a lot more muscle, not to mention the little matter of being twenty years younger.

Woods threatened, "You have no idea who you're messing with, son."

"Neither do you."

When Jake didn't elaborate, I realized he wanted to keep his identity as a U.S. Marshal from the detective for a little longer. Although, now that Woods was aware of Jake's connection with me, all the detective had to do was ask around town, and the truth would come out.

The older man glared at Jake, fingering his gun, but finally took an infinitesimal step away. Then with his muddy brown eyes flat and hard—like a rattlesnake ready to strike—he said, "Just answer the question. What were you doing nosing around the crime scene?"

I searched Jake's face for a clue as to what I should say, but before I could figure it out, he put his arm around me and kissed my cheek. "Go ahead, sugarplum, tell him what we were doing at the Parkside." Jake chuckled, "Just don't tell him everything."

Ah. So that was how we were going to play it. "Well, okay. But he has to promise not to say anything to anyone." I fluttered my lashes at Jake before saying to Woods, "We were there for some privacy."

"Really?" The detective furrowed his forehead. "Then why didn't you stay the night? You checked out after only a few hours." Woods jerked his chin at Jake. "Was that all he had in him?"

"Don't be silly. This big guy can go all night. It was my fault we left early." I chose my next words carefully, knowing that a good lie contained a hint of truth. "I was worried about leaving my grandmother alone overnight."

Woods snorted his disbelief. "Then where's the dear little old lady now?"

I knew the detective would probably check my story, but I hoped not too thoroughly. "Turns out she decided to go with a friend on a casino trip, so we could have stayed." I leaned my head on Jake's shoulder and smiled contritely. "Sorry, sweetheart."

"No problem." Jake pulled me closer. "I was worried about Uncle Tony, too."

"How sweet." Woods made a gagging sound. "You expect me to believe it was purely a coincidence that you were not only at the same hotel but also in the same room as Joelle Ayers, exactly a week after the murder took place?"

"Yes." I barely kept myself from cringing. Yuck! It hadn't dawned on me that we were in the suite on the one-week anniversary of her death. "No one ever told me the name of the hotel."

"And," Jake added, "I booked the honeymoon suite so our time together would be special. Nothing's too good for my sweetie pie."

"Of course." Woods's pupils dilated. "You two must take me for an idiot."

I bit my tongue to stop myself from agreeing.

Jake must have realized how close I was to losing it and telling the detective exactly what I thought of him, because he said smoothly, "The Parkside is one of the best hotels, and we were celebrating our new relationship. Don't you believe in love?"

There was a moment's silence; then Woods started to applaud. "That was some performance. You had me going for a second or two." He hitched up his pants and moved closer to me again. "I might even buy your story if there wasn't a dead body in that room a week ago. A woman who was killed with items from your perverted gift basket, and who just happened to be the fiancée of your ex-boyfriend."

271

"Which might have given Devereaux a motive," Jake interjected, "*if* she still had feelings for Underwood and was intent on getting rid of the competition." He gave me a hug and beamed down at me with such love in his eyes, I almost believed the line he was giving Woods.

The detective tried to interrupt, but Jake continued. "However, as you can clearly see, she's in love with me now and had no reason to kill that woman."

"So you say." Woods's voice was skeptical. "This great love of yours seems very handy to me."

"Yes, and your knowledge of our whereabouts seems very handy to me." Jake narrowed his eyes. "Were we being followed?"

"No. We got an anonymous tip this morning." Woods shook his head in disgust. "I only wish the department had those kinds of resources. Hell, between the bean counters not approving surveillance and the lawyers telling me I can't say she's a suspect, I might as well retire." Woods shot me a look of pure loathing. "And I would if I still had any retirement money left."

I started to apologize, but Jake cut me off, intent on gathering more information. "Who tipped you off? Man or woman?"

"Couldn't tell," Woods answered automatically, obviously responding to the command in Jake's voice. Then he caught himself. "Now wait a goddamn minute—I'm the one asking the questions, so tell me again why you were at the Parkside."

"We already told you." Jake faced the detective and crossed his arms. "So unless you have another relevant question, I suggest you leave."

Woods didn't blink. "How long have you two been going out together?"

I waited for Jake to respond since I didn't want us to give different answers. Heck, I wasn't even sure how long he'd been in town.

"A month." Jake's tone was confident. "We met the day after I arrived at my uncle's."

"How convenient." Woods's smile could have cut through a sheet of metal. "I don't suppose there's anyone who can corroborate that."

"My grandmother," I said.

"My uncle," Jake said at the same time. Then he added, "We kept our relationship quiet at first, but recently we shared it with Devereaux's friends Boone and Poppy."

Wow. Jake was smooth. I needed to remember that he was an even better liar than I was.

As Woods took another step closer to us, a voice exploded into the foyer and Birdie burst from the kitchen into the hallway, holding a rolling pin in her raised hand. "I want you out of my house! I know my rights. Unless you have a search warrant, you need to leave right now and quit bothering these two lovebirds."

I froze. *Shit! Shit! Shit!* I had been hoping to

keep Gran in the dark about all this—especially the part where Jake and I spent an evening in a hotel room alone together. How had I missed the sound of the bad muffler on Frieda's old Chevy Impala? I had to have been really distracted by Woods and Jake.

Gran was still wearing her coat. She must have returned from the casino, seen the police car—even unmarked cars had a distinctive license plate—and come in through the back door.

"Now, Mrs. Sinclair," Woods said, retreating a step, "I'm just asking a few questions."

Birdie darted up to the detective, a righteous grandmother protecting her young. She waved the sturdy wooden dowel at him. "And these kids answered you, so now it's time to leave. I won't ask you this nicely next time."

I caught Jake's eye and tilted my head questioningly. All I needed was for Woods to take Gran into custody.

Jake shrugged, but he was grinning and didn't appear worried.

"Fine." The detective took another step back, plainly making sure he was out of rolling-pin range before adding, "But I'm going to get her this time. I'm this close to arresting her." He held his thumb and index finger together with barely any space between them.

"What's changed?" Jake demanded. "What new evidence do you have?"

At first, I didn't think Woods would answer. Then with a great deal of pleasure he said, "The same person who told us Ms. Sinclair was at the Parkside yesterday told us they saw her there the previous Saturday night as well."

"That's a lie!" I looked at Jake. Did he believe Woods?

Jake smiled reassuringly at me, but before he could speak, Birdie screamed at Woods, "Sweet Jesus! Did you even stop to think your anonymous tipster is probably the real murderer?"

He ignored Gran's question. "You can't protect your granddaughter forever, Mrs. Sinclair. No one can."

"Maybe. But I'll die trying." Birdie looked him up and down. "And I might take you with me since without Dev I have nothing to lose."

"All of you are crazy!" The detective's bellow made the glass knickknacks on the hall table rattle. He turned to Jake and me. "This isn't over."

"No, it isn't." Jake's expression was implacable. "And here's something for you to think about on your way out. Maybe your immediate superior knows about your bias in this matter and doesn't think it's affecting your investigation, but it's time to take the issue up the food chain. Do you think the chief of detectives will allow your personal vendetta against Devereaux to continue?"

Woods's face turned the color of a ripe eggplant. He sputtered, spun on his heel, and flung open the front door. "You just made a dangerous enemy, pal." He stomped out, slamming the door behind him.

# CHAPTER 23

"Well." I blew a curl out of my eye. "That was certainly fun."

Gran had disappeared into the kitchen with a wink and a nudge. No doubt she was already on the phone to Tony, spreading the news of Jake's and my romance.

"Yeah. Real amusing." Jake stood with his hand on the doorknob. "Woods's guitar strings are tuned a little too tight."

"Uh-huh. Let's just hope we aren't around to get hurt when they break." I felt awkward with Jake after all that had happened, both last night and this morning. "So, are you really going to notify the chief of detectives about Woods's prejudice against me?"

"Yes." Jake grimaced. "I didn't do it earlier because going up the chain of command is the last thing a law enforcement officer wants to do to a fellow officer—it's a good way to get labeled a snitch—but I think it's time."

"I can have Boone make the call," I offered, not

wanting Jake to ruin his reputation on my account.

"No. It'll be more effective coming from me."

"Okay. Thanks." I didn't have the luxury of turning down his offer. If I went to prison, Birdie would end up in an assisted-living facility. And after spending her whole life in the same house, she'd hate that. "And thanks for coming over so fast."

"No problem." Jake's tone was distracted. "Good thing you phoned when you did. I was getting ready to leave for St. Louis. I got a message that I need to be at headquarters Monday at nine o'clock, so I'm driving up today and spending the night at my apartment."

"Is it about your injury?"

"No." Jake twitched his shoulders. "A case I worked on a couple of years ago, involving a guy who escaped from prison and took a Sunday school class hostage, is finally going to trial, and they need to prep me before I testify."

"Right. You don't want a scumbag like that getting off on a technicality." I hoped my voice didn't sound as forlorn as I felt as I added, "So, you'll be gone a while."

"Not too long." He shrugged. "A day of prep and a day or two at the trial. I should be home by Wednesday, Thursday at the latest."

"Oh." At least he had said he'd be home, implying Shadow Bend was where his heart was.

"While I'm there I'll see if Meg's had any luck finding out Joelle's real identity."

"Great." Yeah. Just peachy. He was going to spend some quality time with his ex-wife. Even though I was confused about my feelings for Jake, there was one thing I *was* sure about. I didn't want him alone with Meg. "While you're gone, I'll find out if Poppy ever talked to Cyndi Barrow."

"Good. And if you get a chance, check out the housekeeper, too." Jake opened the door and stepped outside. "We'll tackle the mayor and Underwood together once I get back. I don't want you interviewing them alone, since either one could be the killer."

"I can understand that." I recognized his concern, but I wasn't making any promises. Not after Woods's claim that he was close to arresting me. "Have a good trip."

After Jake left, it took me a while to answer all Gran's questions. As I explained everything, I tried to dissuade her from the idea that Jake and I were an item, but that was a futile effort. She'd heard what she wanted to hear, and wasn't willing to let me change her mind.

Finally, a little after noon, I got a chance to shower, dress, and call Poppy. She apologized, telling me she had never caught up with Cyndi, but asked if I could meet her at Brewfully Yours in a half hour. The Country Club Cougars would be there and we could talk to Cyndi together.

When I pulled up to the coffee shop, I was surprised to find the parking lot nearly full. A Sunday afternoon crowd was unusual, but the banner over the doorway announcing a tasting explained the café's sudden popularity.

For twenty-five dollars, half of which went to the animal shelter south of town, thimble-size cups of coffee were passed around and folks pretended they could tell the difference between Folgers and some expensive-label beans. The real reason everyone was there was for the brownies and other pastries that were being served along with the coffee. Since the goodies were considered a palate cleanser, and the event was for charity, the women felt free to eat. Guilt-free calories are hard to come by.

Poppy met me at the door and we walked in together. She was right; the Cougars were out in force. We paid our money, slipped on the lime green wristbands that indicated we weren't deadbeats, and headed toward the women.

It was clear who was who in the social hierarchy. Anya and Gwen were seated in two armchairs with their backs to the wall. Half a dozen women, those next in the pecking order, had arranged the café's wooden chairs to face them. Among those I recognized was the petite blond Country Club Kitten who had been clinging to Noah at the shelter committee meeting.

A couple of wannabes, including Cyndi Barrow,

sat in the last row on metal folding chairs. Poppy and I took the two seats on either side of our quarry, bracketing Cyndi like hunters running down a wild boar.

I made the mistake of murmuring hello to Cyndi while Anya was speaking, and she and Gwen swung disapproving gazes in my direction. A calculating look settled on both women's faces, and after a silent communication, Anya gave Gwen a slight nod.

Gwen homed in on me like a stealth missile. "I can't believe my eyes," she said. "Devereaux Sinclair—you never hang out with us. What brings you here today?"

"This wonderful cause, of course. What else?" I bared my teeth in a fake grin. "I wouldn't miss it. I'm a big animal lover."

"And not just the four-footed variety." Gwen's smile was full of innuendo. "Word around town has it that you've been taking a walk on the wild side with Tony Del Vecchio's hot nephew."

I would have let that comment pass, because even annoying people can be informative, but Poppy said, "Maybe she has. But at least Dev's not giving guided tours of the jungle like I've seen you doing at Gossip Central."

Gwen sniffed, turned to Anya, and whispered furiously in her ear, all the while darting vicious looks at Poppy and me.

"Was that really necessary?" I hissed at my friend.

"Definitely."

"You're really good at making enemies, aren't you?" She could be so exasperating.

"Yep." Poppy smirked. "Which is why I'm divorced, unlisted, and own a gun."

While the coffee samples were being served, I studied the beautiful vacant faces of the women who'd gathered there. They chatted among themselves as they sipped, but they quieted immediately when either Anya or Gwen spoke.

The event was winding down, and I was wondering how we would get Cyndi alone so we could question her, when Poppy got up and wandered over to Gwen and Anya. She leaned close to them and spoke for several seconds in a voice too low for me to hear. I was thinking about moving nearer, but whatever Poppy was saying launched Anya and Gwen to their feet.

They swept the circle of women in front of them with twin glares, scooped up their Louis Vuitton bags, and marched out of the coffee shop. The rest of their entourage followed closely on the heels of their Prada peep-toe platform pumps.

When Cyndi tried to join the others, I put a hand on her arm. "Do you have a minute? I wanted to talk to you about Blood, Sweat, and Shears."

"Sure." Cyndi's smile was tenuous as she sank back into her seat. "Is there a problem with the group? You're not kicking us out of the dime store, are you?"

"Of course not. Your group does such wonderful work for charity." I patted her knee. "I just wanted your opinion."

"On what?"

"Uh . . ." I thought fast. "What kind of serger to buy for the store."

"I think the best brand is Brother, though some people like Singer." I could tell from Cyndi's voice that she wasn't expecting anyone to give much credence to her suggestion. "You really should check with Winnie."

"Thanks." I looked at Poppy as she rejoined us, indicating she should take over. "I'll do that."

"So what do you think got Anya and Gwen in such a tizzy?" Poppy asked. "I was trying to apologize to Gwen for the snarky remark I made earlier and all of a sudden they both ran out of here like I had shot them."

"They don't really forgive and forget very easily." Cyndi's brow furrowed. "She and Joelle and Gwen always said forgiveness is for priests and losers."

"Wow!" Poppy's angelic face shone with false innocence. "That's way harsh."

"Yes. Yes, it is." Cyndi leaned forward, closing in on her point. "I thought they might have been kidding when they first said it, but they really meant it. You don't want to make a mistake around them."

"Were there women in your group that they wouldn't forgive?" I asked. "Maybe someone who became angry enough to kill Joelle?"

"No." Cyndi chewed a thumbnail. "No one ever dared cross them."

"Were Anya and Gwen jealous when Joelle snagged Shadow Bend's most eligible bachelor?" I asked, forcing a giggle.

"Oh, yeah." Cyndi giggled with me. "You could see they were hopping mad, though mostly they pretended not to be. At least they pretended when Joelle was around."

"What did they do behind her back?" Poppy asked.

"For a while they were hell-bent on finding some dirt on Joelle to show Noah's mother." Cyndi shook her head. "But they must not have ever found anything, since Joelle and Noah were still engaged when she died."

Poppy had to get back to her bar by three, but before she left, we sat in my car chatting. First, she told me what she'd really said to Gwen and Anya to make them so angry: that if they didn't pay their bar tab by the end of the week, they'd be cut off. For the next half hour, I updated Poppy on Woods's visit and what Jake and I had discovered on our visit to the hotel. After that, I spent the rest of the time fending off her interest in my love life.

Finally, Poppy had to leave. As she got out of the Z4, she said, "Those Cougars need to be taught a lesson. They think life is just a bowl of cherries. What they don't realize is that life is really a can of hot peppers. And what you devour one day will scorch your ass the next."

I nodded my agreement, and with a promise to keep her informed, I drove away.

That morning, Gran had told me that Joelle's housekeeper was Irene Johnson and that she lived a few miles north of town. When Gran had described the property and given me directions, I'd known exactly where she meant because Irene's place had always reminded me of a dollhouse. It was painted a delicate butter yellow with sage green trim and a white porch. It was tiny, but every detail was perfect.

It took only a few minutes to reach my destination. After parking my car on a concrete apron beside an immaculately maintained older-model dark blue Taurus, I made my way to the front door. I could hear Billy Ray Cyrus singing about his achy breaky heart, but there was no response when I rang the bell.

*Hmm.* Maybe Irene couldn't hear me over the music. I tried several more times with the same result, then followed the sidewalk around to the back door. I cupped my hand and peered through the window. Mr. Coffee's ON button glowed red and a big pot of something was cooking on the stove, so Irene had to be home.

I tapped my knuckles against the wood, then knocked harder. A second or two later, Irene hurried into the kitchen. She was a tall, solidly built woman, and she leaned against the doorframe before she asked, "Can I help you?"

"Ms. Johnson, my name is Devereaux Sinclair. I'm Birdie Sinclair's granddaughter." Everyone knew Gran. "She told me where you lived."

"Oh, sure." Irene opened the door. "You bought the old dime store. Everyone in town was so relieved that a local took it over and that you kept it like it always had been. We all just love that store."

"Thank you. I love it, too." I flashed a big smile. "If I'm not interrupting anything, Ms. Johnson, could I talk to you for a few minutes?"

"Sure, and call me Irene." She motioned me inside. "Have a seat. Can I get you anything?"

"No, thanks." We exchanged pleasantries for a few minutes, then I said, "I understand you worked for Joelle Ayers before she died."

"Yes." Irene's expression was puzzled. "She was one of the ladies I did for."

How to explain why I was asking questions? "Even though I didn't know her very well, I was devastated to hear she had been killed with the contents of a gift basket I put together for her."

285

"That must have been awful for you." Irene patted my arm. "But you really can't blame yourself. Once your baskets are out of your hands, you have no control over what someone does with them."

"I'm trying to remember that." Too bad Woods didn't feel that way. "Gran suggested that maybe if I knew more about Joelle, it might help me come to terms with what happened to her." Okay, that was lame, but at the moment it was the best I could do.

"Sure." Irene didn't look completely convinced by my explanation, but she was clearly too polite to say how crazy the idea seemed.

"Would you be willing to tell me a little about Joelle?" I asked.

"Well . . ." Irene got up, opened the refrigerator, stared inside, then closed it, chuckling. "Why do I constantly go back to the fridge? Do I truly think something new to eat will have materialized since the last time I looked?" When I didn't answer, she nudged the refrigerator door closed with her rear end. "Ms. Ayers was a real private person."

"Oh?"

"Yeah." Irene stood with her hands on her hips. "One time when I was cleaning, I wiped down her computer monitor, and she carried on like I had read her diary and published it on the front page of the paper."

"That must have been awkward," I said sympathetically. "What was on the screen that was so top secret?"

"Just some e-mail from a guy named Etienne." Irene moved over to the stove and stirred the contents of the pot, sending up an enticing aroma of homemade vegetable soup that made my stomach growl. "That's French for 'Steve,' right?"

Nodding, I asked, "Did you notice his last name?" I held my breath. "Or his e-mail address?" Was Etienne someone from Joelle's past? Could this be a clue to her identity?

"Can't say as I did."

"Did anything else odd happen during the time you worked for her?"

"The last time I was there cleaning, Ms. Ayers got a call that really upset her. She took it in the bedroom with the door closed, so I didn't hear anything, but she was meaner than a skillet full of rattlesnakes for the rest of the day."

"So Joelle liked her privacy," I said casually, watching Irene closely. "Was she secretive with her girlfriends too? I understand she had a lot of them."

"As far as I could tell, she hardly ever had anyone over to her condo. But one time when I was there, a lady friend of hers dropped by and she wouldn't let her in."

"Who was that?" After what Cyndi had said, I was betting on Anya or Gwen.

"I never saw her." Irene shrugged. "All I heard was her voice on the intercom and she and Ms. Ayers arguing about her coming up."

"I wonder why she allowed you in her condo, but not her friends."

"Cleaning ladies aren't a threat." Irene shook her head. "And believe you me, she kept a close eye on my every move. I was never there alone."

"Anything else you can think of that would make Joelle more real in my mind?"

"She was pretty and liked pretty things." Irene paused, then added, "And she got lots of magazines about rich people."

"Interesting."

Irene looked at me expectantly, but I couldn't think of anything else to ask, so I excused myself to use the bathroom. She pointed me down the hall, and on my way I peeked into the living room.

There were several items that didn't seem to go with Irene's appearance or her lifestyle. A silver tray with crystal goblets and a decanter, a cut-glass ashtray, and an ivory-handled letter opener looked particularly out of place next to the framed paint-by-number picture hanging over the TV and the bright aqua fish-shaped platter displayed on a side table next to a china dog.

Had the expensive pieces been Joelle's? Maybe Irene had been stealing from her employer and had to kill her when Joelle discovered the thefts. It was a long shot, but I had to check it out.

My hostess was still at the stove when I returned, and I knew I was running out of time. In the living room, I had noticed a thick stack of unpaid bills on the coffee table, along with a calculator and a checkbook.

That gave me an idea of how to broach the question of stealing to Irene. "I imagine it's tough financially losing one of your clients. Have you been able to find someone to fill that slot?"

"Not yet." Irene gazed out the window. A few snowflakes drifted through the twilight. "With the bad economy, not as many can afford a cleaning lady. People are taking care of their own houses now."

I took a breath; the next question was hard to ask. "So it must have been sort of tempting to take a few of Joelle's pretty things—once you found out she was dead and there was no next of kin."

"What makes you say a horrible thing like that?" An ugly flush stained Irene's already ruddy cheeks and she banged the lid down hard on the pot she'd been stirring before turning to face me. "Has someone claimed that I'm a thief? Is that why you're here?"

"No, no. Not at all." I quickly backpedaled. Was her reaction normal outrage at being falsely accused, or guilt? I couldn't tell. But by the set of her chin, I knew I wouldn't get anywhere else on that subject and had overstayed my welcome to boot. "Sorry."

After I said good-bye and was driving home, I realized that Irene hadn't actually denied having stolen from Joelle.

# CHAPTER 24

Okay. This was so not good. Jake had been gone for less than twenty-four hours, and already I missed him way too much. Monday was crawling by like a slow driver in the fast lane. I had delivered the fund-raising flyers to Mrs. Ziegler at the high school, then completed two basket orders before the store opened at twelve. And even though we were busy from noon until closing time, my thoughts returned constantly to Jake, wondering what was happening in St. Louis.

I checked my cell so often that Hannah started wondering aloud about my sudden interest in the phone. When Jake hadn't called by closing time—and since I was still stinging from Woods's crack about my needing a man to rescue me—I decided to go see the mayor by myself.

I couldn't wait, not with the police closing in on me. Although the mayor wouldn't be in his office this late—he left promptly at four—I knew where to find him. The good old boy Tuesday night poker game in the back room of the feed store was a Shadow Bend institution, and it started at six thirty.

Not being a complete fool, I texted Boone, explained what I was doing and where I would be, and arranged to call him and leave the line open while I talked to His Honor. Backup in place, I caught Geoffrey Eggers as he was entering the rear door of the store. He protested, but I pointed out to him that chatting in my car would be a lot better for his political career than our having this conversation in public.

As he settled into the passenger seat, I punched the speed dial to Boone, then accused His Honor. "You lied to Poppy and me about where you were Valentine's Day weekend." I hit him with his falsehood first thing to throw him off balance. "You were staying at the Parkside, the same hotel where Joelle was murdered."

"You're mistaken." His Honor crossed his arms. "I said that I had recently begun dating a lovely young lady and we were together that evening. You never asked where we were."

I let him get away with that, although he had distinctly said they were in town that night. It was always good to have something in the bank with the mayor, so the next time he morphed into an obnoxious politician, I could cash that check.

"I need your girlfriend's name." My tone was unyielding. "And her contact info."

"And if I refuse, will you run to your pet U.S. Marshal?" Geoffrey's smug expression made me itch to slap him.

"No, but I will check with the KC police and see if they're aware that one of Joelle's ex-lovers was checked in to the hotel that night." I stared him down. "They don't know that, do they, Mayor?"

"My girlfriend will kill me if I tell you who she is," His Honor whined. "You know how hard it is to get any privacy around here. We just wanted a chance to see if our relationship would work, before everyone in Shadow Bend weighed in on it."

I was sympathetic, but the best I could do was promise, "I'll keep the information to myself unless it's connected to the murder."

"She doesn't like excuses."

Where had I heard that before? "Give me her name and number, I'll call, she'll confirm your alibi, and that will be that."

"Well . . ." He hesitated, then shook his head. "No. I think she might be Miss Right and I'm not going to risk it."

"But if you were with her from the moment you checked in to the hotel until you checked out the next day, you're in the clear," I coaxed. "Were you together that whole time?"

"Not exactly." Geoffrey's face flamed an

unhealthy shade of red. "We met at the hotel a bit after six. But after I checked in, she remembered that she forgot the . . . well . . . some personal items that she'd said she would provide, so she had to run to the drugstore."

"How long were you alone?" I asked.

"I'm not sure." Geoffrey shrugged. "I fell asleep watching TV and she was back when I woke up."

"What time was that?"

"Around eight."

"Do you have any proof that you remained in your room that whole time?" I questioned.

"No." Geoffrey frowned. "But I'm telling the truth."

"Then give me the name of your girlfriend so I can confirm it, and I won't have to involve the police."

"No." Geoffrey got out of the car. Just before he slammed the door, he muttered, "She'd never forgive me."


"What do you think of the mayor's story?" I asked, speaking to Boone on my cell while I drove home.

"Even if his girlfriend confirms his version of events, it's not much of an alibi. We need to see if the hotel records show when he entered his hotel room and if he reopened the door during the time the woman was gone."

"I'll ask Jake to check on that the next time I speak to him."

"Right," Boone agreed. "Even if it only took the girlfriend a half hour for her trip to the drugstore, that leaves His Honor with enough time alone to kill Joelle and get back to his room." I could hear the frown in Boone's voice. "But how could the mayor know he'd have those thirty minutes free?"

"If it was a crime of passion, which is how it looks, he could have run into Joelle in the hall. She invites him in for whatever reason and does something to inflame him, so he kills her."

"So, the mayor remains on our list of suspects?" Boone asked.

"At least until Jake can confirm with the hotel what time he entered his room and whether he stayed inside until his girlfriend returned like he claims."

It was eight o'clock and Gran was snoozing in front of the TV while I pretended to watch a rerun of *Law & Order*. I was starting to get irritated. Surely Jake wasn't still at headquarters. Was he having such a good time with Meg that he couldn't spare five minutes to let me know he was okay? Granted, he'd never said he would call, but it was just common courtesy. Right?

Wrong! I was acting like a lovestruck adolescent, and worst of all, I had no right to behave that way. Fine. I jumped to my feet, grabbed my laptop, and powered it on. Instead of wasting time mooning over some man, I would make a list of what I had learned yesterday from my interviews with Cyndi and Irene, and what I had found out from the mayor. I needed to figure out who killed Joelle more than I needed a guy in my life. No matter how hot he was.

Cyndi had confirmed that Anya and Gwen were extremely jealous that Joelle had snatched Noah from Shadow Bend's tiny pool of successful single men. She had also claimed that they were looking for dirt on Joelle to stop her from marrying Noah. But had they found anything? Surely if they had, Nadine would have mentioned it when we talked at the fund-raiser. Was there some reason Anya and Gwen wouldn't have told her?

Irene's comment about Joelle's extreme privacy issues went along with the victim's secret identity, but was that all she had been hiding? Had the police checked her computer, traced her calls, and really searched her place, even the second time? Somehow I didn't see Woods as being all that thorough. And which of Joelle's friends had tried to get into her condo the day Irene was cleaning?

I included His Honor's version of what had happened Valentine's night, and added my list of questions. Then, as the ten o'clock news was coming on, I e-mailed what I had found out to Jake. I clicked SEND and stood, stretching the kink out of my back.

Gran woke up a few minutes later, and once we had watched the weather report, we went to bed. I heard snoring coming from Birdie's room a few minutes after I crawled under the covers, but I tossed and turned into the wee hours.

When my phone rang the next morning during breakfast, I tried not to snatch it up like the last piece of candy in a Godiva chocolate box. From the smug grin on Gran's face, I knew I'd failed.

"Why the hell did you talk to the mayor alone?" Jake's anger vibrated through the speaker of my cell.

"Because I'm fully capable of conducting a simple interview on my own. I arranged for backup." My irritation matched his, but I gritted my teeth and explained nicely, "I know you're busy and I understand, but I can't sit around and wait for Woods to arrest me."

"You have no idea how fast a one-on-one confrontation can go bad." Jake didn't give an inch.

Neither did I. "It turned out fine."

"This time."

We fumed in silence for a couple of seconds; then Jake said with grudging admiration, "You've got guts."

"Thank you."

"I'm glad a bullet didn't splatter them all over the inside of your car."

Letting that comment pass, I asked, "What are you doing today?"

"I'm testifying, so I won't be able to have my phone on. I should be through by four and I'll call you then."

"That works for me." I kept my tone neutral. "Since you apparently saw the e-mail I sent last night, what did you think of the other information I found out?"

"All good points, although even if the housekeeper was stealing, my guess is it was after the vic was dead. Besides, the way Joelle was killed doesn't really jibe with a thief committing murder to cover up her pilfering."

"Yeah. I thought that, too."

"Yesterday was a madhouse around here, so I didn't get a chance to phone the chief of detectives about Woods's bias, but I'll do that, and get on the rest of the stuff as soon as I can." Jake's voiced dropped. "Meg's funneling all the data to the KC cops, but so far no one has shown a lot of interest." He paused and I could hear someone talking to him. "Sorry. I've got to go. Talk to you this afternoon."

After I hung up, Gran tried to question me about Jake, but she gave up when I answered in monosyllables. How could I explain things to her that I didn't understand myself?

• • •

A final lingering customer brought her purchases up to the register, and as I bagged her items, I forced myself to act friendly rather than push her out the door. At last, the store was empty, and I flipped off the OPEN sign. It was six and Jake hadn't called yet. I was toying with the idea of phoning him when my cell rang.

Even though he was all business, Jake's voice sent a ripple of happiness through me. "The police still have no clue about Joelle's identity, and Meg has come up empty, too. I think our best bet may be that e-mail the housekeeper saw. Etienne is a fairly uncommon name, at least in the United States."

"True." I had thought the same thing. "Do you know if the cops examined Joelle's computer or her phone records after she died?"

"They claimed to have done both, but it was before they knew she was using a stolen identity." Jake lowered his voice. "After I got your e-mail, I asked Meg to check if they had reexamined that evidence once Joelle's false identity was revealed, and she just told me there was no record that the KC police took a second look."

*Hmm.* I sure wished Jake's contact at the U.S. Marshal's office wasn't his ex-wife, but beggars couldn't be choosers. "Can you request that they do?"

"Meg's getting the phone and computer records for me, but we may have to take a look at Joelle's condo ourselves."

Before I could ask if that was legal, Jake said hurriedly, "Sorry. I've got to go. It looks as if I won't be home until Thursday. Sit tight until I get back. Do not talk to Underwood by yourself."

I hadn't planned to talk to Noah alone, but as soon as Jake ordered me not to, I realized it was exactly what I should do. Despite all indications to the contrary, I knew in my heart that Noah was not a murderer. In fact, he might be holding the one piece of evidence that could reveal the real killer.

# CHAPTER 25

I had already rung the bell three times when Noah jerked the front door open. His usually perfectly styled hair fell across his forehead and into his eyes. He needed a trim—and possibly a shower. I wrinkled my nose. A stale odor that reminded me of an old gym locker wafted from him.

Adding to my sense of unease was his attire. The Noah I had known in high school, and observed from a distance for the past thirteen years, was always immaculately dressed. Tonight he wore navy sweatpants with bleach spots down one leg and a T-shirt that might have been red at one point, but was now a washed-out pink.

The most worrisome part of Noah's appearance was the confused expression in his eyes. He almost looked drugged.

Scrubbing his face with his fists, he asked, "Dev, what are you doing here?"

"Uh." Noah didn't seem happy to see me, and for a split second, I wondered if maybe I *should* have waited to talk to him until Jake returned.

"Dev?" Noah's voice had warmed up, and now it held a hint of concern. "Are you okay?"

"Sorry. I'm fine." Mentally, I gave myself a good shake. This was Noah. He was not on drugs. And he wasn't any threat to me. I'd probably just woken him up. "But I do have a couple more questions for you. Can I come inside?"

"Sure." Noah tried to hide his confusion. "Come on in." He moved out of the doorway so I could enter. "Let's sit in the den."

This was the first time I'd been in Noah's home, and as I followed him a few feet down the hall, I wondered what the rest of the place was like. The little I could see was beautifully decorated, but appeared cold and uninviting. Was Noah as lonely as his house implied?

Noah interrupted my thoughts. "Would you like something to drink?"

I declined his offer of refreshment and settled on one of the leather club chairs facing the sofa.

A tan Chihuahua stared at me from his place on the matching chair.

Noah must have noted my interest because he explained, "Lucky was Joelle's. She named me his guardian in her will."

Although I already knew that, I pretended not to, and said, "He seems like a nice little dog."

"Yeah." Noah plopped down on the couch. "It's been tough on him. Chihuahuas are one-person animals, so he's still adjusting to me."

"Poor thing." I noticed the remains of a frozen dinner on the coffee table. The food was barely touched, but the beer bottle next to the white plastic tray was empty. "Well, anyway, the reason I wanted to talk to you is because an issue has come to light since Jake and I spoke to you about Joelle's murder, and I wanted to hear your side of it."

"Sure." Noah reached for the remote and turned off the TV set, which had been playing a *National Geographic* special on the wildebeests of the Serengeti. "What's up?"

Noah still seemed foggy, and judging from the pillow and afghan lying at one end of the couch, I was betting he'd been awakened from a deep sleep. It finally dawned on me that it had been only ten days since Joelle's murder, and because her body hadn't been released yet, there hadn't been a funeral. To Noah, it probably felt as if she'd died just yesterday.

A part of me sympathized, but the other part, the one Woods was trying to convict of murder, said good. It's easier to get the truth from someone who's vulnerable. And although I didn't think Noah was guilty, he might have information about the person who was.

"Actually there are two things." I forced myself to relax against the back of my chair.

"Yes?" Noah's pearl gray eyes met mine, and a sliver of our old chemistry feathered up my spine. "What do you want to know?"

I hoped none of that attraction showed in my expression as I gazed steadily back at him. "Your nurse told Jake that you let your entire staff leave last Saturday while you were waiting for your emergency patient to show up. That seems odd to me." I tilted my head. "Why would you do that? Weren't you afraid you'd need assistance?"

"A little." Noah twitched his shoulders. "But by the time I let Eunice go, it had been over a half hour since the call. I think I already suspected the patient would be a no-show." He rubbed the bridge of his nose. "I hated to keep her from her holiday plans for a false alarm."

"Really?" I deliberately injected a modicum of skepticism into my tone.

"Really." Noah tapped his fingers on the arm of the sofa. "You said you had two questions?"

"I did." My voice sharpened. "The other matter is a bit harder to explain away."

"Yes?"

I sat forward. "How come you told us that you didn't arrive at the Parkside until seven thirty last Saturday night, but hotel records show you parked in the garage well before six?"

I watched carefully for Noah's reaction. He had never been a very good actor. In high school, drama was about the only class in which he didn't excel. I was sure I could tell if he was lying.

"I have no idea." He frowned. "I hadn't even left Shadow Bend by six, so there's no way it could have been me. Maybe the Parkside had a computer glitch."

"There's no evidence of that." I willed him to come up with the same explanation I had.

"There must be some mistake." Noah wrinkled his forehead, thinking hard. "I just don't know."

I waited, hoping my guess was right, but reluctant to put words into his mouth.

Abruptly he smacked his forehead with his palm. "In fact, I never parked in the garage at all. The police had the whole area cordoned off when I arrived. I had to park on a side street and walk to the hotel."

*Yes!* If he was telling the truth about his arrival time, that was exactly what I figured must have happened. "Do you have any proof of that?" I asked, knowing Noah's word alone wouldn't convince Jake. "Did you see anyone before leaving Shadow Bend?"

"No. The area around the clinic was deserted." Noah slumped. Then a moment later he jumped to his feet, walked to the desk, and handed me several yellow slips of paper. "I got three parking tickets. I didn't have any change and planned to go back and feed the meter once I got some. But—" He stuttered to a stop and swallowed hard.

"That's interesting." I glanced at the tickets and saw the seven forty-five time stamped on the first, eight forty-five on the second, and nine forty-five on the third. "Though it doesn't explain why the records show you parking in the garage from five forty-five until eleven the next day." This was the part I hadn't been able to figure out before, but now an idea popped into my head. "Is it possible someone switched key cards with you?"

"I suppose." Noah's eyes lit up with a hint of hope. "Joelle left the key card for me at the clinic's appointment desk. My receptionist, Madison, called me on the intercom and told me the key was there. I told her to leave it on the counter and I'd get it when I had a chance."

"So"—I beamed at him approvingly—"it sat on the counter, in plain sight, for several hours?"

"I suppose so . . . until I walked out the door." Noah's smile matched mine. "In fact, I almost forgot it. You could confirm it with Madison."

"You don't still have the key card, do you?" I asked, thinking the police had probably taken it or Noah had turned it over to the hotel when he left.

"I might. I just might." Noah nodded slowly. "I put it in my jacket pocket that night, and I don't remember ever taking it out."

"You've had it in your pocket all this time and never noticed it?" I asked.

"I wore my leather jacket last Saturday, and I've been wearing my wool coat since then," he explained. "Let me check."

He disappeared down the hall, with me trailing him. It took only a few seconds for him to find his coat in the foyer closet, and when he faced me, he was triumphantly waving a white plastic rectangle.

Why was my life always full of more speed bumps than a church parking lot? Although I was pleased to have proven Noah's innocence—at least it would be proven as soon as the KC police confirmed his story with Madison and the key card in his possession was shown not to open the door to the suite the night Joelle was killed—I was no closer to removing myself from Woods's Most Wanted list. I needed to find him a viable suspect soon, or I would end up in jail becoming acquainted with a woman named Bad Betty in an up-close-and-personal way.

When I arrived home, a note on the kitchen table weighted down by a cupcake-shaped saltshaker didn't improve my mood. Gran had gone to bed with one of her sick headaches, but she wanted to remind me that I had promised to take her to see my father Sunday afternoon.

I never went into the prison to visit him myself, but I always drove Gran back and forth. In view of my current precarious position with the law, I really didn't want to be anywhere near a penitentiary, but a promise was a promise, and I certainly couldn't let her go alone.

After a quick bite to eat, I plopped down on the couch and spread my notes on the case all around me. There had to be something I was missing. I had been at it for about an hour, and was going over the hotel's garage parking data again, when I finally spotted it.

According to that list, early on the evening Joelle was murdered, at five forty-five p.m.—the same time Noah supposedly arrived—someone named Etienne Aponte had parked in the hotel's garage. The e-mail that Irene had seen on Joelle's computer had been from an Etienne.

Considering that Etienne was an extremely unusual name, at least in the Midwest, it was unlikely that an Etienne who was unrelated to the case chose that day to stay at the Parkside Hotel. This Etienne had to have had something to do with Joelle's death.

My first inclination was to call Jake, but after some thought I decided to e-mail him with my discovery instead. I wanted to include all the information I had gleaned from my visit with Noah, and I knew Jake would be unhappy to learn I had talked to my ex-boyfriend alone. My hope was that he would have cooled off before we spoke on the phone.

My cell rang the next morning at seven. Thankfully, I was in my car driving to the store early in order to work on several basket orders, because I didn't want Gran overhearing what Jake had to say. Especially since the first few minutes of the conversation were an unpleasant replay of yesterday's call.

"What part of '*Do not* talk to Underwood without me' did you not understand?" Jake's fury throbbed through the little phone's speaker.

"I understood your order; I just chose not to follow it." I barely stopped myself from saying *because you're not the boss of me*. "Nobody likes to be told what to do, least of all me."

Jake grunted, or maybe growled. I know I heard teeth grinding.

Finally I said, "As you must know, since you obviously saw my e-mail, I was sure Noah was innocent and now I have proof."

"The only reason you were convinced he was innocent is because you wanted him to be."

Jake's words seethed with exasperation. "Just admit you're still in love with him."

My annoyance matched his, but I ignored his taunt, held on to my patience, and asked in as civil a tone as I could muster, "What about Etienne Aponte? Were you able to find out anything about him?"

Jake was silent for a couple of seconds, then grudgingly said, "He's Joelle's husband."

"What!" I shrieked before I could stop myself. "But she was going to marry Noah."

"Not legally." Jake's voice held a hint of satisfaction. "Your precious doctor was about to enter into a bigamous union."

Instead of responding to Jake's crack about Noah, I demanded, "Tell me everything."

"Joelle Ayers is really Jolene Aponte. About a year and a half ago she won half a million in the Louisiana lottery and disappeared."

"Wow."

"Yep," Jake agreed. "She spent the next nine months or so transforming herself. She bought colored contact lenses, dyed her hair, had plastic surgery to enlarge her breasts and remove her wrinkles, and took speech lessons to improve the way she talked. Once she was transformed, she assumed an identity that was ten years younger than her real age."

"How did you find all this out so fast?" I had sent him the info only eleven hours ago.

"Etienne Aponte filed a missing persons report when his wife vanished," Jake explained. "Once we found that, the rest unraveled quickly."

"What rest?"

"It turns out Etienne's fingerprints are in the system because he applied for a job as a bank security guard," Jake paused, then delivered the coup de grâce. "And they matched the print found on the champagne bottle stuffed in Joelle's mouth."

"Oh, my God!" Now I remembered that Woods had never answered my question about whether there were other prints besides mine on the murder weapons. "Why didn't they run those prints right after the murder?"

"They did, but Aponte's prints are what they call 'civil fingerprints,' so they're not in the criminal databank."

"Oh." After thinking about it for a minute, I asked, "So how did they find them now?"

"The FBI doesn't advertise this, but they've started to retain the fingerprints of employer-conducted criminal background checks." Jake lowered his voice. "So, when I heard that Aponte was a security guard, I called in a favor and asked a friend at the bureau to run the print on the bottle through those records."

"And it was a match." I blew out a long breath of relief. "Which means Aponte is the killer, right?"

"That's the way the KC cops are figuring it. Joelle ran away rather than divorcing Aponte so she wouldn't have to give him half the money from her lottery win. According to her friends in Louisiana, she always dreamed of living a different life, of being a country club lady with designer clothes and fancy cars." Jake took a breath. "And since Joelle's will is not in her real name, and she's still married to Aponte, he's her legal heir. The theory is that he tracked her down and killed her for the money."

"Wow!"

Jake added casually, "I made sure the info went to Woods's chief of detectives so he couldn't bury that evidence."

"Thank you." Those two simple words didn't seem sufficient, but they would have to do until I saw Jake in person. "So, I'm no longer a suspect?"

"That would be my guess."

"Were there any prints on the shoe?" I knew mine hadn't been on the stiletto because it wasn't part of the basket's contents.

"Let me check." Jake rustled some papers. "Nope. It was wiped clean."

As I pondered why one weapon was wiped clean and one had prints, Jake was called away. He hung up before I could say more, but I didn't care. Joelle's killer had been identified. And it wasn't me.

At the end of our conversation, Jake had sworn me to secrecy, so I couldn't share the good news with Poppy or Boone, but he had allowed me to tell Gran. He understood that it wasn't fair to let her keep worrying about me.

On my way home from work that night, I stopped at the grocery store and bought two filet mignons with all the fixings, and she and I celebrated my freedom. But after supper, as we watched TV together, questions began to plague me.

How had Etienne found Joelle? If law enforcement couldn't trace her true identity, how had he located her? Someone in town must have tipped him off, but how had that person known who she really was?

Four people would benefit if Joelle's secret was revealed, and all of their motives revolved around preventing her from marrying Noah. Nadine didn't think Joelle was good enough for her son, the mayor wanted Joelle for himself, and Anya and Gwen each wanted Noah for herself.

Nadine and presumably the mayor had alibis, but not Anya or Gwen. My money was on one of them. During the next commercial, I told Gran I was going to the bathroom, and then phoned Jake.

Once I had run my theory past him, he said,

311

"Even if you're right, and one of those two women told Aponte where he could find Joelle, it isn't important right now. The police have him in custody and he's been charged with his wife's murder."

"But how about Noah's key card? Shouldn't someone check it out to see if someone really switched cards?"

"Yes. An officer from Kansas City has already picked it up from Underwood and talked to the doc's receptionist, who confirms his story." Jake's tone was soothing. "I'll pass your theory about Anya or Gwen informing Aponte about his wife's whereabouts on to the KC cops so they can strengthen their case, but you're in the clear. You can leave the rest of the investigation to the police."

# CHAPTER 26

I woke up the next day smiling. I was a free woman. I had been instrumental in clearing my name, and I hadn't waited for a man to rescue me. To top it all off, Jake was coming back to Shadow Bend. He'd said he'd probably get into town around one, but he wanted to check on Tony and do some chores at the ranch before picking me up at six to celebrate my newfound freedom.

Since the store closed at noon on Thursdays, I used the afternoon to work on baskets, take inventory, and pay bills. Although only the first task was fun, I found myself singing along with Lady Gaga on the radio while doing the others. I even boogied a little. And believe me, I never dance.

It was almost two o'clock when my cell signaled that I had a text. Once I found the phone hidden under a stack of order forms on the counter, I saw a message from Poppy that read: 911 . . . GC . . . NOW!

*Oh, my God!* What kind of emergency could there be at Gossip Central?

Instantly, I grabbed my coat and purse, locked up the store, and texted back: OMW. Then I was in my car heading to Poppy's bar.

What in the world could have happened? It couldn't be man trouble. Poppy wasn't involved with anyone currently. If she was being robbed, she'd have called the county sheriff. Maybe she'd had an accident, phoned for the ambulance, and been told it could take a long time for the EMTs to arrive since they were already tied up with another emergency.

It had been snowing for a couple of hours, and the temperature hovered a few degrees below freezing, making the roads slick. Shadow Bend had only three ambulances—and the news of one being in the garage for repairs had made the front page of the paper. If there had been a multicar crash, the other two units would be unavailable. I just hoped that I could make it to Gossip Central without becoming another weather-related casualty.

Torn between the need for speed and the knowledge that my little car wasn't built for icy conditions, I finally compromised by going faster than was completely safe but slower than I wanted to go.

When I turned into the bar's parking lot fifteen minutes later, Poppy's SUV wasn't in sight. In fact, the only vehicle in the lot was a bright yellow Corvette that I didn't recognize. Maybe someone had stopped by, seen that Poppy was sick or injured, and driven her to the hospital in the Hummer, which could handle the bad weather a lot better than a 'Vette.

The snow was coming down heavier than when I left the store, and the sign over the Gossip Central's entrance was crusted in white. I hadn't bothered with a hat, scarf, or gloves, and when I sprang out of my car, the icy flakes drove into my exposed skin like a thousand tiny bee stings.

Shivering, I sprinted up the steps. The door was wide open and a snowdrift had formed over the threshold. Something was seriously wrong. As I rushed inside, I felt a prickle at the back of my neck, which turned into an all-out shudder when

314

I heard the sound of the dead bolt sliding into place behind me.

I wheeled around just in time to see Anya Hamilton level a gun at my heart.

Jake felt a twinge of unease when his cell rang. Who would be calling him from County General Hospital?

"Jake, this is Poppy. Where are you?"

"I'm at the ranch."

"Thank God."

"Why?" Jake's heart stuttered. "Has something happened to Devereaux?"

"I hope not." Poppy faltered. "But you need to go to my bar immediately because I think she's in big trouble."

"I'm on my way." Jake jammed the phone between his ear and shoulder and shrugged on his jacket. "Now tell me what's happened."

"Gossip Central doesn't open until four p.m. on weekdays, but everyone knows I'm usually there doing paperwork, cleaning, or stocking the bar several hours before then," Poppy explained.

"I see." Jake knew that witnesses had to tell their stories in their own way, and trying to hurry them just made the process take longer.

"About an hour ago, there was a knock on the door and when I opened it, Anya Hamilton was on the step. She said she had stopped by to pay her bar tab, so I let her in." Poppy snorted. "That should have been my first clue that something was up—Anya never pays until I'm almost ready to sic the bill collector on her."

"Right." Jake jammed his key in the truck's ignition and sped down the lane.

"As soon as she was inside, she asked to use the restroom. Then while she was gone, I got a call from the hospital saying my father had had a heart attack." Poppy paused to take a breath, then continued. "Anya was still in the bathroom, so I shouted for her to lock up, threw a key on the bar, and left."

Jake turned the pickup onto the main road and mashed the accelerator to the floor.

"When I got to the hospital, no one knew anything about my father, so I started to phone my mother and realized the call about my dad had come in on Gossip Central's landline. I never even thought to grab my cell before I left."

"Uh-huh." Jake swerved around a slow-moving Buick.

"The hospital let me use their telephone to call my dad, and he's fine. But when I phoned my mom, she knew right away I was calling from the hospital, which made me realize that on the call I received at Gossip Central, there was no name on the ID, just 'Missouri caller.' "

"That is odd." Jake glanced at his watch. He was still a good five minutes from Gossip Central, and Poppy had to have been gone from the bar at least a half hour before she called him.

"Somebody wanted me out of the bar." Poppy's voice was a mixture of fury and fear. "And I'm pretty sure it was Anya. I think she shut off the ID thingy on her cell and called me from the bathroom."

Jake felt his insides clench. "So what makes you think Devereaux is in danger?" As the words left his mouth, he recalled Devereaux's conviction that either Anya or Gwen had tipped off Aponte as to his wife's whereabouts.

"What if Anya killed Joelle?" Poppy asked.

"Someone has already been arrested for that murder."

"But it's possible the police have the wrong person in custody," Poppy pointed out. "And if Anya is the killer, and her next target is Dev, what better place to lure her to than her best friend's empty bar? Dev wouldn't hesitate to go to Gossip Central, and there are no nosy neighbors that might notice something unusual happening."

"Why would Anya want to kill Devereaux?" Jake asked.

"Because, the other night in the bar Anya was raging that no one was getting between her and Noah now that he was up for grabs again. And when Gwen suggested the good doctor still had a thing for Dev, Anya went berserk. She poured a whole container of margaritas over her friend's head and threw the empty pitcher against the wall."

"Son of a b—!"

"Exactly." Poppy paused, then added, "There's a key to the back door in a fake rock next to the steps."

"Where's Poppy?" I demanded. Had Anya gone crazy and killed her? "And what's with the gun?"

I noticed that Anya was wearing a leopard-print T-shirt with the words YOU SAY PETTY & VINDICTIVE LIKE IT'S A BAD THING written across her impressive chest. That message scared me almost as much as the pistol she was waving in my face.

"Shut up!" Anya stepped closer, grabbed my arm, and turned me around. Pressing the gun into my back, she forced me to walk past the bar and across the dance floor into one of the conversation areas. This one was a favorite of the Country Club Cougars, since it was decorated in pink and blinged out with fake jewels.

"What's going on?" I stopped at the entrance, not wanting to be trapped in such a small space, but Anya pushed me toward the opposite wall. She shoved me down on a rose velvet chaise longue and stood facing me as I asked, "Is Poppy okay?"

"Your friend is fine. I just arranged for her to be gone for a while so we could have a nice chat in private. She was kind enough to leave her cell phone so I could use it to text you." Anya's hazel eyes were filled with a childish resentment. "And I told you to shut up. Why can't any of you people do as you're told?"

"Any of us?" If Anya was going to kill me, I didn't plan on going gently, or silently, into that good night.

"Joelle. Etienne. Noah." Anya waved the revolver around wildly. "Everyone."

"I don't understand." Actually, I was afraid I did understand, but I wanted Anya to say it. If I was going to die, I wanted her to be caught, and I was counting on Poppy's concealed voice-activated listening devices to pick up her confession.

"I planned for Noah to marry me, but then Joelle flounces into town and steals him right out from under my nose." Anya's red face clashed with the pink decor. "And now that I've cleared that obstacle away, you think you're going to snatch him up?"

"No." Now that she reminded me, I had heard that Noah had taken Anya out a couple of times, but I was pretty sure they were never officially a couple or someone would have mentioned it to me. "I'm not interested in Noah. I'm going out with Jake Del Vecchio. Remember, you were teasing me about him at the coffee tasting?"

"You might be screwing Tall, Dark, and Hot— I saw you at the hotel Saturday night—but you've got your eye on Noah for the altar."

"Were you the one who called the tip in to the police about me being at the Parkside?" Everything was coming together. "You've been following me, haven't you?"

"Of course." Anya raised a brow. "Ever since you and Noah had that lovely long talk at the Manor the other day, and I heard he'd been saying such nice things about you."

"Our conversation was about Joelle's murder. Nothing else."

"You can't fool me." Anya shook her head stubbornly. "I saw you go to his house Tuesday night."

"That was about Joelle, too." I could see I wasn't convincing Anya, so I switched gears and tried flattery. "How in the world did you pull off Joelle's murder? You must be a genius."

"It wasn't easy." Anya cradled the pistol to her breasts like a puppy, and said thoughtfully, "It all started when Joelle and Noah got engaged. Up until then, I thought he'd get over her like he had all of his other little flings."

"But he didn't." I knew that Noah had dated quite a bit, although usually not the same woman more than once or twice. "How did you figure out that Joelle wasn't who she said she was?"

"I was looking for something to discredit her, and I was suspicious that she was so secretive about her past, so I broke into her condo."

"Without her knowing?" I peeked at my watch. It had been nearly fifteen minutes since I had arrived. Maybe if I could keep Anya talking, Poppy would come back or a delivery guy would show up.

"Sure. It was simple to get in. Joelle had the kind of lock that if you turned the inside knob, it opens, which meant that if you stuck a credit card between the door and the jamb, and jiggled it, the lock button pops up." Anya smiled meanly. "The only thing a cheap, wooden hollow-core front door and a button popup lock are good for is to keep the Jehovah's Witnesses out."

"Wow." I made sure my tone was admiring. "I had no idea."

"Yeah, well, I dated a locksmith once," Anya explained. "It took me less than an hour to find Joelle's stash. She had rolled all her old identification papers and stuffed them into a hollow shower rod."

"So once you found out, you contacted her husband?"

"Yep. I e-mailed him from Joelle's own computer, then erased any evidence of the message so no one could tell it had been sent." Anya's tone was smug. "I thought he'd contact her and all hell would break loose."

"But it didn't?"

"No." Anya frowned. "So when nothing happened, I suggested a romantic Valentine's

Day weekend for her and Noah at the Parkside and helped her set everything up. Then I contacted Etienne and arranged for him to come to Kansas City the same day."

"Why?" It was clear that Anya wanted to tell someone about her master plan and I was willing to listen. Maybe she'd talk herself into an arrest.

"I had dated the head of security at the Parkside, so I knew how to disable their cameras." Anya shrugged. "I figured either Noah would find out Joelle was already married or, since I heard Louisiana men had hot tempers, Etienne would kill her. Either way, she'd be out of the running for the title of Mrs. Underwood."

"Why didn't you just let Nadine in on Joelle's past?"

"I thought about it." Anya pursed her mouth, then shook her head. "But I was afraid that psycho old pageant queen would twist things. That she'd somehow use the fact that I was the one to tell her about Joelle to poison Noah's mind against me."

"I see." I could certainly understand Anya's point about Nadine. "So, what happened?"

"I met Etienne at five fifty-five, let him into Joelle's suite using Noah's key card. I had swapped mine for his when I followed Joelle to his clinic earlier that day. She left the card for him on the check-in desk, and as soon as the receptionist stepped away from the counter, I made the switch. Then I hightailed it down to the lobby to meet Geoffrey."

*Ah.* So Anya was the mayor's secret girlfriend. What he'd said about her not forgiving him if he told me her name made sense now. Cyndi had said Anya didn't forgive or forget.

Anya continued. "Geoffrey registered. Then on our way to our room I told him I forgot to bring the condoms. I left him and went to check to see if Noah had discovered Etienne."

"I bet you also arranged for the call from the patient who never showed up, which delayed Noah at his clinic. You intended for him to find Etienne and Joelle together, but you didn't count on traffic, or that Noah would wait as long as he did for the emergency patient."

"That was a miscalculation on my part," Anya admitted in an annoyed tone. "Etienne was gone by the time I got back to Joelle's suite, and all he'd done was handcuff Joelle to the bed and stuff a champagne bottle in her mouth."

"So when Noah finally arrived, she could have claimed she'd been assaulted."

"Exactly." Anya nodded approvingly. "So I had to improvise."

"You drove Joelle's high-heel shoe into her heart?" Looking at the petite woman in front of me, I found it hard to believe she was strong enough to do that.

"I play tennis." Anya flexed her right arm. "I

have a wicked backhand. The tricky part was wiping off my fingerprints without getting any blood on the washcloth."

"Amazing." I was running out of questions. "Well, I certainly understand your motives. In fact, I sympathize with them. Back years and years ago, when I thought I was in love with Noah, I probably would have done the same thing. But now that I've met Jake, I've realized that any feelings I once might have had for Noah are long gone. Joelle was a tramp who had to be eliminated. I totally understand and promise to never tell anyone what you did." I tried to get up, but Anya pushed me back down.

"Sorry." Anya's beautiful face showed not one iota of regret. "You need to kill yourself because you couldn't live with the guilt after you murdered Joelle."

"No. Really. That's not necessary." As I looked frantically around for something to defend myself with, I saw a movement behind Anya, but couldn't make out what it was in the dark bar.

Anya dug into the pocket of her designer jeans and threw a small leather memo pad with an attached pen at me. "If you write a suicide note for me before I shoot you, I promise not to kill your grandmother."

*Kill Gran!* Okay. Now I was mad. I was taking this bitch down.

As I pretended to write, I watched Anya for my

opportunity. When a board squeaked behind her and she turned her head to look over her shoulder, I launched all my not-inconsiderable weight at the tiny woman.

We both toppled to the floor, and as I lay on top of Anya, fighting to keep her pinned to the ground, I tore at her gun hand, panicking when I couldn't free her clenched fingers from the pistol.

A nanosecond later Jake ran in, pressed his revolver to Anya's head, and said, "Drop it."

Anya stared at Jake for what seemed like an hour before she released her weapon.

I crawled off of the downed woman, and Jake flipped her over onto her stomach and cuffed her hands behind her back.

After he Mirandized her, I asked, "How did you know I was here?"

"Poppy figured it out and called me."

"Did you hear Anya's confession?"

"No." Jake shook his head. "I came in when she was planning your suicide."

I explained about Poppy's hidden recording devices and he grinned.

While Jake made arrangements to bring Anya to the Kansas City PD, I telephoned Poppy to assure her that I was fine. It took me nearly as long to tell her what had happened as it did for Jake to explain everything to the KC cops.

Once we were both finished with our calls, Jake heaved Anya up from the floor, marched her outside, and deposited her in the passenger seat of his truck. He handcuffed her to the grab handle near the door. Then he helped me into the backseat and climbed behind the wheel.

Despite Anya's constant chatter—she kept trying to explain her motives for killing Joelle—I spent most of the trip in a near comatose state. Fighting for my life had exhausted me. When we crossed into the city limits, Jake caught my eye in the rearview mirror and said, "After we turn Anya over to the Kansas City cops and you give them your statement, we need to talk."

# EPILOGUE

The past couple of days had been surreal. Everyone from the Kansas City police to Etienne Aponte had wanted to talk to me. Some, like the cops, I couldn't avoid. Although to be fair, finding out that Detective Woods and his immediate supervisor were under investigation for their actions on the case was worth the trip into the city and the six hours I spent telling my story again and again.

I managed to steer clear of everyone else by putting Xylia and Hannah in charge of the dime store, holing up at home, and refusing to answer either the door or the phone. I really had no choice. Between my own precarious emotional state and Gran needing my full attention, I didn't have anything left for the rest of the world.

Gran had not reacted well to my near-death experience—okay, neither had I—and she needed repeated assurances that I was fine. But by Sunday morning she seemed back to her old self, insisting I go to work the next day and start seeing people again. She was also adamant that we visit my father as originally planned.

Although she tried to convince me to go inside with her, I resisted her pleas. My original jail phobia had increased a hundred percent, and I still blamed my father for ruining our family name. It would be a cold day in hell before I voluntarily set foot on the prison grounds.

But Gran never gave up, and the drive home was filled with her blow-by-blow account of her conversation with my father, including his claim that he had a lead on how to prove his innocence. Finally, about a mile from home, she fell silent. When we drove up to the house, I knew why. Parked side by side were Poppy's Hummer and Boone's Mercedes.

Avoiding my gaze, Gran said, "Did I mention that I invited your friends over for supper?"

"No. No, you didn't." I narrowed my eyes. "What's the occasion?"

"Your rejoining the land of the living." Gran patted my hand. "I know you needed time to regroup; so did I, but you three have been friends for nearly twenty-four years. You can't shut them out just because there are things you don't want to face."

She was right. It hadn't been very nice of me to ignore their calls and refuse to see them, but I hadn't been up to rehashing Thursday's events. After a brief hesitation during which I tested my emotional state, I realized I was feeling better, and now was as good a time as any to discuss what had happened.

As Gran and I got out of the car, I couldn't decide if I was relieved or upset that she hadn't included Jake in her little party. Maybe he was still out of town. Friday morning, he had left me a voice mail saying he was on his way to St. Louis. The prosecutor was putting him back on the stand to testify about some additional evidence that had come up.

I hadn't heard from him since then, although to be fair, I'd silenced the ringer on the house phone, turned off my cell, and hadn't checked either for messages.

When we walked in the door, Poppy and Boone rushed me. In between their hugs, and my thanking Poppy for sending Jake to rescue me, I noticed Gran escaping into the kitchen. I hoped it was to cook dinner and not stir up more mischief.

Eventually Poppy, Boone, and I made our way into the living room, and I began to answer their questions.

Poppy started out with, "If Joelle or Jolene, or whatever her name was, wanted to keep her background a secret, why in the name of God did she go after a guy like Noah? She had to realize that marrying one of the town's most eligible bachelors would cause a lot of jealousy and someone was bound to look into her past."

"It was a calculated risk." I settled into a corner of the sofa to relate everything I'd learned from Jake and Anya since we'd last spoken. "She had spent most of the lottery money she won reinventing herself, so she needed to marry someone rich before she ran out of cash. There were only three guys in town who met her criteria. She dated His Honor and Vaughn Yager, but they made it clear they weren't interested in marriage. Which left Noah."

"Who was ripe for the picking." Boone sneered. "What kind of 'rescue me' fairy tale did she tell him?"

"I have no idea." Noah was another person who had been trying to talk to me before I went incommunicado, but I knew I was far from ready for that conversation. What if he wanted to try to resurrect our high school romance? At this point I had no idea what I wanted, and I didn't think it was a good idea to discuss the matter until I knew my own heart. Maybe in a year or so Noah and I could talk, but not now.

"How about Anya?" Boone leaned back in

329

Gran's La-Z-Boy and levered the footrest up. "Why was she willing to kill to get Dr. Dreary? Or was she just psycho?"

"She was definitely Looney Tunes, but her reason for wanting Noah was the same as Joelle's." I had decided it was easier on all of us to call Jolene by the name we had known her. "Anya's almost out of the money she got from her last divorce settlement, and she needed a rich guy fast," I explained. Anya had talked freely to Jake on our drive into Kansas City, so I had heard all her excuses.

"I suspected as much." Poppy smiled meanly. "I noticed she'd stopped getting Botox and all her expensive jewelry had disappeared."

I continued to answer their questions until Gran called us to supper. She had made fried chicken, green bean casserole, mashed potatoes, biscuits, and gravy.

In between bites, Poppy said, "Who would have ever guessed that women like Joelle and Anya could be so desperate?"

"Yeah," I agreed. "This whole situation sure taught me a lesson. I'm going to quit comparing myself to other people. Even though you might never see it, they are probably more messed up than you are."

"Amen," Boone and Poppy said simultaneously.

After dessert, I walked Boone and Poppy to the door. He had some work he needed to finish before the next morning and Poppy had to get back to her bar. Hugging them, I said, "Thank you both for understanding that I needed a couple of days before I could talk about all this. I sure wouldn't want to damage our friendship."

Boone shook his head. "Darlin', we'll be friends until we're old and senile."

"Yeah." Poppy grinned. "Then we'll be new friends."

Gran must have turned the telephone's ringer back on when we got home, because as she and I were finishing up the dishes the phone rang. She raced past me, elbow-checking my midsection in order to answer before me. "Yes. Uh-huh. Good."

As she hung up, I asked, "Who was that?"

"Jake. He's coming over for pie and coffee." Gran yawned loudly. "Sweet Jesus! I'm bushed. I think I'll take a nap." She disappeared into her bedroom and closed the door with an emphatic click.

Fifteen agonizing minutes later, Jake showed up. I hadn't noticed that it had started snowing again, but he stomped his boots on the welcome mat and clapped his Stetson against his thigh. We both seemed a little tongue-tied and unsure what to say to each other after having spent a couple of days apart.

"Hi," I finally said, breaking the awkward

silence. "Let me take your coat and hat." Once I had hung his jacket in the hall closet and placed his Stetson on the shelf, I asked, "When did it start snowing?"

"About a half hour ago. Just after I got back from St. Louis." Jake looked around. "Where's Birdie?"

"She claimed to be tired and went to take a nap." I raised a brow, indicating my doubt, then asked, "Kitchen or living room?"

"Living room." Jake winked. "You told me Birdie's bedroom is next to the kitchen, and we wouldn't want to disturb her rest."

"Right." We settled on the sofa, and I asked, "How did the trial go?"

"We convicted the scumbag." Jake's voice was almost savage in its triumph.

"That's great."

"Yeah. It felt really good hearing that guilty verdict." Jake smiled widely. "He was a bad one."

We sat in another awkward silence for a while, and then I said, "Hey, did you hear Woods is in trouble?" When Jake shook his head, I explained. "Internal Affairs is looking into both his *and* his immediate supervisor's behavior during the murder investigation. It turned out Woods's supervisor also lost money with Stramp Investments, which is why he did nothing when Boone called him regarding Woods's bias against me."

"We should have guessed that." Jake stretched out his legs. "I tried to talk to Woods after we brought Anya Hamilton in, but, as Tony would say, he had a lot of bull for somebody who doesn't have any cattle."

Snickering, I felt myself relax. Jake must have noticed, because he tried to take me into his arms, but I moved out of his reach. I knew that once he touched me I'd be lost, and I still had a lot of questions for him, some of which I doubted he could answer.

I started with an easy one. "Hey, why do you think no one ever asked us why we were talking to them about Joelle?"

"For the most part, I don't think anyone cared. She didn't have any true friends, and her death barely made a ripple in Shadow Bend."

"That's really sad." I thought about it for a minute, then moved to the harder issue. "You mentioned that your ex-wife was the one who left the marriage. What happened?"

"Do we have to discuss this now?" He frowned, clearly unhappy. When I nodded, he said, "Fine. Eighteen months ago, I was involved in a case where a seventeen-year-old girl who was on trial for killing her stepfather escaped from her guards. I found her. She convinced me she was innocent, and I tried to help her. Turned out she was a sociopath and she shot me with my own gun."

"Oh." I was silent for a moment, then asked, "Is she the one who caused your current injury?"

"Yes." Jake nodded. "Between the multiple surgeries and rehab, it's been over a year since she shot me."

"But what does that have to do with your marriage?" Had he had an affair with the girl?

"After the first surgery, when I was still groggy from the anesthetic, Meg told me she couldn't stand being married to a cripple. She walked out of the hospital and filed for a quickie divorce."

"What a bitch!" *Oops!* I hadn't meant to say that out loud.

"I found out later the doctors told her that I'd be in a wheelchair for the rest of my life."

"Obviously they were wrong." I thought about what I'd overheard and Meg's actions, then asked, "Does she want you back now that you're able to walk?"

"Maybe." Jake shrugged. "But I'm not interested."

"Even if you're able to return to active duty?" I highly suspected that Meg would do her damnedest to win him back, and if Jake was with her every day at work, she'd have ample opportunity to seduce him.

"No." Jake's tone was firm and he scooped me into his lap and whispered into my hair, "Because I've found someone so much better."

I wrapped my arms around his neck, savoring

his words and the warmth of his embrace. But in the back of my mind, a basketful of niggling doubts remained. What would happen with Noah now that he was available and I had good reason to believe he still loved me? What would happen if Jake left Shadow Bend to resume his old job? Would Jake and I turn out to be like Gran and Tony? Why hadn't she waited for him?

My last thought before Jake's lips claimed mine was that I was glad Gran was in the next room. I could enjoy this moment and think about the rest tomorrow, but having a seventy-five-year-old chaperone a few hundred feet away would keep me from going too far.

## Center Point Large Print
600 Brooks Road / PO Box 1
Thorndike ME 04986-0001 USA

(207) 568-3717

US & Canada:
1 800 929-9108
www.centerpointlargeprint.com